D1135503

I KNOW
WHAT I
SAW

I KNOW WHAT I SAW

IMRAN MAHMOOD

RAVEN BOOKS

LONDON · OXFORD · NEW YORK · NEW DELHI · SYDNEY

RAVEN BOOKS
Bloomsbury Publishing Plc
50 Bedford Square, London, WC1B 3DP, UK
29 Earlsfort Terrace, Dublin 2, Ireland

BLOOMSBURY, RAVEN BOOKS and the Raven Books logo are
trademarks of Bloomsbury Publishing Plc

First published in Great Britain 2021

ISBN: HB: 978-1-5266-2762-9; TPB: 978-1-5266-2763-6; EBOOK:978-1-5266-2764-3

2 4 6 8 10 9 7 5 3 1

Typeset by Integra Software Services Pvt. Ltd.
Printed and bound in Great Britain by CPI Group (UK) Ltd, Croydon CR0 4YY

To find out more about our authors and books visit www.bloomsbury.com
and sign up for our newsletters

To Dad (Poppy)

Without you, the world still turns but it turns more slowly
and in much less light.

I miss you

To Shahida who gave me life
To Sadia who changed my life
To Zoha who made my life
To Shifa who completed my life

'We are healed of a suffering only by experiencing it to the full'

Marcel Proust

1

Tuesday

The sky is a bruised sea. It threatens to burst and split the night. There is a children's play park nearby. The gates are shut but unlocked and they push open easily with a gentle squeak. Of course, at this time of night it's deserted, and I know that I can sleep here until light. Time as it ticks on a watch is not as useful to me as how the light looks when it waxes or wanes. For me the time is hidden in shadows and in the lengths they cast on the ground. I think about earlier today, about Amit and the fruit now warm in my pockets. That at seventeen years old he thinks about me at all is a surprise. I've known him a summer, an autumn and now most of a winter. And he brings me oranges when most people bring nothing but chaos and dirt.

The ground here is covered in woodchips, making a decent mattress under the slide where it is dry, shaded from the elements by the wide tin slope. Before, when I knew too much about numbers and nothing about living, I tried to sleep in the tunnel, to use its seclusion, but the curve is death to sleep. Now I crouch under the slide and tear out sheets of newspaper, rolling them into apple-sized balls. I can't read the financial pages any more so the pink ones are the first to go. Each one is forced into the gaps in my coat sleeves, the wool inflating until I am like the Hulk. And then I do the same to the legs of my jeans. In no time air is trapped in pockets and my body warms – the paper clings on to the heat. The remaining balls I arrange into the carrier bag from Amit's oranges, and convert into a pillow. I lay the oranges by my head because the scent of them comforts me.

From here all I can see in the blue moonlight is the dulled metal underside of the slide. The position of it, sloping towards me upside down, gives me a sensation of vertigo. Vertigo. Mum wrote a paper about *Vertigo*, the film, and Proust, and how much the one had borrowed from the other. Madeleine Elster was Hitchcock's heroine's name. The connection was obvious, Mum said. Proust's madeleines and his painter, Elstir, combined into one. And then, wasn't *Vertigo* just a yearning for lost time? Wasn't it the yawning abyss that caused the vertigo?

Mum was an academic above everything else, the kind of person who could only escape the gravity of life by manipulating herself with art. Rothko was her thing. I hadn't really ever got on with the abstractness of him. It didn't make sense to me, having a painting of just four colours. *'But isn't that just the incredible thing about him, Xander? That a person using four colours and no repre-sentational effort can paint oblivion? Don't you find that amazing?'*

She was the kind of person who looked up to rarefied heights, but down was where I wanted to be, with my nose in the dirt and the physics.

'And you're sure that you want to read the sciences?' she'd said once. 'You're not exactly your father, you know.'

'I know.' Then I wondered how she couldn't see that that wasn't what I wanted at all. I didn't want to be him. Not in a million years. Even so, I slid into Cambridge with four As to read Mathematics. Not science exactly, nor a degree to capture the imagination, but at least it meant something to other people, even if it meant nothing to me.

'Fuck out of my patch.'

I sit up so quickly that I bang my forehead on the underside of the slide and then there's this sickening thud in my ears as a wet boot strikes my temple. I cry out and try to focus but all there is is searing pain. It pounds and beats, freezing me even though I need to get myself ready to fight. I claw through the pain, waiting for my firing synapses to create space for me. My eyes shut until the ache recedes a little, just enough for me to move.

I look at him through screwed eyes and see that he's smaller than me. He in turn rolls his eyes up and down me until he realises the same thing. I have always been big. I've taken up a seat and a half since I was fifteen. Never fat, or even muscular. Just big. Bones like old iron.

People avoid me on the streets. There are pockets of men here or there, malignant in places, benign in others, but they react the same. Usually they circle around me, never getting too close, in case they fall all the way in and down into the drain. And I don't mind the wary distance. I don't want them near me anyway. I don't need the company that they all seem to crave in one another. So they leave me alone and I leave them to their hot clusters – of drugs, alcohol and hacking laughter. And if I miss the chance for conversation, I remind myself that I wouldn't seek it amongst them anyway.

'My fucking spot,' the man says. His voice is so deep that I can feel it vibrate in my chest. It curls at the edges in drink. He is perhaps forty but it is hard to tell – street years carve deeper into the skin. In any case he is shades younger than me for sure. I look through the gloom into his eyes for some sentience but I can tell that he's half-soaked.

'Not tonight,' I say, looking him dead in the eyes. My head pounds but I hold his gaze, because I know I have to.

'Yeah?' he says, his voice lifting now. 'I know you. You're the weirdo.'

He steps towards me and I see something winking in his hand.

My brother once said that statistically speaking the difference between winners and losers is that, over the longer term, losers give up.

'Put the knife down,' I say.

His eyes are rimmed in watery fury. There are tears streaming down his cheeks in rivers. No, not tears, rain. It has started to rain. That kick to the head must have been hard. Adrenaline is in play, I can tell, because my focus is too tight. I need to see the wider picture, but the periphery is stepping back into shadow, further and further.

'That's my fucking spot,' he says again and then lunges at me.

My heart starts to race as the chemicals brim. Everything around me slows down. The surge gives me a kick of energy, of life, so that my eyes pop open and I feel myself stepping into the warmth of a chemical power. He comes towards me but I step to the side, dodging the blade easily.

He stumbles so I take the advantage and use his weight to push him to the ground, and then I kick him. These boots are made for kicking. Steel toes behind thick leather. He grunts. I kick him again in the ribs and then, before he has a chance to catch his breath, I drop to my knees and rip the knife out of his hand. It is just a small lock knife, fancy, but the blade's sharp. I hold it under his chin and poke just hard enough to let out some blood.

He freezes.

'You had enough?' I say, my heart loud in my head.

'Yeah,' he says, nodding.

I get to my feet, the knife still gripped in my hand.

'I'm keeping this,' I say, and fold the knife and put it in my pocket. My heart is still racing. I make an effort to breathe slowly so that the one, the breath, can regulate the other, the heart.

'It's my fucking spot,' he says again but he is crying now, real tears not just rain. 'You took my spot.' He rubs under his chin at the spot the knife pricked and for a moment I wonder whether I should just leave and give him his place back.

But winners never give up.

I watch him roll on the woodchip and push himself to his feet. He holds the edge of the slide for support as he sways from booze or pain. Then he roots through his clothes and tugs out the familiar shape of a quarter bottle of whisky. He empties what little there is into his mouth as his eyes drench me in hate.

'Cunt,' he says. I turn away but then catch a glimpse of something spinning in the air. Instinctively I shield my eyes but then I feel the thick heel of the bottle crack into my skull. I yelp and drop to my knees, still clutching my head. The pain is dull and sickening and I try to breathe through it, but then out of the blackness, a knee crashes into my temple. I drop to the soft ground, the tang of wet earth filling my nose. And then his limbs are over me, searching for the knife.

'I'm going to fucking kill you,' he says.

'I'm stronger than you, Rory!' I scream. It escapes from me, that name. He's always there, finding a way in, in these unguarded moments. Or, I wonder, is it the blow to my head that has derailed me?

'Rory?' He looks at me, confused. 'Psycho bastard,' he adds, backing away.

'Rory!' I shout and then I stagger away, unable to control my steps as I zigzag into the slicing rain.

2

Tuesday

The sound of sirens splits the night. I stop for a second. Triangulating, calculating. That Doppler effect – is it getting nearer or further? Who are those sirens for? Me? Are they coming to rescue me, or catch me? My logical brain takes over and calculates the variables. I have to get out of the park. Maybe you'd think he won, scared me off his pitch, saw me off. But in this world strength means more. I won. I have the physical strength and he knows I can return. These guys, they hunt in packs sometimes, and there could be another one not far behind.

In my mind's eye is the zonal map of London I carry in my head. Red Zones are the areas I stay away from now: Camden, King's Cross, Dalston, Bow, Mile End, Peckham, Old Kent Road. There are air holes there which are safe but those aren't places I can be in for long. Those streets have been colonised by gangs that will stab a person to earn ranking points. I could head for the neutral Blue Zone: Vauxhall, Camberwell, Elephant, Oval. I can be in those spaces and stay unmolested for a time. The Green Zone, where I am now, is supposed to be fine: Dulwich, Chelsea, Fulham, Westminster, City, Holborn. But I was attacked right in the middle of it. Nowhere is completely safe. It's a question of playing the odds. For example, I stay away from the Purple Zone, the truly unpredictable spaces: Paddington, Edgware, Caledonian Road, Seven Sisters, Tottenham. Safe, if you know what you are doing, but take a wrong turn or even the right one on the wrong day, and there's no telling what will come for you. I breathe and push through the metal gates. The sirens are following.

The rain is coming down in sheets. I need shelter. I need to get somewhere dry, to give myself a chance to heal and recover. I consult the map in my head. Walworth Road leads to the Elephant and Castle. The Elephant to St Georges Circus. St Georges to Waterloo. Waterloo to the Strand. I am grateful for my head when it works. That this map is here, always ready to use, dry and crisp, the Zones pulsing. I look around and slowly through the throbbing in my head I come to a realisation – I don't know where I am.

I try to recalibrate. Where was I? I had been in Hyde Park. It feels like a certainty until suddenly, it no longer does. Have I been running or hobbling in this rain, in this dark, wet cloak of a night, for this last chunk of time? I can't tell. This pounding in my brain is relentless, a dull, thick fog that I cannot reach through. That boot to the head has really done some damage.

I feel myself panicking now. The sirens are still chasing me. The rain is throwing itself down and all I can feel is the slick soak of my clothes. I have to get dry. I have to find some shelter. This has happened to me before and I nearly died from the pneumonia. You could recover from it, this cold and this rain, but for me it would take days for these clothes to dry out. I couldn't survive it in my state. I'd drop into a wet death like that.

Where am I? There's a couple there just ahead, leaning into one another for cover under a blue and yellow golf umbrella, I mouth words at them as they walk by but they hustle past, heads down. There was a definite look from the man. He wrinkled his face away from me and I think even this rain can't rinse the stench from my body.

I need a sign.

I trudge through puddles that I don't see at first and curse, because these boots sponge up water. Reaching into my coat sleeves I pull out the balls of paper that are now sodden and pulpy and slop them on to the ground. I can stop racing now, I think. Whatever was pursuing me isn't any longer. He won't have come all the way here. Over my shoulder I see that the road is clear. The sirens have died away to a whisper, catching or saving someone else. The first street I see is South Street. The sign says W1 Westminster – I'm in Mayfair. Green Zone. That's right, I remember now. I had been in Hyde Park. I think.

The road is quiet. I know these roads from before. In a previous life, these roads were soft to the touch. I know that if I walk along here the road will adopt another identity and become something else. South Street and its high-faced mansions recede behind me. And yes, now here is Farm Street emerging under my feet. I think there's a church here, or at least there is in my memory. Perhaps a library – something established and permanent.

As I lumber on through the rain, I see with a sinking feeling a flash of light, blazing blue in the pavement. Then, seconds later, a deep roar of thunder before the heavy rain turns, just like that, into a deluge.

I duck under the great stone steps of one of the houses and wait in the shelter of the cavity. Despite the cold there's nothing for it but to take my coat off and wring it out. Rainwater runs through my fists as I squeeze first the sleeves, now the flanks. When I put it back on, it's a pound or two lighter and my hands are raw.

I reach into the lining then and find my dry pocket. I shut my eyes as my fingers fumble for my cigarettes. I pull them out and open the box. Thank God, they are dry. Fighting frozen fingers, I tap the box against my palm until a cigarette magically rises. I mouth it, light it and take in a lungful of smoke. A spike of pain comes driving into my brain, causing me to clutch my head.

I freeze until the pain subsides and then when it does, through the smoke I see a door. It is black, painted in high gloss, as the others are in this road. But it's smaller than the main one at the top of the stairs. Maybe it had once been a tradesman's entrance, or an annexe or a flat? I try to wipe the rain from my eyes, but it clings, blurring my vision. Something doesn't feel right. And then I see it.

The door is ajar. Just.

3

Tuesday

There's no light coming from the gap in the door. In that infinite bordered space, there is nothing and everything. I rub my left eye to clear the smears but the mist lingers.

My head is still thumping, and between the waves of sickness, I tug at the memory of what happened. Rory attacked me. No, not Rory. A man. Just a drunk in the park. I dig the tips of my fingers hard into my temples. For a moment the pain subsides, but then returns and with it comes other pain that I had relegated to the edges. My ribs ache. My legs are trembling. I take a final drag of my cigarette before flicking it into a storm drain. I look up.

The darkness in the gap behind the door pulls at me. I could go in, I think. I could. It would be dry. Just for a few minutes. I push the door slowly, keeping my ears pricked for anything beyond, any voices, or even a television, but there's nothing. Then I pause. I can't go into someone's house. It's illegal. But still, I keep pushing. I could shelter in the hallway, just until the rain stops? The door gives way smoothly under my touch and I step into the space behind it. There's a smell that I

11

recognise. A kind of 'closed-up' odour that develops in empty houses. It's as if the absence of a person from a house, even for a day, begins a kind of decay. As if the separation from its heart makes the house die a little. Inside, I shut the door behind me, softly. The darkness begins to recede as I blink furiously. It's not warm in here, but not cold either and not wet. I want to sink to the floor and rest just a little, in this covered nook that's resolving before me into a narrow, tiled corridor. Clearer with each passing second.

'Hello?'

I throw my voice deep into the hallway. If it catches a person, if there's someone there, I can explain I found the door open and was just passing. That I'm just warning them against criminals, warning them against myself in different circumstances. There's no answer so I call out again, but only the silence comes ringing back.

Hopefully, I feather the wall with wet fingers until they find a switch. The hall fills with light and Victorian tiles appear at my feet arranged symmetrically, intricately, black on white. A huge gilded mirror glares at me from the left with Tiffany wall lamps on either side. The house of an old dame.

A pause. My heart quickens with the waiting. If there's anybody beyond this hall, these lights will alert them, so for seconds or minutes I am frozen. Waiting. Until … nothing.

Finally, I sink to the floor, my back against the heavy wooden door, and breathe. The pain kicks up again as the adrenaline dissipates. And then I begin to shiver. My heart drops in my chest. It is beginning. If I don't get dry soon and warm, I am going to get very ill. I rub life into my cold fingers and then when the dexterity returns to them, I unpick the laces of my leather boots and tug them off. Rainwater has pooled inside them so I upturn them against the door to drain them. I stare at my feet, which are covered in plastic bags for warmth. I pull them away and then peel off the damp socks beneath them. The skin of my feet is pale, deathly. I look away from the blisters and the blackness that rims the nails. It always shocks me that my own body sickens me like this. On the cold tiles I stand and take off my coat, shaking it out before wrapping it around my boots and socks. Newspaper I had missed earlier falls now to the floor in sodden balls and the cold begins to climb from there into my bones. I shiver. I watch the other black door at the far end of the corridor, waiting for it to spring open and for anger to appear in its light. I strain my ears for sound but all they pick up is the rain outside. I rub my temples again but the pain refuses to be eased by touch.

If only it will stop for a moment, so I can think.

I gather my coat-boot bundle and walk towards the other door, catching my face in the mirror. It startles me, this face that I know but don't recognise. My cheeks are burned from weather. The beard is the most striking thing – it's the thing about me that I forget most often. But the real surprise is in the eyes. And not just that the left has swollen almost shut, but the impression they give: they seem lost, somehow innocent. And then as I am puzzling this, my expression catches me in a flash of anger that I didn't know I was carrying.

Before I turn the handle on the door, I call out again.

When I step in the smell from the room hits me in a wave so I am reminded of Proust and his madeleines. It's the wax, the scent of it transports me, capturing memories and then scattering them. Is it Mum waxing banisters that I remember now, or is this just the smell of art galleries? I can't remember precisely but Mum is definitely there, hovering, remote, aloof. I think she's warning me.

It takes a minute to adjust to the gloom but slowly the room crystallises. There's a large square bay window and then I see leather chesterfields along two walls. I look to the right and start at the sight of a tall, square-shouldered man in the corner. But it coalesces, into a grandfather clock. At the far end of the double room, there is a dining table and chairs, neatly tucked in. I stand still, listening, with the thumping, rhythmic beat of my heart playing in my ears.

Books and records are stacked on shelves either side of the fireplace, in neat rows safely behind glass. I crouch down, spreading my hands on the floor. This carpet is unfamiliar. It is silk. Otherworldly under my skin.

My head drops against it as I lie down, and I breathe. After a few breaths I double over as tears spill from my eyes. Soon, though, I sleep.

When my eyes snap open, I don't know how long I've slept. Something I cannot now process, something in the past, has jolted me awake. I sit up. There must have been a sound. As soon as I scramble to my feet, I clamp a hand over my mouth to give my ears space to hear.

Voices in the hall.

I freeze.

The front door slams and I hear the click of heels against the tile. Two voices blow in, a man and a woman, and suddenly it's clear that I have to move. I don't know what's upstairs, or even how to get there. Maybe the way up is there to the right of the dining table and chairs. Could there be a nook there where perhaps stairs are nestling? I can't be sure, I know only these connected living rooms down here. I should have gathered myself earlier and explored my surroundings. That's what I do when I find somewhere new. I look around to make sure that the place hasn't already been cuckooed. I make certain of my exits and of all the weak spots so that if I have to I can make a run for it. Why didn't I do that? How badly did he hurt me?

The voices are near now. In a second that door will open and they'll burst in. After that, the lights will blaze on. A nano-second later, I will be trapped in that light, frozen in view. Caught with no way out.

Across the darkness I leap on to the sofa before I see my boots, bundled in my coat, there in the middle of the floor. Somehow, I spin around and scoop them up, just as the door opens. I leap and in a blink I am behind the sofa. The voices – louder, still jolly – trail in. My eyes, adjusting to the darkness, are helped then by the light falling in from the opened door, but there's nothing to see here, trapped behind leather.

'Ha,' I hear the woman say. 'Like you would!'

The light clicks on. And everything is bright.

4

Tuesday

I left my life to be alone. When I think of it, phrased in that way, I feel like an idiot. To be *alone*. The idea that I once thought I could find solitude on the streets! When the drunks don't piss on you and the police don't move you on and the people don't look through you in that way, there's still the sky. For you the sky is freedom. It's your endless, unconfined self. But for me the sky is a shroud. It wraps me. It binds my eyes and mouth so that I can't breathe.

I can't breathe. My eyes are wide now as I force myself to connect my body to my surroundings. From behind the chesterfield I can see nothing but parts of myself. The dirt under my fingernails, the grime burned into the skin of my hands, the sleeves of my jumper, baggy and bobbled with pilling. I've made the mistake of holding on to my breath for fear of being noticed. And now that I am safe and hidden and I can breathe again, I have held on for too long. I lower my head so the coat-shoe bundle is tight to my face and breathe out into it.

'There's a bottle under that cupboard,' the woman says. 'You open that up and I'll put on a record.'

I track the sound of their bodies as they separate and bustle in different ends of the room. My heart is still beating too quickly and I worry that I am going to hyperventilate.

'This Gamay?' he asks, his words muffled but he stretches out the vowels just as my father used to.

From the sound of his voice, he is at the far end of the room by the dining table. There must be a cupboard there. His voice is low, on its knees. I concentrate on the words so that I can control my breathing and stave off the claustrophobia that threatens.

'Or shall I get the champagne?' he asks, his tone oily.

'Champagne?' she calls out. 'What are we celebrating?'

'Nothing,' he says, to the sound of glass kissing from being handled. 'Just, you know, there is the money.'

She laughs but there's uncertainty in her voice.

'I'm kidding,' he says and then to fill in the space, he adds, 'The Gamay then.'

'Any of the reds will do.' Her tone is rich and velvety. Loud. She's near. Then her voice drops and becomes shaded as if she too has crouched down. 'What about Jack T?' she asks.

'Bit bluesy,' the man says, his voice getting louder now as he walks back towards her. There is a clink of glass and then silence. A hiss, then suddenly the room fills with sound, in stereo.

Then came the night they came
That was the night they took you …

The music masks my presence here which is good for all kinds of reasons, not least that I need to move. My thighs are beginning to burn from crouching so long, so I wait till the music builds to a chorus and then I shift to lie flat, wedged in. I stare at a ceiling that is now bathed in light. The bass beats through the floorboards into my flesh. And then as the sound of their voices murmuring through the music filters down to me, I begin to relax. They are close to one another. Their voices are soft and intimate.

At least they are not on *this* sofa.

The album continues to play.

Naming birds in our tree
When you were with me
Listing all the things they'd see …

Then that same hiss, like waves throwing up surf. Every few minutes a spray of words reaches me, distinct before ebbing away.

'Wait,' she says. 'Let me flip it over. Still haven't worked out where that smell's coming from.'

A few seconds of silence. I hold my breath before the music comes again and I can breathe again. That smell – does she mean me?

Another song plays but now gives me a rush of memory. From *before*. Grace.

We were in the bowl of a boat. It was dark but there was warmth in the air. It was summer and we had found a small rowing boat on the edge of the Thames as we were walking back from somewhere near Kingston. Laughing, we dipped the boat gently into the water and kicked off from the bank quietly. She had a half-drunk bottle of rosé in her hand and giggled at the idea that we were in someone else's boat. *Stealing*, she said. We weren't stealing but borrowing, I told her as seriously I could. And she sang it then, that song.

There's trouble on the uptrack
And trouble going back
And quite clearly not one train will move today ...

'Your train is ready to depart, ma'am,' I said, mock-bowing.

I close my eyes and the rhythm rocks and lulls me back and forth. I weave between flashes of what might be dreams or some long-gone reality until I drift further and further away. When I open my eyes again, the couple are still murmuring but the light has now dimmed to an orange flicker across the ceiling. A warmth begins to rise over me and I realise that somebody has lit a fire.

All I can do is wait this out. At some point soon, the couple will leave. Then I can slip out of the door, along the hall and out again into the air.

This song. It's *that* song I think. The one that has something to do with a film we watched once. The one she liked. Her face now comes into my mind but I clench my eyes to shut her out. Not now, I can't indulge this now. I need my wits about me. I have to be ready to move.

The record has ended and is hissing in its orbit. As soon as they go, I'll go.

'Not again,' he says when, after a pause, the music starts up once more.

'So grouchy!' she says and laughs. In my imagination, she is young and blonde and is nestled under his arm.

'Not again, I said,' says the man. There's an undercurrent of something, bristling.

'Just once more,' she replies and her laugh tinkles under the bristle.

A beat.

'It's like you deliberately ignore me,' he says. 'Fuck's sake.' Then a scrape as the record is wrenched from the player.

'Careful! You know how much—'

'How much what?' The wine is in evidence in his vowels.

'Nothing. Forget it.'

There is a sharp snapping sound and a light thud.

'What did you do?' she exclaims. Her voice is shrill. Indignant.

'Accident,' he says bitterly.

'You broke it!' She shifts on the sofa. 'You broke it. Idiot!'

'I'm an idiot? It's a fucking record. Get over it. I'll get you another one.'

'Yes, but it wouldn't be *that* record,' she says, her voice dropping at the end.

'What? You mean it wouldn't be *his*?'

She sighs, deflating as if she is tired of this.

'Oh, just forget it,' she says, and as she does her voice trails off, as if she's moved across to the dining area. She seems disembodied without the sound of her feet to tether her voice.

'No, no, no. Not forget it,' he says, his voice pursuing her, breathy and urgent.

'Get off me.' Her voice is distant. She is deep in the other end of the double room, from the sound of it.

I roll quietly on to my side so that I can look out into the room beyond the edge of the leather sofa. The area at the far end is in shade. The dying light from the fire can't reach it but I can still make out their legs. He's wearing suit trousers. She's in stockings or tights. I look up but the dining table is still obscuring a lot of what would be visible. I strain until I can see flickers of movement.

He's holding her by the wrist but she is tugging it away. There's no fear in her demeanour. She knows him. She's safe.

'Precious fucking boyfriend record,' he says. Some of what he is saying doesn't reach me. 'Knew all that time – keeping – the things in there – quiet just like—'

'Oh, for goodness' sake,' she retorts. 'You're drunk.'

I blink away spots appearing before me. She says other things that I don't catch.

Her voice is sharp and rises to the ceiling and then scatters around me like fallen glass.

'You know how I feel about – getting my father – and at this time – when …' His voice rising and falling, makes its way to me in incomplete packets. If I could only hear more.

'If you sorted out your issues, maybe you wouldn't—'

Then more noise.

I crane my neck for a better view. I see a cloud of dark hair.

'Shut. Up,' he says.

He has leaned her back over the table, and is covering her mouth with his hand. I can see her struggling, fighting to get upright, fighting to get his weight off her body. Fighting to get his hand off her mouth.

My heart starts to race but I am paralysed. *Stop now!* I say under my breath. *Enough.*

Her legs kick out but reach only air.

Don't! She can't breathe.

Her voice is trying to escape from her lungs but he smothers it, pressing his hands on her face. I have to get up now and *do* something, but I am rooted to my place. I'm not supposed to be here. I've convinced even myself I am not here. And yet I am. I have to get up. I have to run and pull him off before …

I take a breath and force myself to my knees. From here I can see that she is failing. Her face and her neck are changing colour. Her hair falls softly around her face but something about it is grotesque. I will some movement into my legs but they are stuck.

I cough. It distracts him but then, just as he turns around to look, I drop back behind the sofa, unable to hold my ground. I am terrified of being found here in this house, but she has to be more important than that and I am furious that I can't control my instincts. But I see that he's released her now. He turns back towards her, then the shock of what he has done – *is doing* – seems to hit him. She gasps, clutching her throat, and levers herself off the table, breathing hard.

He seems to have forgotten what distracted him and is now holding her gently by the forearms.

'I'm so sorry, darling. I'm so … I'm drunk. And you just – you know how much I hate being compared to him. If you hadn't—'

'*Me?*' she exclaims. 'Me? You nearly killed me! What the hell's wrong with you—'

I peer round the edge of the leather sofa in time to see her spin around and launch a flat hand at his face. As soon as the blow lands, almost before the sound ripples to my ears, he reacts, as if bound by the laws of physics – every force has an equal and opposite reaction. The moment her hand whips his skin, he swings his fist into her face. They are like two table tennis players who play just one shot each. It is that quick.

Her head snaps back with a crack. She freezes then. Her face is a pale, perfectly still surprise. My heart stops. My head pounds, and in that gap when all things still remain possible, my life flashes before me in a kaleidoscope.

Bright light moments. Heavy sadness. Regrets, mainly.

My mind gathers as many strands of my life as it can in that divided infinite sub-second, like it's fleeing from a burning building. My last possessions.

The woman's knees buckle as if the bones in her legs have vaporised. She drops. Then there is another dull crack as her body pulls the back of her head down hard on the edge of the table. And then, finally, another thud as she lands scattered on the floor.

I can't believe what has happened. I'm cemented in place, supine, like her, the air trapped in my lungs. He is stuck in his frame too, the man. He stands over her body, holding a hand to his mouth. A heartbeat, maybe two and then he's moving again. He falls to his knees and appears to be whispering her name. I can't hear clearly from here and all I can think is *shit*, what just happened? This can't be happening. I start to pat myself down, getting ready to move but then I realise I can't. I can't take my eyes off him and what he's doing. He's stroking her cheek gently and calling what must be her name over and over, desperately. *Chelle, Chelle, Chelle.* And then he is tapping her cheek harder with his palm, but her head lolls. He looms over her for a second before he puts the side of his head to her mouth, listening for breath. Five, six, seven seconds he is there, searching, before he's up again. Then his hands cloak his face as he lets out a scream.

A beat and then he moves.

I see him from my place and he is frantic. His arms and eyes dart out as far as they can reach. His movements are erratic, random almost. He rushes back into my part of the room and swipes up his shoes before returning to the dining room to pick up something that chinks. Keys, maybe. Now he's back, rummaging, and all the while I want him to just leave so that this can be over. He has a jacket in his arms. He runs back into the dining area before circling round again where I see him stoop out of view. Then he loops back to the far end of the room, with a glass which he then manages to drop. It shatters and he swears before gathering the pieces up with his hands into his jacket. I see it all from the leather-edge of my hiding place.

A panic seizes me. I should stop him. But it's too late now. The police should be called. I turn on to my front, preparing to get up but something keeps stopping me. I don't know this man. How can I know what he is capable of? I cut off the thought at its roots. It's me I'm terrified of. I know what I am capable of. And yet I have not moved.

He stands over the woman, his head dropped on to his chest. He is muttering something but I can't make it out. Then his head snaps up. He pulls a handkerchief out and begins to wipe a bottle that is now in his hand. When he finishes he places it carefully on the table, studying it for a second before changing his mind and picking it up again. He considers for a moment and then pours some of the contents over the woman's body before crouching next to her and putting the neck of the bottle in her hand. He straightens again and looks critically at the scene. His frantic quality has gone now and in its place a kind of coldness has descended.

He steps back. Looks. Then takes another step back. Looks again. He leaves. The door at the end of the corridor slams. As it does, at last, I too am slammed, back into existence.

I am here in this room with a woman who is dead.

5

Tuesday

The blood flows back into my legs as I step out from behind the chesterfield. The room seems different. A tableau altered by two or three brushstrokes. There on the other sofa is a pale, soft pink jacket, draped across the backrest. A record sleeve is laid carefully on the floor and not five feet away is the record itself, split in two. The record player is hissing determinedly, as if crying for attention.

The pounding starts again in my head and with it my heart begins to thud. I run over to the woman and reach for her neck, hoping for a tiny beat of life. The skin is still warm under my fingertips but despite that I know as soon as I touch her that she is dead. I should leave because this is now a crime scene, a murder scene, but something about her holds me back. I stand to look at her. Her mahogany hair makes her seem alive, the way it covers her face with curls. Her white shirt is spattered in places, making a map in red wine. I want to neaten her up, straighten her skirt – twisted, like her legs.

The silence in the room begins to make itself heavy. I have to leave. I look around, just as the man did, and suddenly I am in his loop, riven with his urgency and guilt. I have to escape. I cannot be here with a dead body. I mean, look at me, I'm a homeless man, I'm an easy person to point fingers at. I run back to the sofa and pick up my coat and shoes. I look around desperately for anything else I might have left. But I have nothing, just this, what I stand in and what I have in my hands. I almost step on something and bend to pick it up but I mustn't disturb the scene.

I take a last look her. She is, *was*, beautiful from what I can see of her face, shrouded as it is in reddish-brown curls. As I turn to the door, my eyes fill and I don't know what to do. The tears run down my cheeks. I didn't know her but I could have. I might have liked her.

I race through the hallway, surprising myself once again at the mirror. Me, still. But changed somehow. Younger? No, less distinct, perhaps. I pause and then run back into the room to wipe down the things that I have touched. The handle, the sofa. There's nothing else that I can remember so I shut the door behind me and wipe that handle down too, all with the edge of my damp coat.

My heart skitters as I stand on the cold tiles in my bare feet. The police, I think, if the guy calls the police, and I am found here in this state, I will be undone. I'm sure I can hear a siren in the distance. I must move.

I unravel my coat, letting my shoes drop to the Victorian tile. There is the cold of something hard and flat against my skin but I pull my coat over it, wrapping myself up. Its dampness and weight gives me the sensation of walking through mud. I pull open the door with the edge of my sleeve and I am outside. The cold night air washes over my face and into my lungs.

I breathe once, then, keeping my head low, I run. I have to hide. A man like me knows about hiding, but tonight I have to hide from myself because I can sense it coming upon me. A feeling of claustrophobia, of meeting myself in my head, and when that happens, I'll have to leave myself, become nobody. I'm not hiding from the police, it's not that at all.

Before. Before, when I was like you, I had your problems and your conveniences. I know you think that we spontaneously appear, caked in dirt, and that we just materialise on the street, but we don't. Remember, we bring ourselves here from some warm place. We only come when the balance weighs in favour of leaving, when the problems of staying outweigh the rest. I was like you, before. For example, I used to have a brother.

I stop for a breath as I round Hyde Park Corner Tube. I drop my head and hurry towards Westminster – Green Zone – each stride stretching sinew so that I can cover as much distance as possible in the wet.

I had a brother. Have. Had?

As I hit Pimlico the traffic begins to thin. This is London so it never spreads so thinly that it has the feeling of winding down. There is only a shift in patterns. The tempo is reduced by the tiniest fraction. The urgency is less. Commerce is plying its night shift where the demands are different. I remember the thrust of commerce, how it felt under one's arm, pushing forward.

Memory and history are not the same thing.

When I remember my life before, I am really reimagining it, in flashes, in tiny abstract glimpses. And in that memory, I compose my own rhythm, close enough to match the original percussion, but far enough to be no better than an improvisation inspired by it. But in the end, I always wash up in the same place with the same question. How did it all begin?

Dad, for instance. Could you say, it all began with him?

'Xander,' he said once. 'You're so bright. Why do you have to be so disruptive?'

He spoke to me, away from Rory. He convinced himself it was so that he didn't embarrass me, but I knew the truth was that he didn't know what I was capable of saying.

'Maths is boring,' I told him. His brown eyes, large and cow-like, made me despise him.

'You need the maths to understand the physics,' he said.

But Mum overheard this and hovered close.

'Proust. Try Proust, if you're bored,' she said.

Only an academic would think of saying something like that to a child, I think now.

As I step on to the bridge, the sound of police sirens makes my heart flutter. If they are racing to her, they're too late. And I wonder then about that. I was too slow to affect anything. I was much too slow. If I had done something, maybe she would be alive.

The pain asserts itself again and is now a cage over my head. For a minute I wonder if my mind is playing tricks on me. Did I really witness a woman being killed? And then I think of it. Yes. The crack, the thud and spilled blood. I know what's coming next. It's knocking. It announces its arrival so mundanely, the guilt. I tense my body against all that guilt, coming for me.

Having crossed the bridge, I'm now skirting the back alleys and cobbled side roads that my body knows intimately. In the Blue Zone there are squats where I could stay but I don't want to. Homeless communities are everywhere and I know about the sorts of lives that people have survived. I see how the chaos seems to cling to them. I can't take up their share of space. And I know they'll try to exert a kinship over me, and I'll want to tell them to leave me alone, that we are not the same. That above all I did this to myself, *for* myself.

My immediate viable choices then are to find a dry space in the park or under a bridge, or to walk all night until it becomes light and then sleep. It is halfway to dawn. The adrenaline leaving my body has caused other chemicals to bring on sleep. I pass a navy metal stand, piled high with free newspapers, and pick up four *Metro*s without breaking my stride.

I skirt around the Elephant and Castle and take a seat on a bus – the driver turns a blind eye. There are no more than a few passengers, each of them in his own pocket of life, misery or joy. My left eye is still misty but is now beginning to burn. I press it gently against the cold window to soothe it and see that the rain which had let up has started again.

I don't have a clear idea of where I'm going and begin to drift in and out of sleep. Then as the bus shudders over some pothole, I'm jolted from sleep into another oblivion and I remember the house again and that a woman was killed. And that I was there.

The night spins around me. This pain, this rain, the tiredness. A swell of nausea builds and makes me retch. I have to find somewhere soon. Just to rest. I press the bell again and again for the driver to stop but he drives on. 'Just let me off,' I shout. He glances in a mirror and finally he opens the door.

I find a doorway on the street and lean my weight against it. The space between action and inaction stalls my thoughts. I can see her face in front of me, frozen as it was then. Still. If I had acted she might be alive and yet I wonder if I would have been. Or him, if he would have been.

There is a drip from the ceiling of my tiny patch of shelter that lands in maddening spots on my knee. I separate my legs to make room for it but then it taps on the tile. The rhythm begins to soothe me and I fall into a kind of trance. Sleep paws until I am asleep.

6

Wednesday

One Friday each month, Dad, who was a physicist, would sit us around a table and set us a random topic of discussion. He'd listen and occasionally mediate, and then at the end he'd hand out a prize for the best ideas. Answers, he told us, weren't important. To think, that was the important thing. The prizes weren't particularly exciting by today's standards – an Airfix model airplane once, a small electric motor and some circuits another time. Once there was a skateboard – that was mis-judged. But the prizes, like all prizes, were icons – declarations of superiority.

Of the two of us, Rory was the genius. I was the impressionist – a fake. He had the beautiful brain. I had the right arrangement in my head, but it didn't produce the same music. And Dad, though he loved us both, loved perfection and purity most of all. He loved maths. When he saw numerical puzzles, he some-how saw the Universe in a way that I couldn't – but Rory could. Rory was a pure mind. But he was younger than me, so for a while I could mask the symptoms of his genius. I remember how urgent it was that I hold him back to give myself a chance of winning something. Maybe just love.

The Fermi paradox: that was the one, now I think back, that changed everything. You'll know the one, Fermi, a physicist, asked about extraterrestrial life: *If there are so many trillions of planets in the observable universe and billions of Earth-like planets among them, where are all the people? And why haven't we heard from them?*

When he set the discussion, Dad played at being the casual benign professor, as if the questions spontaneously occurred to him. But I'd known for some time that they came from the back of a monthly physics magazine. So I occasionally went to the local library when the new issue came out and had a quick preview. And one day there it was: Fermi. Rory loved space and astrophysics and there was no way of beating him without a head start. So, I cheated. For a week I read everything I could on the subject at the school library, and even spoke to the physics teacher after lessons.

The day of the test came and I remember Rory had been up in his room doing some computer programing. I had had to call him twice, to get him to come down.

'So,' Dad said when Rory floated in. 'Where are all the aliens?' He held up the prize. A lock knife with a dark, polished wood handle. I salivated as Rory rubbed his chin, oblivious.

Though there are plenty of Earth-like planets – enough to guarantee that there's intelligent life out there – the Universe is so vast that the likelihood of finding them is vanishingly small. Aliens living, say, only ten million light years away would need to travel at the speed of light for ten million years before they reached us. Which means they'd have to leave their home planets before humans came into existence. And then head over to us on a huge cosmic gamble.

'But what if they mastered interstellar travel?' Rory asked.

I smiled.

'Not possible,' I said. 'The amount of energy, even if somehow there was a way around the limits on the speed of light, you would need – would be – well – astronomical.'

'But an advanced civilisation, with technology expanding in accordance with Moore's Law, could tap the energy.'

'What?' I sneered. 'Fusion?'

'Well, maybe fusion. It doesn't matter. If you could harvest all of the energy on the planet, that would probably be enough.'

'Not enough. Not if you calculate the rate at which you'd be using the energy and multiply it by the distances you'd be covering.' I knew this. I'd researched it. Type I civilisations. That's what he had stumbled on, just from *thinking*.

Dad smiled and then winked at me.

Rory scratched his head.

'Could harness the energy of your star. That would be enough.'

'What?'

'A planet would need a star to sustain life. If you could collect all of the sun's power, that would be enough.'

And now through pure thought he'd stumbled on Type II civilisations. I stopped smiling.

'You couldn't do that. It's impossible,' I said.

Dad rubbed his hands and smiled at Rory.

'Or is it?' Dad said, arching an eyebrow at Rory.

Rory raised his eyebrow with his finger. It annoyed me that he couldn't do it without physically pushing it with his finger.

'Wait. What if you, I don't know, built a thing around the sun that captured all of the energy, or most of it? Then you could have something that self-replicated using the sun's energy.'

I pushed my chair back along the tile and stood up. I gave him a hate-filled look and left. Later, after I'd accused him of cheating and he'd convinced me that he hadn't, he said, 'Statistically speaking, the difference between winning and losing is that over the longer term, losers give up. You give up too quickly,' he added plainly. He wasn't being mean or smug or irritating; he was just saying it, as an observation.

'And that's how you win, is it?' I snapped.

'I don't care about winning. You can have the knife,' he said, holding it out to me.

'Then what is it?'

'It's solving the equation. Sometimes you have to keep going to solve it. You give up. There's no fight in you.'

There's a tapping on the crown of my head. It is sharp, icy, as if needles are being driven in. My eyes flicker but I'm in the warmth of a dream that draws me back.

'Okay, fella,' a voice says now. My eyes open reluctantly and I am drawn from one place to another, colder one. A figure looms heavily in the doorway and for a moment I feel as if I am about to be attacked.

Static. A flash of fluorescence on the sleeve.

'PC 375 X-ray Tango. Calling for assistance on Lordship Lane East, Dulwich. LAS.'

The police.

My heart begins to race. Somehow, they have found her dead body and have already connected me to her.

'I didn't do it,' I say to him. He puts his hand out in the direction of my face and continues to speak into his shoulder.

'And uniform. Roger that. Sir, we have paramedics on the way. Can you give me your name?'

'What? Xander Shute.' As soon as the words leave my mouth, I curse. If I'd been even a little more awake, I would have given a false name. But he's caught me under the vapour of sleep.

'Okay, Xander. Just have a seat where you were and keep your head up. They'll be along any minute.'

I try to blink some sense into my brain.

'Paramedics?' I say at last. The sun has just begun to paint light into the sky and the gold gives everything a dreamlike tint.

'Yes, sir. You've had a nasty injury there. Just keep your face turned up,' he says and gently eases my head back.

The bottle. The idiot who threw the bottle. The cut must have started bleeding. I touch my head gently, fingers hovering in my hair. The tips come back red. I struggle to my feet but then the world begins to spin, forcing me back down.

'Officer. Wait,' I call out to his luminescent back.

He dips his face into the radio on his shoulder. 'Just sit still. Try not to move, sir,' he says, making a half-turn away.

'Really,' I say. 'I don't need paramedics. I'll be on my way in a second.'

He continues to mutter into his shoulder, holding a palm out towards me to pause me. Then when he has finished his call, he crouches over me.

'They're on their way now. I'll just take some details while we wait. Address?' he asks and then, catching up to the dirt and the tatters, he adds, 'Or is there somewhere you can stay?'

I shake my head and he ticks a box on a pocketbook form he is holding.

'Date of birth?'

'Thirty, seven, sixty-nine.'

'Family? Next of kin?'

'No. Mother's dead. Father too,' I say.

'Okay, fella,' he says and then takes a serious look at my head. 'What happened there then?'

I stumble around in my head trying to remember. It just happened, but I can't immediately catch it. There was a man. A bottle.

'Tripped,' I say. The woman in the house obscures everything else, but I can't tell in this spinning state whether I have done something I need to hide. I could have saved her. Does this make me guilty of some kind of manslaughter?

He writes something in his book, licking the tip of the pen as he does.

'Where?' he says.

I straighten up against the door to get a better look at him. He is young. His face has the glow of youth.

'Where did I trip? I have no idea.'

He looks at me suspiciously.

'In the park,' I say then. 'Hyde Park.'

He smiles a little and rubs his hair. The blond is gold in this light.

'How did it happen?'

'I told you. I fell,' I say, feeling my temper rising.

He swallows and looks at me again, pen poised.

'How though?' he says. 'What made you fall?'

'I don't know. It was wet. I fell.'

'What did you fall on?'

'The ground.' I narrow my eyes at his persistence. 'Does it matter?'

'On the grass?' he continues.

'Yes,' I say. 'Look. I'm feeling better now, Officer. I think I want to go,' I say and make to get to my feet. I catch the eye of a young woman as she passes. She is no more than curious – probably on her way home after a party – but still I feel the connection she is creating with her passing glance.

'Hold up, there's the paramedics now,' he says, and waves at the ambulance flashing towards us. He helps me back to the ground and continues with the questions as the vehicle draws to a halt. 'I don't get it,' he says then, sniffing the air.

My heart misses a beat. 'What? Get what?'

'How did you cut yourself by falling on grass?'

I close my eyes. 'I fell on the grass but I hit myself on the corner of a bench on the way down,' I say. And as I say that, the image flashes into my mind of the woman falling, her knees collapsing beneath her weight. Her head smashing into the corner of the table. He notes down my answer before going over to introduce himself to the paramedic team. They are a man and a woman, their demeanour curiously casual. They seem too upbeat for ambulance people.

'Hello, Xander, is it?' the woman says brightly, coming next to me. Her eyes join her smile so that I am drawn to them a little – green flecks in brown irises. 'Just going to ask you a few questions. Do you know your name?'

I sigh. 'Why do I need to know my name when you know it already?'

'I'll put you down as conscious responsive,' she says brightly and starts to check my pulse with a plastic clip she attaches to my index finger.

'Well, we're just going to run you up the road for a quick once-over at the hospital. With head injuries it's always better to be safe.'

I pull my finger from the clip and get to my feet. All this commotion, the flashing lights, the noise, it is all making me queasy, dizzy.

'Do you need my consent?'

'Yes,' she says. 'But the sensible thing for you would be to—'

'Great,' I say, wrapping my coat around me. 'Then I'm not going.'

7

Wednesday

I sit perched on the edge of a hospital bed as a nurse swabs around my head. She disappears and then returns with a small surgical-looking pack. Her eyes are so blue. If I had managed a few more steps before my legs gave way again, I wouldn't be here.

'Just going to pop some stitches in that for you,' she says. Her tone is chirpy, chirrupy even; designed to neutralise fear. 'Hopefully, it won't scar too much, my love. Just hold still. There.'

'Thank you,' I say. 'It wasn't necessary really.'

'Actually, that was a bleeder, that one there. You'd have got it all over your clothes,' she says. By the time her thoughts have caught up with her voice, it's too late. She pretends that my clothes would have been worse for a bit of bloodstaining.

My jeans were in decent condition when I pulled them out of a recycle bin at the supermarket. Clothes seem to be turned out nearly new these days – rejected just to make cupboard space. This large red-checked shirt wasn't missing a button when I found it. And this grey jumper, ridiculously, is cashmere, from my life before. I keep it because it's warm – there's no room for sentiment. My greatcoat is from a charity shop. It was a bitter winter, colder than this one when I went in with a little begged money, looking for socks. I came out with this coat, heavy, woollen. The staff took pity on me and I was too cold to be proud.

'So have you got far to be getting home to?' she says as she works away.

She stops suddenly and closes her eyes slowly.

'Well, the world's my mattress,' I say, as brightly as I can. I wince and the paper on this gurney tears as I shift on it.

'I'm so sorry,' she says. 'Is there nowhere you can go, for a night even?' she adds as she finishes up.

I slip off the bed and rub my hands. I want to shake hers but there is so much dirt on my skin that I daren't. I see a tiny basin in the corner and go over to wash my hands, turning the levered taps with my elbows. Brown water streams on to the white porcelain.

'Thank you for this,' I say, pointing to my head. 'I'll be fine now. I've got a friend I can stay with who lives nearby.' I did once have a friend nearby.

He is smiling – Seb. We were throwing a frisbee across an ancient, serious courtyard. His arms were brown from a summer at the family villa. When he threw the disc, it floated high and then coasted past me, sliding to a stop at two pairs of feet. Nina and Grace. It seems too long ago to reach.

I close my eyes.

'You might feel a touch groggy for a day or two but there's unlikely to be any lasting damage,' the nurse says and then I'm back here. In a hospital bed.

I wipe my eyes with my sleeve. The woman from the house fights her way into my head, scarlet blotting her white shirt.

'Ooh, careful there,' she says. 'You'll pull away the stitches.'

'Oh,' I say, sitting up. 'You stitched my eye?' I feather my brow with the tips of my fingers.

'Yes. Don't worry. You might have some gaps here and there in your memory. But it'll come good, don't fret yourself.' She smiles at me.

'I should have done something though,' I say.

She looks quizzically at me.

'I let her die. I watched as she was murdered,' I say.

She walks to the door. 'I'll just see if there's a doctor about for that scan,' she says and steps out.

I glance into the corridor. A different police officer from the one who had brought me is there. His face has the expression of a man used to killing time, scrolling through a smartphone with the expression of a child. He shifts in his bulky police gear as he sees me.

'Done,' I say, peering out.

'Oh,' he says, standing. 'Good. Do you mind if I ask you a couple of questions?'

I return a look that must be more alarmed than I'd intended.

'Just for my notebook. Have to account for the time that's all,' he says, tapping his notebook.

There is a TV screen above me, playing some old show. A wisp of music snakes out. *Ma belle amie. You were the beat of a drum and a symphony.*

And that music, through some path I can't untangle, takes me back to Grace and when I first saw her. It was Freshers' week. Arriving at the college, I had the sensation of having finally sloughed off a battered old skin. There was no sadness in leaving Mum, Dad and Rory behind. In no time at all I was at a desk signing up for a student union pass. I had just put the pass into my pocket and turned around when I saw her. Just there, standing behind me.

'Grace Mackintosh,' she said. The person at the desk checked her name on a long printed sheet and frowned. She repeated her surname and he found it.

'Oh,' he said, looking over at me. 'You're in the same class.'

I froze. She smiled at me and all I could do was stare at her, a white-blonde sun. That was how it felt, as if I was being bathed in her radiance.

'Hi,' she said, 'I'm Grace. This is Nina.' Nina was the darkness to Grace's light. Sharpened slate, to Grace's softened curve.

'Hi,' I said. 'I'm Xander. Xander Shute.' And once again I couldn't move.

'Xander Shute?'

I look up.

'I am arresting you on suspicion of assault occasioning grievous bodily harm. You do not have to say anything but it may harm your defence if you fail to mention when questioned something which you later rely on in court. Anything you do say may be given in evidence.'

'What?' I say.

'Sorry, sir, I am going to have to place you in handcuffs for your own protection.'

I recoil but his movements are so practised that my resistance is futile. The cuffs are heavier than I had imagined they would be. As they go on, the cold steel makes me shiver.

'I am now going to search you. Do you have anything on you that could cause either of us any injury?'

'What?' I say again. 'No.'

He gets down into a crouch and begins to pat around my legs moving slowly upwards.

He stops. He takes some surgical gloves from somewhere and puts them on. I do not know what he thinks he has found. My lighter?

'Charlie,' he says down the corridor to another police officer I have just noticed. 'Get me a weapons tube. I've got something.'

My heart skips. The knife. The old drunk's knife.

'That's not mine,' I say, too quickly. 'I found it in the park.'

A few minutes later the other officer returns with a Perspex tube. He deposits the knife into it. Evidence. How have they connected me to the woman's murder so soon?

'What's going on?' I say, but even as I say it I know something is wrong. *Grievous bodily harm.*

She must be alive. Still.

8

Wednesday

In the car on the way to the police station, I go over the events, scrabbling for details. A woman dead. Not dead though now, but alive. But harmed. Grievously. I try and think, late twenties, was she? Thirty? Dark hair, in curls. She was wearing a pink skirt, I remember now how it twisted around her waist. And that white shirt, the spilled wine, making maps on her body. A broken record. But the man who was there is more important right now. I'll need to give a description of him with clear details so that when I deny it, it has the ring of truth – or if not truth, then plausibility. Plausibility: so much more important than simple, ordinary, mundane truth. Especially for a person like me.

I cast my mind back to him. It was difficult to judge from my vantage point on the floor, but I guess him to be about five feet eleven? Six feet? Trousers. He had trousers, of course, he had trousers but what were they like? Suit trousers I think, dark grey maybe. But what else? The details elude me and I screw my eyes hard in remembrance, but his face is lost to me.

'You okay there, sir?' the officer in the passenger seat says – the younger one.

I nod but keep my eyes shut. If there is memory to squeeze out, I must do it now. The police will be setting traps. They will roll out barbed questions and watch as my words catch on their sharp points. The car turns a corner, sending me rocking against the fabric seats.

What did he look like?

By the time we pull to a halt, I have gathered no more than a few wisps of memory. I remember her hair, the curls and how they were arranged across her face, covering part of it. The rooms too, the quality of light in them, the precise texture of that silk carpet. This is uselessly committed to memory, but him? Thirties maybe, early thirties, late twenties? Brown hair? Possibly, but who could tell in that light? I was on the floor for most of it. He was obscured by the edge of my sofa.

At Paddington Green Police Station, I am processed in a way that seems casual: my fingerprints rolled lazily on to sticky film, photographs taken without ceremony or flash. The contents of my pockets: lighter – one, cigarette ends – four, pound coins – three, belt – one, laces – two, key – one, placed into a brown paper bag with a window at the top and then locked into a cupboard. Then I am introduced to the custody sergeant and shown to my cell. It happens, all of this, in a smear.

Minutes or hours pass – in a room without windows, it is impossible to tell. It is deliberate, it seems to me, this sensory deprivation. There's only hardness in here, and smoothness. Concrete floors and walls and this concrete bench for a bed. Steel lavatory. Iron door. Me. The feeling it creates is one of separation from reality. Nothing in nature, out there in the world, is so hard to the touch and so devoid of texture.

It is disorientating to be in a room alone. Since I left home in favour of solitude and freedom, I haven't had walls. Whatever safety they once provided is a memory. There's no safety here, there's only the rationing of space.

I hear a rattling at the door and I jump to my feet. Two officers enter the cell, carrying bags and a roll of paper. One sets the paper on the ground as the other begins to open a plastic bag with the word 'EVIDENCE' written in blue across it.

'We are seizing your clothes as evidence.'

I watch as the officer with the bags holds one open.

'Coat,' says the other and mumbles a number which he writes into a record book.

I stare at him in disbelief but he is not putting up with any nonsense. He just shakes the bag at me impatiently until I take my coat off and roll it into the open sack. Before long all of my clothes are arranged in plastic sacks on the floor. I stare at my arms. I'm not used to seeing my uncovered flesh. It's bright in patches and then suddenly dark with dirt. The smell drifting off my skin is so strong that one of the men covers his mouth with his hand.

'What am I supposed to wear?' I say.

The one with the bags hands me a pair of grey jogging bottoms and a sweatshirt along with a pair of black plimsolls.

'Am I supposed to go out into the world like this? Without a coat?'

They say nothing. They simply gather up my clothes and give me a sheet of paper explaining the circumstances in which I might get them back. They leave.

I sit staring and willing the door to open. I have to leave here soon, the pressure is building. Then minutes pass and an officer's voice leans in to ask me about a meal and a hot drink. More time drifts by until another officer comes by to advise me about my rights to a solicitor.

'Have you had a chance to read that leaflet? Do you want to take up the offer of free legal advice?'

'Yes,' I say to him.

'Anyone in particular?' he says, plunging his meaty arms into his pockets.

'No.'

'Then I'll get the duty,' he says and leaves on soft-soled shoes.

I remember how I did nothing, just stood by, watching, when she died. Even if they believe me, I'm guilty of that. They won't take any account of the fact that I was afraid of what I could have done to him, if I had let go of myself. Whatever condition she might now be in from the delay – from the hours wastefully passing, while I was running – that was me. I caused it.

Another bang of metal brings me back to myself. The door swings open to present what must be the duty solicitor. She is slight, with dark auburn hair tied back in a high ponytail. She mutters something about an interview and although I haven't fully absorbed what she is saying, I nod. She has bitten nails. Something about them, those nails, bleeds away any confidence I might have had in her. That and the faded suit.

'I don't want you!' I say at her.

'Sorry?' she says. The northern vowels make her sound slow and even as I am thinking that, I know that it's unfair. She looks at me again, confused.

'I don't want you,' I repeat.

'Sorry? What?'

'I don't want you. I don't want you. I. DON'T. WANT. YOU!'

She stands back, a little shocked.

'Fine,' she says and bangs on the door until it is opened. 'Good luck then,' she says to me, not unkindly. Then as she is let out, she says to the officer, 'He's on his own.'

I stare at the door that has just closed. A scratched PIG on the blue paint makes me suddenly laugh.

Moments later, an officer opens the door and nods at me.

'Interview,' he says.

My heart starts beating again. I haven't been able to distil the events into any order. What am I supposed to tell them, that I lay cringing in a corner? If I come clean about being there, what does that say about me? That I am a man who is not above breaking in and being somewhere uninvited? That I violated someone's home and lurked in its dark corners? What kind of man will I become by admitting that?

What kind of man am I if I don't admit that?

9

Wednesday

When he was fourteen, Rory won a prize – a real one. It was the equivalent of a child's Nobel prize for science. I remember seeing him walk on to the stage of a university lecture hall, a small huddled figure in that vast space. He smiled coyly as he shook the Dean's hand and I looked on, slowly warming through with jealousy until I was glowing white. It was a prize I was too old for. People clapped. A man spoke about the 'completely innovative' approach to one of the world's most complex theoretical physics questions. The maths in it was difficult but the truth was that he was so bright that he could slice straight into the physics while the others were still stuck on the numbers. But that wasn't the only reason he'd won. It had been *my* solution, from one of Dad's monthly debates. And though I'd harvested it from some other physicists I'd been researching in answer to the debate, Rory didn't know that. As far as he knew he'd just stolen my answer.

I was made to go along to the presentation. Afterwards, Dad had promised us, him, a steak at a new South American steakhouse. Later, once the steak had been eaten and he'd been slapped on the shoulder by Dad – later, once we were back at home watching Dad drink whisky and Mum wine – later, once the trophy had been nudged into centre spot on the mantel, Rory, to whom I'd said nothing all evening, walked up to the fireplace and picked up the trophy and placed it at my feet.

'This is yours,' he said, avoiding my eye. 'Dad,' he said then, still looking at the floor. 'This is his. It was his answer.'

Dad nodded and took a sip of whisky. 'It belongs to you both. Not for the science – but because you improve each other.'

I tried to rationalise what he'd done. He was younger. He was allowed to make mistakes like this. I might have done the same in his position. In fact I never reminded myself that I'd cheated him. Or that he'd have won anyway. Instead I sat with the trophy at my feet, ashamed of it and me and him all at once. Hours later, Dad was sleeping in his chair, snoring, his glass balanced on his chest. Mum, watching Dad closely, put down her glass and came to me. She took my face in her hands and then turned to do the same to Rory. Her hair was greying, I noticed, and she had started wearing her glasses permanently then.

'I won't leave you,' she said. 'Not ever.'

I opened my mouth to say something but the words wouldn't form.

'You don't have to say anything,' she said, smiling sadly.

'... but it may harm your defence if you fail to mention when questioned anything you later rely on in court. Anything you do say may be given in evidence. Do you understand?'

I'm here again with a jolt. I nod. I wrap my arms around my body and huddle. If I create enough warmth, it might help with the pain.

'For the tape,' he says.

I haven't seen this officer before. There is something in his eyes that telegraphs dullness. He blinks slowly as if the wheels are moving through sludge. But there's also something else there, humanity maybe? Suppressed, but there, blistering the skin, waiting to break free but being held back by stupidity. I wait, expecting the bubble to burst so I can be honest with him. But I don't know if I can just say to him that I did not attack her. That I only watched. That yes, I failed to act, but I did nothing. That that was my crime and I'm prepared to suffer the consequences of that inaction.

'You have to say it out loud, for the tape.'

'Yes,' I say. 'I understand the caution.'

'Do you know why you have been arrested?'

'Yes,' I say.

The officer looks unsurprised by this. Maybe everybody who is arrested knows why they have been taken.

'Tell me then. Why do you think you've been arrested?' he says, then looks across at his partner.

I have barely registered her presence. She sits at his side, hair pulled back from her face. I'm not sure what her official title is but it feels as if she is in deference to him, this man who she must know can't keep up with her. The intelligence in her eyes shows the advantage she has over him.

'The murder. Or the attempt, however you want to define it. But I didn't do it,' I say, looking at my hands. I shrug in my clothes and suddenly, in this confined space, I feel the urge to run. The room is too small for three of us really. It's tiny, just enough space for the table and chairs. There's certainly no room to spread.

'Okay, well, we are here to listen. We aren't making any judgements, are we, Rochelle? Just tell us what happened from your point of view.'

Rochelle? I wonder. Might that have been *her* name too? The name brings a rush of familiarity. Perhaps I heard it, that night. Was that the name he had been calling out? Over and over.

'I didn't do it. But I was there. I saw it happen,' I say.

'You saw what happen?' she asks. Her eyes narrow and I can see they are processing something I am not included in.

'The attack. I saw her being attacked. I was in the room.' I look up then at the faces of the two officers in front of me. They look at one another. Disbelief? No, not that, something else. Confusion.

'Her? Did you say *her*?' she asks, her eyebrows contracting.

I nod. 'The woman. In the house. I saw her being strangled. By her boyfriend.'

They look at one another again. The silence grows, expanding until it fills every speck of space. He is confused and irritated with himself and with me, because of something he hasn't understood.

'This interview is being terminated. The time is 22:22 by my watch,' he says and presses a button on the machine.

'What's going on?' I ask. They look at one another ominously.

'We are just going to get the custody sergeant to speak to you again. You might need an appropriate adult,' the woman says and pushes off from her seat. I have forgotten her name already.

'An appropriate adult? I'm not a child. Wait. I'm not mad either. I might look odd,' I say, 'but there is nothing wrong in here.' I point to my right temple.

'It won't take a moment but it's best if you don't speak until he's seen you.' She holds the door open and motions for me to leave.

I am ushered back to my cell and left to wait. They are concerned for my mental health. Out there it happens every day. Even as people walk past, covering their mouths and noses, the eyes are there communicating pity, and disgust. But here, I have the power of speech. I have the opportunity to speak and be heard. They have to hear me. When you hear me, you don't leave thinking I'm crazy I promise you.

I hear the door to my cell clang open.

'Mr Shute, I'm the custody sergeant.' I look up and see the officer from before. I stand to speak to him so I won't be at a disadvantage sitting.

'Just a few questions,' he says, rubbing his white stubble self-consciously. I wait for him to run through them and answer them all. No tricks in these questions at all. 'Are you currently or have you ever had treatment for any mental illness?'

'No.'

'Have you ever been sectioned under the Mental Health Act?'

'No.'

'Have you ever attempted suicide or are you feeling suicidal at the moment?'

'No.'

'Okay. I don't think you need an assessing psychiatrist at this time.'

Now I am back in the interview room and this time I listen to their names: *Rachel* Blake, not Rochelle. And Simon Conway, detective inspectors, both of them. The interview starts again from the top. The initial statements are all the same, as if I am caught in a system glitch: introductions, caution, the right to a solicitor, all explained meticulously once again. I avoid their eyes through it all, concentrating my gaze on my fingers.

'Just before the break,' says Rachel Blake, 'you were telling us about witnessing an attack. On a woman.'

'Yes,' I say. I am still puzzled about why they'd decided that I was mentally unwell. Nothing that the custody sergeant asked me gave me any hint.

'Well, I'm going to be asking you about that later. For now, I want to talk to you about the attack on a gentleman by the name of Kenneth Squire. Does that name sound familiar to you?' she asks.

'No,' I say. This is plainly a mistake. 'Who is he?'

'He is a person, like you, shall we say, of no fixed abode. If I may show you a photograph? The suspect is now being shown exhibit RB/1, a photograph of the victim. Do you recognise this man?'

I stare at the picture and my blood freezes. It is unmistakeable – it's the man from the park, the drunk. A shot of his face, with his eyes closed. There's a long surgical scar running along his throat. But it is him.

'Er, yes. I. Well. No, I don't know him as such but I do recognise him,' I say slowly.

'From where?' Blake asks, her voice flat.

'I'm not sure,' I say. 'Just from around.'

She continues. 'Mr Squire was found earlier this morning in Hyde Park. He was stabbed in the neck and would have died if he hadn't been spotted by a runner. Do you have any idea how he might have received that injury?'

'No,' I say.

'That cut on your eye, Mr Shute. How did you get it?'

I put my fingers to it. The stitches lie proud of the surface but I resist the urge to scratch them.

'I fell,' I say. They know more than they are saying, but at this moment I cannot fathom what they know or how they know it.

'Fell where?' Blake says, her voice even and steady.

'I don't know,' I say. 'People like me fall. We fall and we get up and we fall again. East Dulwich? Camberwell, maybe. Who can say?'

'You, Xander, you can say. In fact, you did say – to the police who took you to the hospital – that you fell in Hyde Park.'

My memory of the detail of that conversation is patchy. I could have said that to the officer, I probably did, but I can't remember.

'That's it then,' I say, hiding my fists beneath the desk.

'Is there a reason that you didn't remember? I mean, after all, it only happened today,' says Conway.

'Concussion?' I venture.

'Concussion?' says Blake. 'Not amnesia?'

'I forgot. What can I tell you? I hurt my head. I was taken to hospital. How am I supposed to remember all these details you're throwing at me?' I say.

Conway shifts in his seat. 'If we were to examine your clothes, would we find any blood belonging to the victim?'

'No,' I say and then repeat the answer with more confidence. There can't be any of his blood on me. 'No. You won't. So, do your tests and let me go now please.'

Blake seems relieved by my answer and nods meaningfully at Conway.

'Okay, so before we terminate the interview, you were saying something about witnessing a murder,' he says. Whatever fight he had seems to have burned away like morning mist.

My brain is telling me to say nothing because I will end up incriminating myself. All I would do is build their case from nothing. They've got nothing. They don't even know about this woman. They can't put me at the scene. And then it occurs to me: I assumed they were arresting me for what happened to her. That simple, stupid fact has led me wildly into error. I've assumed that she was still alive because they didn't arrest me for murder. But she could be dead.

If her body is found, then what? What if someone saw me? What if I left a print somewhere? They've now got my prints from the arrest and my blood will be everywhere at the scene from this wound – the bleeder – the cut above my eye. They are going to nail me to the wall. I know how this works. I have to say something. Besides, I am committed now. I started my interview telling them about seeing a woman being attacked and I can't now undo that.

'Yes,' I say. And then before I know it, I'm telling them about the murder. I tell them about the Victorian-tiled hall and the Tiffany shades. The silk rug that I lay on. How the couple came in, she with her voice tinkling like glass. How I hid while they drank and then argued. How she looked, afterwards, broken on the carpet. How he ran. How I ran.

'Murder?' says Conway at one point. 'You didn't say it was murder at the start of the interview.'

'No. I. I thought this was why I was here. For her. And you said grievous bodily harm and I assumed she was alive still,' I say, stumbling over every word. 'I'm still not certain. She could be alive, you have to check.'

'So, she was dead? Then alive and then dead and now alive again?' Conway says, looking sceptically at Blake.

'No. I don't know. When I left she looked dead, but she could be alive. You have to send an ambulance. Do something.'

'She *looked* dead?' he says.

I glare at him.

'The address you gave, Farm Street? In Mayfair?' Blake asks, cutting in.

'Yes,' I say, '42B. Black door.'

It's only when they have stopped the tape that I realise I am crying. The tears have been silently streaming down my face and ponding on the table, drop by drop – cohesion and adhesion. Suddenly the exhaustion overtakes me and I collapse into the grief. Blake and Conway say nothing for a beat and then finally I hear the scrape of a chair as Conway gets up.

'Okay, Mr Shute, we are going to continue our investigations into this assault. We'll be following up some of what you have told us about your whereabouts at the time of Mr Squire's stabbing and I'm authorising the sending of your items for forensic testing. Till then you'll be released on police bail. We need a bail address.'

I look at Conway. 'Bail address?'

'We could always hold you here in police custody if you'd prefer, sir.' The eyes have lost whatever kindness I thought I had detected in him.

Blake gives him a look and then softens her eyes for me.

'Is there anyone at all you could stay with? Temporarily?' she asks.

I think for a moment, but there's no one.

'No,' I say. I am led quietly back to my cell. As the door shuts I call out to Blake, 'How long are you going to keep me here?'

The hatch opens with a clunk. 'Mr Shute. We need an address. If you can't give us one, we have no way of making sure you'll turn up when we need you to come in again.'

My heart begins to race. 'You can't keep me here,' I say.

'No. Not indefinitely. But without an address we might have to hold you and let the magistrates decide bail. And to be honest, Mr Shute, without an address I don't fancy your chances.'

'Wait,' I say, desperate now. 'If I just don't have an address, I don't know what you expect me to do.'

'Without an address I don't know what you expect *me* to do,' she says, and closes the hatch.

10

Thursday

When I shut my eyes, these walls move silently towards me, to compress me. And then as I flick open my eyes, they move soundlessly back. They won't be caught out. They are relentless.

This time when I open my eyes, I shall keep them open. The air in here is stale and smells of disinfectant. My stomach turns a little when I absorb this. I have to get out of here. There is air outside, just feet away, clear and crisp and wet and fragrant. Cold February air.

Though a February night is not a night to yearn for. The ice in the air can freeze everything useful on a human in minutes. But when the fingers begin to sting with cold, everything in the world vanishes. That's a good thing. I need to get out of here. I can't be here for another hour, let alone a day or more. I wouldn't last a day.

I close my eyes from tiredness, but when I open them I see the ceiling recede back into place. A second longer and it would have been too late. It would have crushed me.

When I saw him over her I could have done something.

I sit up at once. When I blink rapidly she appears in the creases of the darkness, her face familiar now.

'Let me out!' I shout. 'Let me out!'

The pounding in my head returns. If I call for a doctor, perhaps somehow he could explain to them why I need to be out of here, and how it will corrode me if I am left any longer. Soon the hatch will open so they can check I am alive. If I scream when it opens, would that get me out?

Minutes drip by.

Then there's a noise at the door. I make ready to scream at the hatch but it's not the hatch but the whole door that opens. The light blazes on causing me to shield my eyes.

'Come on, Mr Shute. You can go.'

I look through my fingers. It's Blake.

'What?' I say, getting up.

'We have an address for you,' she says.

When she sees the look on my face, she adds, 'Thirty-two Cross Street. SE22.'

'What?'

'That's the address we have on the PNC,' she says. 'You were arrested in 1989 for Common Assault. Cautioned.'

I know that address. It rattles in some hollow place in my brain. 'But that's not my house,' I say.

'I know,' she says, her tone flat. 'It belongs to a Sebastian Matthews.'

That name and a catalogue of memories it spins with come crashing around me.

'I'll take you back to get your personal property. Don't forget your return date in two weeks,' she says and hands me a paper with the date on it. I take it and crumple it into the pocket of my tracksuit bottoms.

If I keep quiet I can leave. There is no need to upset every-thing with truth – the truth that I don't live there and that I don't know him any more – that he wouldn't want me there. I'll walk out of this police station and straight to some sheltered nook or station waiting-room. I don't need to upturn this tiny conspiracy we share. She knows I won't go to that house. She knows it's not an address I can use. She's just finding a way to help me.

'And count yourself lucky we haven't charged you with Being on Enclosed Premises. Don't go breaking into any more houses, even if you think they're empty,' she says.

Blake leads me out to get my things. The fag ends are the only things that I can see through the window of the paper bag they hand me.

'I am sorry,' I say at last to Blake as she turns to go. 'Tell her family I am sorry.'

She smiles but there is no joy in it at all.

'I can't go out in these,' I say indicating the jogging pants and thin grey sweatshirt they have given me. The plimsolls are the things that make me feel most vulnerable. 'Can I at least get my boots back?'

'Evidence,' Blake says, shaking her head.

I am about to protest when I remind myself that she has pulled strings to get me out of here.

'Thank you for finding a way to get me out,' I say at last.

She frowns a little at this as if confused. 'Don't thank me. Thank him,' she says, nodding at the space behind me.

My breath catches as I chase her meaning. I look across the low aluminium gate and see him for the first time in years.

'Seb?'

'You look like crap,' he says.

11

Thursday

It is 03:11 according to the clock. The warmth of the car and the smoothness of the ride cajole me into sleep, but I can't let go yet. I look across to Seb who holds the wheel with confidence. His sleeves are crisp, cufflinks glinting gently in the street lights as they pass. He stares straight ahead at the road in concentration, though the traffic is light on Crystal Palace Road. It seems as if he's keeping his eyes occupied just to avoid me.

We go over some speed bumps and then pull off to the right and down a row of smart terraced houses. Memories rush in but in no kind of order. I know this place. The car draws smoothly to a halt and a button is pressed for a handbrake. When did this happen to cars?

'This is us,' he says and steps out. He looks the same, still handsome, greyer. He's a touch more drawn around the cheek but something gets us all. I climb out and follow him to his door and wait while he unlocks it. He presses a switch to flood the hall with soft amber light. The walls are painted in muted shades but the light dances off the polished wood handrails and antique sideboard.

'Come in,' he says, waiting.

'I can go,' I say, looking at the dirt on my hands. 'I won't stay.' The cold drops over me and irritatingly I shiver.

'Don't be silly,' he says. 'Come. You're letting the weather in.'

I shiver again in these thin police-issue clothes, and suddenly whatever power there was in my legs has gone. My knees buckle and I'm falling against the door, but he catches me just in time. Everything becomes murky and then there is nothing.

I wake up and gather fragments of memory. There's Seb half-dragging me inside his house, up the stairs – soft cream runners against dark, polished wood. Me, stumbling, being ushered like a drunkard to a bed and the sensation of my 'cell' clothes sticking to my skin as they are pulled away. The smell as the garments come away and how it stains the air. A towel is laid out on a chair through patches of vision. Then I feel warm air slowly wrapping my limbs. Then darkness and oblivion and finally sleep.

When morning tears open my eyes, I stall for a few moments, trying to remember where I am. My head is throbbing. I get up out of bed and partially draw the curtain across the low morning sun. From the clock on the bedside table, I see it's just after eight. I open my eyes and listen for sounds because I don't know anything about the life of the man whose home I'm in. I don't know if there are any children in the house, or a partner, or friends.

There's some distant clinking, like the sound of breakfast being laid. I look for the tracksuit I'd been given but I can't see it anywhere. Seb must have taken it away for washing. He's left me a change of clothes, laid on top of a white towel. Dark red trousers, blue-checked shirt, some new underpants still in the box, socks and a crew-neck sweater. These are his clothes, clothes in current use – not spares. I take the pants from the box. They are pristine in my stained hands. It has been years since I've worn pants; they aren't necessary. The whiteness of the cotton stares out at me. I can't wear his clothes without a bath.

I wrap the towel around my hips and walk along the corridor, taking in the bookshelves crammed with books. The mix of French literary fiction and pulp is disconcerting until I remember I left the French books here long ago and Nina always loved cheap and easy thrillers. I also remember now, randomly, that she smelled of roses. I wonder if she's still with Seb. The bathroom door has been left ajar as an invitation. I go in and stare at the polished bath. It's been so long since I've been in one. I reach across to the taps but hesitate. It feels like an intrusion, but in his house, his clothes, it also feels like the least I can do. A few minutes later I am lying in the water and watching the dirt as it runs off my body and sinks to the bottom. I find a nail brush and scrub away what I can without losing my mind. Then the hair. Not until I soak it do I become aware of how long it is. Finally, I scrub my face until it feels as if it is pink again. When I drain the bath I'm shocked by the grime lining the bottom.

When I walk out I catch sight of someone in the mirror. Someone from a nightmare. Of course, it's me, but the face staring back at me is running with blood. I realise with a dull ache that I have scrubbed away my stitches. I sigh and clamp the towel to my face until I find plasters with cartoon pigs on them. So he has children? I manage to staunch the flow with three of them overlaid one across the other and take a last look in the mirror. I look clean but faintly ridiculous.

'Oh. You found the plasters,' he says with a smile when I walk into the kitchen. They tingle a little on my forehead. 'Nieces. There are eggs and bacon there.' He points to a covered plate. 'And fresh coffee in the pot.' He is wearing a grey suit with a Prince of Wales check, a pale blue shirt and a crimson tie with tiny elephant motifs on it. He takes me in, dressed in his checked shirt and red trousers, and smiles. Then he stands and gathers his keys from the table. The smell of bacon turns my stomach on and off again. But I need to eat.

'Thanks,' I say, sitting down. He looks at me as if he is about to say something but changes his mind.

'Listen, I have to go to work,' he says, looking at his watch. It's a Rolex Milgauss. I had one once – because it was named after the mathematician.

'We can talk when I get back. Should be back around six. Help yourself to whatever you want,' he says. He pauses when he sees the agitation in my expression. 'It's fine, it's just me in the house.'

'Thanks, Seb,' I say. 'But I'll get out of your hair. And I'll get these back to you if you can show me where you put my other clothes.'

He stops in the doorway and turns to face me. His smile doesn't quite reach his eyes.

'Xander. No. Please. Just stay.'

'I don't know. I find being indoors – it's hard for me.'

He stops and then fumbles around in his pocket until his wallet appears in his hands. I recoil but he isn't giving me money.

'Then take a walk. Jump on a bus, get some air. Here, take my old Oyster. There's thirty quid or something on it. But stay – at least till I get back,' he says.

I nod, but I am sure I'll be gone for good when he returns. Besides, he hasn't given me a key.

Once he's gone I sit and shovel food into my mouth. I pour some coffee and take a deep draught. The caffeine circulates warmly through my body until cell by cell my body shakes itself free from sleep. As the energy returns to my muscles, I go into the living room which is pale and bright. Polished surfaces wink at me from every sharp edge. All this new furniture but I know this room, this house – I know its bones, even if the flesh is new. I look for more signs of Nina, but find none. What happened to her?

A television set the size of a Rothko decorates one wall, a set of stereo equipment with tubular speakers lies beneath. I find just one picture of Seb on the mantel. In it he's twenty-two maybe, his cheeks pink against an azure sky. There's just the faintest impression of a college building in the background. And there at the front is Nina, and next to her, Grace.

I think I remember some of this day. I was there during this picture, I am sure of it, though I am not in it. Maybe I'm behind the lens. The odd thing is that in my memory of this picture, I *am* in it. I can visualise the expression I held, impatience I think it was, because I didn't want to be in it.

Seb looks the same. Perhaps he's rounder in the cheek in the picture than now, and less grey. But the eyes are the same shade of blue. And although it shouldn't, this surprises me. The hands, they're the same too. And he, above all, is the same. There's still this current of beauty.

The sofa gives way under the weight of my body. I am sinking into it and the sensation is foreign and alarming. I get up quickly and lie instead on the carpet. The moment my head touches the twisted wool, pain erupts, images of that night cascade. The man is standing over her, pressing his weight on her as she kicks and struggles. I can see it from where I am on the floor, but fear or cowardice binds my hands and mouth.

If I had stood up, then what?

The edge of her face flashes before my eyes in the dying light of the fire. Her skin is already flat, pale. The red stain on her shirt is still spreading. It travels until it reaches her neck and then it spills over, pooling in the dips created by her throat. And then it rises and rises until it is up to her chin. It brims over her lips for a second and then her eyes snap open. She screams as the blood fills her mouth.

I open my eyes and catch the ceiling as it begins to drop on to my head. The walls begin to move, too. I have to get out of here.

Once opened, the front door lets in a wave of cold air that forces me to shut it again. I can't leave in this weather without better clothes and shoes. I go up to the bedroom I slept in and root around the wardrobe there. A few old suits hang from the rail along with a few white and some pastel-coloured shirts. There are some polished Oxfords and Monks at the bottom but nothing you could wear for long in the cold and the wet. There are some brand new walking shoes with the labels still on but I leave them there and try his room instead.

Seb's room, softly lit, is laced with the scent of lime and basil. I flick the hangers along, looking guiltily for a coat. There are new cashmere and wool ones, but I take a heavy wool one instead. I try it on and find that it fits nicely enough even though he is a little thicker and shorter than me. His clothes, all those chinos and pale shirts, haven't changed a bit, either. His life has cocooned him.

I worry about taking them but he has more clothes than he can wear. It's fine. I look down at the brogues and keep tight hold of the thirty pounds of Oyster. At the end of everything, I know he is my friend. Or was my friend. But friends, real ones, like siblings, can't be lost through the effluxion of time. They are stars, still in their places, whether you look at them or not.

I walk quickly down the stairs and pause at a mirror by the front door. I peel away the plaster from my face. In less than a day, I have become reborn. Almost thirty years of living have been wiped out with cotton and wool and a bath. Except inside, where I know the layers are tougher and the marks run more deeply.

12

Thursday

In these clothes I can visit the places that my ordinary life prevents me from accessing. I walk into the grounds of the Dulwich Picture Gallery, pulling the velvet collar of my coat to my face. I think I'm here because I need a kind of privileged space to think in peace and comfort. Walking liberates me. It frees me from the oppression of stasis and that feeling of being locked in with myself. But when I move across open space, it's as if the locks come undone and I can bear to be with myself a little longer. The longer I am free, the easier I find my shadow as company. I'm less fraught, less … chemically volatile.

I wonder about what the police said about this man, Squire. Those pictures showed him as pretty badly attacked. He wasn't when I saw him though, was he? I'm sure they've made a mistake arresting me for it. I would have remembered doing that or anything like that to him. But then, do the police arrest people for no reason at all? Though they do have targets and clear-up rates and papers to think about. Or is there another reason that they arrested me? Could I have lost time, like I did at the hospital? But even if I had, I wouldn't have blocked the whole thing out, something would have stayed with me. I look around the grounds and feel some satisfaction at coming to this place to reason everything out in peace. It's only when I'm near the café that I realise that we came here once before, Grace and I.

We worked long hours in the City, both of us, occasionally working through till dawn. When we pulled those all-nighters, they'd give us time off in lieu, and on those precious days we made a tradition of heading into south London for some *green*. It wasn't quite the idyll of Cambridge, but it was leafy and philosophically a hundred miles away from our north-of-the-river home. It meant different things to each of us. For Grace being out here met her spiritual needs. 'The grass, walking on it, is grounding,' she'd said. 'It takes up all those free electrons floating about. And in Buddhist philosophy—'

I'd have raised my eyebrows when Buddha was invoked. For me there was a simpler equation in the greenery of south London: it was a break from the grind. I think about this and wonder if that's where it began, this need to escape my life? I don't know. But we held hands here, I know that. 'We should buy a place here somewhere,' she said.

'We should. We really should.'

'Somewhere we can grow old together. And you can garden and I can bake.'

I laughed and drew her into my coat. I remember it now. 'I don't really see you as the baking sort,' I said. She pulled away in mock indignation.

'Hey!' she said, before adding, 'but what about that loaf I made once?'

I marvel at this now when I look back, that she'd loved me. When I examine myself for the same glints of beauty and magic that I saw in her, I can't find them. She said I was honest and gentle. But most of all that I was brighter than her – that's what attracted her most, she said. Clever men were hard to find, apparently. I rough over this memory because I know how fraudulent this claim of hers is.

From the café I circle round and head out towards Dulwich Park just across the way. There's a fence around the perimeter edge but the planks are weather-worn and have come away from their nails. I pull a section back and step through into the vast grounds. I let my feet lead me. As I walk I have the sensation of being followed, but when I glance behind me, there are only trees.

The police seemed more interested in the Squire attack than in the woman lying dead in that house. It can only be because they don't believe me. Did I look unhinged to them? I keep catching myself being hunted by ghosts – is that what they saw in me? I should have insisted on going to the house with them, because what if she's still alive. Is there some sense in calling an ambulance, even now?

I shake some of the fug from my head. There's still pain there but it's ebbing away. To my right the ground climbs up a hill which I follow. The wet grass smells of my childhood and of Rory. If I can help it I hardly ever indulge Rory any more. I push him out whenever he draws close but sometimes, like now, when some scent catches me by surprise, I am taken bodily back to him. This wet grass and suddenly here he is, six or seven and rolling down a hill. Squealing. And then in the next instant, he is no longer six or seven but twenty-six. At the end of his life.

When he was twenty-six, Rory was found dead.

He comes to me like this, the full span of his life in a single slide. Childhood – adulthood – death. When I think of him the memories tug something inside. He fell from the eleventh floor of his apartment block in Holborn, but I'm not sure if I trust all the details of that memory or whether it's a pastiche of imagined and real. But I do remember roaming the parks with him for hours on end when we were children, with a ten-pence piece for an emergency phone call *just in case*.

When I went to identify the body, I was alone. There was nobody left to me, no one to absorb the despair when it flowed over. Dad had been in a care home for over a year. In patches of lucidity he remembered Rory and in those moments, just as the scales fell from his eyes, and he learned again for the first time that Rory was gone, he'd crumble. His face would collapse, then his chest and finally, if he was sitting in a chair, he would sink to his knees and howl. And I would stand there, watching – with pity, but also with bitterness that he couldn't help me. It wasn't consolation, exactly, that I needed, but something to drive away the numbness.

Now as I sit with my back against a park bench, my heart beating fast, that feeling invades me again: the emotionless feeling of isolation. I coax some heat into the sleeves of my coat by rubbing them and think how I am the warmth of my life. How much energy life generates just to be and to continue being, and then when the time comes, as it did for Rory, the furnace just … stops.

I have to beat away the existentialism. Getting up, I tighten the coat around me and trace a path to the main entrance, walking quickly towards it. The ache in my temples has returned and is clouding the few thoughts that I have. She is dead, I know it. I remember now that I felt for her pulse and couldn't find one. So I let her life be taken. The heaviness of that realisation crests over me. I don't know anything about her. Who she was, what she did. What her name was. Her face presses up against my skull, becoming slowly, painfully familiar. I need to know more about who she is – *was*. And who killed her.

I could start by going back there. Maybe by now the police have notified the family and there's someone there I can talk to. I could tell them that I was the one that found her and alerted police. That's not too far from a version of truth and if I can comfort them with some— I stop myself in this thought. It's not succour I have to give them, it's something else – justice, or vigilantism. Because above all, they'd want him found. I want him found.

I quickly leave and find my way back on to the main road and begin to map the route to Farm Street. I can trace a path from Blue to Green Zones without ever having to look up. There is nothing to see out there anyway, I have come to understand that. There's only what is at the feet. Everything else is just glister.

After a few miles of hard walking, I look up and the brass glints: 42B. Within I can see that the lights are on.

When I spoke to the police I couldn't give them a good description of the man, but I can change that. He has to come or go at some point and all I have to do is stay here and watch him do it.

I take up a vantage point just past the sign for what looks like a business property, bordered by railings and sheltered a little from view. I plunge my hands into my coat pockets, forgetting momentarily that it's not mine. My hand stalls in the pouch as it touches something unexpected. I pull it out. A cigarette pack. Seb – a smoker? He never used to be. I tap out a cigarette and seconds later I am inhaling smoke, relief flooding every nerve. It's been some time since I had a clean one.

From here the door to 42B is easy to see and I'll know when anyone comes or goes. The light burns a soft, expensive glow behind the window blinds. I strain to detect motion behind the glass, but so far there's only the odd shadow falling across the pane to indicate life. I wait, and feel the February light running away and in its place, the cold arriving. It is piercing, but I'll wait here all night if I have to – for her sake. What was her name? Did he call something out as he put his ear to her lips? *Chelle*? My heart thuds over something but I am not sure what.

I smoke the cigarette to its embers and flick it into the street. My bones are beginning to seize from the deepening cold. My head drums up an ache once again and I crouch in the doorway to ease the pain. Once the throbbing has died away a little, I lean in against the door in a familiar position. I used to sit this way for hours, in those first days on the streets, when I needed to catch up with the chaos in my head, and to silence it. Eventually the silence descended, on the third or fourth day, in a doorway just like this one. I was watching people flowing past as if they were parts of a river, their legs washing by. Then silence came when I discovered there was only me in the world – me on one side and everything else held aloft on the other. The weight of my existence in perfect counterweight to the entire universe.

I think of Grace sometimes in terms of her weight against mine – hers an equal and opposing force to mine. We were opposites that attracted. For example, I couldn't get on board with the whole Buddhism thing. I didn't understand how a rational, mathematical mind could be so seduced by what was essentially fable and myth-making. But she didn't see what I saw.

'Buddhism is essentially mathematical,' she said once, trying to explain.

'Is it?'

'Yes. Come on, Xander: the Golden Ratio. You were the one who told me about it.'

I probably had, but as I'd tried to explain to her, the spiral of a conch, or the curl of a fern, was just a function of the coding in the cells. 'It looks mathematical because it uses mathematical code,' I said.

'But all that proves is that God or the Universe is a mathematician,' she said. 'You really should come and speak to Ariel about this. You'd like him, Xander.'

'What makes you say that?'

'Because you're the cleverest man I know and he's – he's the most spiritual.'

The yoga teacher was another thing. He was always buying her trinkets or giving her 'amazing' head massages. She couldn't see the jealousy ponding in me so she kept trying to make me meet him. Once, it must have been when we were on our way to work, I tried to tell her.

'What?' she said, skipping a little to catch up. Her perfume tugged at me.

'I don't know. Just. Does he have to keep giving you massages?' I said and then regretted it.

She tucked her spare arm into mine. 'Head and neck massage. It's for pressure points. So I can put up with you!?'

What had she meant by that, I wonder now. She said I could become fixated on things and that made her tense. And now I catch myself in remembrance of that scene, but I'm interrupted when at the edge of my vision, I see the door open. I stand to get a better look as the back of a man pulls the door shut, locking it. I sieve my memory. Could it be him, the man I saw that night? He seems the same build, has the same dark hair. He turns and heads down the steps and I see his face properly for the first time. I'm expecting a jolt of recognition but it doesn't come. Rather it is a dawning – a gentle light spreading. It must be him: same hair, same shape face. He's too far away to make out his features clearly but there's something in his gait and the way that he navigates the pavement that gives him away. And the jacket is the same one, or could be.

Who is he? There is someone there behind the killing, hiding inside him. How is he feeling about what he has just done? I search his faraway features without luck. But there must be misery and regret and shame and guilt somewhere under that face.

And then, just as he walks around the corner and out of sight, I realise: the police haven't arrested him. Is it possible that they haven't seen him yet? I don't know how a murder – even an allegation of murder – wouldn't have had them round here straight away.

But I am here and he's here, or was moments ago, free. And she, the woman, was in there not two days ago. So where is she now? Has he disposed of her? Concealed or covered what evidence there might have been? She is after all *somewhere*, right now, hidden, occupying a place in time and space. But she won't be for long. She is slowly disintegrating cell by cell and becoming less her and more something else. I know this. I know it.

When I buried Rory, he was just five days dead. But for the intervention of the funeral parlour, he would have been black from decay. Putrefaction. His organs would have begun to liquefy. Bacteria would have bloated him around the eyes and to see him like that would have convinced you that he was destroyed, gone. But the undertaker gave him a whiff of life. He looked good enough to breathe.

So now, in that house somewhere, or in the garden or a basement or somewhere, definitely somewhere, she is quietly merging with the earth. Whoever she loved would be frantic. And I – I, who might have changed history – am standing here mute once again. For a second time I have let him slip away unchallenged and I hate how passive I have become.

If I can't chase him then I need to find out who he is.

13

Thursday

When I cross the park, I find myself in a small road, South Audley Street. I see Mayfair Library and that shakes something loose in my head. I've been here before. I push open the door but hesitate, and then I remember I'm clean. The staff blink calmly at me as I pass through and turn a corner. There is a bank of computers to the left and I aim straight for them and sit down. How to begin a search on a man I know nothing about? My eyes lid over and again the pain in my head strikes up a beat.

The sensation of someone before me makes me open my eyes. There's a lad standing in front of me, late teens, in school uniform.

'Here,' he says and holds out a magazine to me. I take it, puzzled, from his hands and see that it's the *New Scientist*.

I sit up and look into his eyes, questioning.

'She told me to give it to you,' he says, indicating the librarian in the next aisle, wheeling a book trolley.

I stand up to get a better look at the woman. She has long blonde hair and a small serious face. She catches my eye and waves at me before walking over.

'Xander!' she says. 'Is that really you? You look so different!'

I stare at my clothes and then at my hands. I *am* different.

'Thank you,' I say, confused for a moment, and then I remember all at once. This is my library. I come here every week, for this magazine and for warmth and ordinary sanctuary. And she, *Hazel*?, has always been nice to me. My heart starts to thump suddenly. How have I forgotten this, even for a second? Is something happening to my brain? I rub my head as if I can massage my brain back to normal. That kick in the head from Squire. What did he do to me?

I stare at the magazine in my hands. 'The Galaxy That is Missing All Its Dark Matter'.

'It's a good one this week.'

Looking up, I see that the boy is still there.

'Thanks,' I say, and fumble for more to say. 'You a scientist?'

'What?' he says and he looks more confused than me.

'Science. Do you like it?'

'Not really. I prefer the arts,' he says. He's confident with me. He should be wary of me, an adult stranger. Don't they teach kids that any more?

'You knew that, Xander,' he says, a little uncertain. I feel like a feral cat that he's trying to stroke.

'Have we met?' I say, alarmed.

He looks at me with a frown, laughing a little. 'Yes, Xander! It's me, Amit. Are you okay?'

I look again at the computer and the blinking cursor. I am a computer expert and I have written hundreds of programs for mining and predicting data streams, but I can't use this thing in front of me. I stand.

'Sorry. I have to go,' I say to the boy. When he turns his head and his hair flicks in his eyes, I suddenly remember him. Amit.

I saw him at the gallery – he gave me oranges, and suddenly I feel a pressing need to remember what happened to them. As I ran from Squire, I left them behind. The thought that they are rotting under mulch makes me unaccountably sad.

'Have you, erm, tightened the loose screws now?' he says, pointing at his head and smiling. 'Remember me?'

'Of course,' I say. 'Thanks for the oranges,' I add as a convincer, and he smiles again.

I make for the exit. The librarian is there at the desk and opens her mouth to say something but whatever it was, I wave it back into her head. I have to go and get this straightened out in person. There should be police there. The man might be disposing of evidence this second. That could even be where he has gone.

Once off the bus I make quickly for Paddington Green Police Station. I walk in and the smell, a cloying tangle of disinfectant and boiled potatoes meets me.

'I need to speak to Rachel,' I say at the desk.

The desk sergeant looks at me. 'Rachel?'

'Or her colleague, DI Conway, I need to speak to one of them.'

He looks blankly at me as if I'm speaking in tongues, before languidly tapping on some buttons on a phone.

'Name?'

'Shute. Xander Shute.'

'You want to be careful with a name like that,' he says, enjoying his own humour. He mumbles into the handset before replacing it. 'Coming now for you.'

Time drags its heels through the silence and I wait, sinking as I do.

'Mr Shute?' I spin around with surprise. I see both detectives.

'Why haven't you been?' I say.

They exchange a look that confuses me.

'We've been trying to get hold of you,' Blake says.

'What for?' I say, following them as they walk to the same room I was interviewed in before.

'Come, we'll speak in here,' Blake says, opening the door for me. The walls, matt black, undulate, making me queasy.

'The Farm Street crime you reported,' she says seriously.

I cross my arms and nod. 'That's why I'm here,' I say. 'Why haven't you got police there?'

'You've been to the address?' Conway says, concerned. 'You shouldn't be going—'

'You don't understand,' I say. 'I saw him, the murderer, he's still there walking around free as a bird. You need to go and arrest him, now.'

They look at one another again but say nothing. Blake opens the file and pulls out a photograph.

'Is this the man you saw?' she says, pushing the picture over to me.

The photograph is blurred like a still image from a video. I wonder whether there is CCTV somewhere that captured him. I look carefully at the face. It's the man I saw earlier this evening, without a doubt.

'That's him,' I say. They make tiny movements of their eyes towards one another.

'Why haven't you picked him up?' I say. 'Why is there no police presence there at all?'

And then I see the discomfort in their faces. Blake gives me a concerned smile. 'Actually, Xander, he's not a suspect.'

'But the picture,' I say, pointing at the image. 'It's him.'

'It's a still from the officer's body-worn camera,' Conway says.

'So, you spoke to him. Someone spoke to him, surely? How did he explain the body? You must have had a team there. Forensics. You can't have let him go. He killed her!' My voice is climbing, no matter how hard I try to ground it.

'Just calm down for a second, Mr Shute. Okay. Mr Ebadi. He's a UAE national,' Conway says, pointing to the image.

UAE? Did that make him Arabic? If he was Arabic I would have noticed. Wouldn't I? But the context maybe confused me. He is light-skinned. I saw him in a Victorian house with a white woman and I just assumed – wrongly assumed. Even so, this is him.

'So?' I say, finally taming my voice.

'So, you didn't mention that he was an Arab gentleman,' Conway says. 'In your statement, you said it was a white male.'

I look at Blake in disbelief. 'But light-skinned or white, what's the difference? He murdered a woman.'

'Well, we don't believe he did,' Conway says, pulling the photograph back.

'He's got an alibi for the night of the murder,' Blake says softly.

'What alibi?'

'He wasn't in the country, Mr Shute. He was in the UAE.' I detect delight in his voice as if he has caught me in something, a lie.

'Anyone can – could say that, have you checked?'

'Mr Shute, we have checked. We've seen his passport, he was good enough to show it to us. And his flight e-ticket,' Conway says flatly. 'We spoke to the airline. It wasn't him.'

I cover my head with my hands as my head begins to pound. It had to be him. It *was* him, wasn't it? Suddenly I am not sure any more. Maybe it was a white male I saw after all. I had it right first time around before they tricked me into this odd admission.

'Then it wasn't him. It was a white male as I said.'

They look again at one another.

'Did you check for other occupants? I don't know if it was that guy,' I say, stabbing at the still. 'But it was *someone*. Someone killed a woman in that house.' My voice is shrill in my ears.

Blake shakes her head sadly and stands up. 'The officers checked that house. There was no evidence of any murder at all.'

No evidence? How can that be? 'So, now what?' I say. 'What's your next move? You can't just let him sit there destroying evidence.'

'Our next move is, do you want to make a withdrawal statement?' Conway says. 'We can't have a murder allegation left hanging in the air.'

'Withdrawal? No, I don't want to make a withdrawal statement. I know what I saw and I can't believe you're not taking it more seriously!'

The file sits tightly under Blake's arm.

'Think about it, Xander,' says Blake. 'You might have made a mistake here. I can understand it, of course I can. You're facing an extremely serious allegation yourself. A man was badly assaulted. He's alive, but Mr Squire had just been minding his own business before he was attacked with a knife. So, I can understand how the stress of that might cause you to deflect the allegation by making another. Believe me, we see plenty of allegations and cross-allegations, but this is too serious, Xander. We are giving you a chance here. Drop it, now, and we can write it down to nerves. Otherwise, I'm afraid we are going to have to charge you with wasting police time. Or perverting the course of justice, if the CPS want it to go that way.'

My eyes travel from one officer to the other. Slowly and deliberately, I cross my arms.

'You better charge me then,' I say.

14

Friday

They're still talking about dark matter in the magazines. The maths is still the maths and the theoretical physics is still as it was, theoretical. The only thing that ever changes is the intensity with which they remind us that we know nothing. When I think of dark matter, it always brings me straight back to Rory and the conversations we had. I didn't have anyone else to talk to about this stuff – only he understood it well enough.

'Ninety-five per cent of the Universe is dark matter and dark energy,' I said to him once. It might have been for one of Dad's 'debates'.

'So?' he said.

'So, none of it's ever been observed. It's pure hypothesis.'

'And?' He was doing that thing I hated, lifting an eyebrow with his finger.

'So er-bloody-go, we only know what five per cent of the Universe is. We don't know what ninety-five per cent of it even is.'

He lets this sink in. 'No,' he says finally, 'that's not the same thing.'

I stare at him.

'It's not the same thing. We don't know what it consists of, elementally, but we know what it is. It's dark energy and dark matter.'

'No. That's just a bloody hypothesis. It's theoretical. It doesn't exist outside some physicist's head.'

Dad had been in the room, I remember, because I was always aware of him. He was reading his paper but he was listening. Mum might have been hovering, glasses hanging from a chain, but equally she might have been in the study, writing a paper.

Dad smiled because he saw something that I didn't and he was enjoying it.

'I disagree,' Rory said. 'It does exist.'

'How do you know that? Has it ever been seen? Has it ever been detected?'

'It could be a weakly interacting massive particle. If it interacted too weakly for detection. What with neutrinos and everything.'

'It's not a WIMP,' I say.

'No, but that's not to say it doesn't exist. It just means that it doesn't interact with light or electromagnetism or any way that we have now of detecting its presence. But neither do thoughts or dreams. All we know is that ninety-five per cent of the Universe isn't ordinary matter. So, it stands to reason that it's *something*, whether it's called dark matter or an elephant, it still exists. If, that is, you still want a standard model of cosmology, which you have to unless you want to throw Einstein out?'

'That's just bloody sophistry,' I said, but I knew he was right. I left the room. In my bedroom I lay down, Psychedelic Furs playing at full volume on my ghetto blaster. Halfway through the first track, there was a knock and he spoke through the closed door.

'I'm sorry. I don't mean to win all the time. It's – just – I know the answers. Sometimes,' he said.

I didn't reply.

He stood knocking at the door for some time. Calling my name but I remained silent.

'You okay? Hello?'

'You okay? Hello?'

I look up and see a face pinched at me in concern. Where am I?

I look down at the pavement before looking up at the face again. The expressions on these faces are all the same – guilt in some form. A woman who has lost her son to the streets or a man who has too much money and too little good to show for it. Even just a girl who has read too many books.

'Where am I?' I say.

The woman is maybe forty years old and looks like a person who has seen a lot and is afraid of very little. She has the face of a market trader.

'Holborn,' she says in a leathery voice.

Green Zone. 'Time is it?' I say, rubbing my eyes against the street lights. The darkness of the blue in the sky makes it hard to tell.

'Just after midnight,' she says and then starts rummaging in her pockets. I am about to stop her giving me money when I realise that she's just fishing for cigarettes.

The evening and a day slot into place with a series of clicks. A charge of wasting police time wasn't serious enough for them to hold me overnight. I'd left the police station and walked and didn't stop. The night was bone cold and this coat of Seb's just wasn't up to the job and I ended up here. I used to come here in the old days when I worked. It's changed a little but the atmosphere is familiar: corporate, safe. Blue Zone. People leave you to yourself here. A doorway here can be yours for an entire night without anybody calling the police to have you moved on. Very few drunks or chancers.

I pull the coat tight around my body and stand. The woman looks up at me and smiles through a mouthful of smoke, showing me the silver in her mouth.

'You're a big lad, ain't you?' she says, cackling.

I give her a half-smile and look around deciding where to go next.

'It's going to drop tonight,' she says, flicking her cigarette away. 'You want to get yourself to a shelter tonight if you can.'

'How did you know?' I say, surprised that Seb's clothes aren't better camouflage.

'Ha,' she says. 'It's the eyes. And the hair.'

I nod my thanks and move off. The shelters aren't for me. I can't take the weight of all those people, circling.

To my left is Tottenham Court Road. To my right, Farringdon. I take the right.

The police went there and spoke to the man, Ebadi – is that what they called him – the same man I saw yesterday? He had an alibi. I don't trust it, though. I don't trust something as flimsy as what they called an e-ticket. Don't those things just come off a printer? And those coppers – I don't trust that they did the job properly. How can they have been and searched the place and not found a body? If they even did search the place. Maybe they spoke to him and were satisfied by his alibi and then didn't bother with a search.

But I do trust Seb, and his friendship even after all these years have passed. I head towards his place and in an hour or so I am outside his door.

My finger hovers over the bell a moment before finally making contact. I grimace as I wait. I don't want to wake him up. It's already been too much of a liberty, using his home as my bail address and taking these clothes – the ones he gave and the ones I stole. And now here I am, waking him at past one.

The hall light blazes and a minute later the door opens to reveal Seb in a washed-out blue dressing gown, squinting against the light.

'Xander, where have you been?' he says.

'I'm sorry,' I say. 'I had nowhere else I could – and I really need—'

He holds up his hand to wave away the explanation. 'No need. Come in. It's going to freeze tonight.'

I expect him to go straight back upstairs but instead he wanders into the living room, turning to me as he walks in.

'Whisky?' he asks, clicking on a lamp to give the room a warm glow.

'Sure,' I say, and follow him in.

'The police called for you earlier,' he says with concern. 'Look. I don't want to pry, but what's going on with you?'

I sit in one of the plush cream chairs. I owe him an explanation but I can't muster the effort that the explanation will involve. 'It's nothing,' I say.

He looks at me, disappointed, before turning to the whisky and pouring an inch into crystal glasses.

'I've reported a crime but the police aren't taking me seriously.'

'Anything I can do?' he says, handing me a glass.

I shake my head and as I take the glass, I'm drawn again to the picture on the mantel. I stare at it as Seb stretches himself on the sofa, bare heels in the soft carpet. Grace peers out shyly from the image. Something about her expression, soft and smiling, is heartbreaking.

'Do you remember that?' Seb says, watching me. 'Nina had just got herself one of those SLR cameras. You know the ones with the fancy zoom lenses.'

I shake my head. There is the frayed edge of a memory there but not much more.

'Yes, you do,' he says, taking the frame into his hands. 'She wanted each one of us to take a picture of the other three. That's the one you took.'

I get up and sit next to him on the sofa to look more closely at it. 'I remember bits,' I say. 'But I have trouble clinging on to much from those days. It's being outside, the exposure. Messes with the wiring, I think.'

Seb nods as if he understands but I'm not sure whether he does exactly.

'I still see Nina from time to time,' he says then.

'Oh. How is she?' I say. And then I wonder about Grace. Has he seen much of her? I want to ask but that thread, wherever it leads, is too sharp. Painful.

'The same. You know what she was like, too clever for her own good.'

I smile. There is Nina at eighteen, out-talking and out-arguing a professor during a tutorial. 'Too smart for you at any

91

rate,' I say. And then I realise I don't know how long they've been apart. Or together.

'I'm sorry,' I say when I see his face fall. 'I didn't mean to.'

'Oh, don't worry. We all knew I was never going to be able to hang on to her for very long,' he says, smiling sadly and taking a sip of his drink.

'How long exactly did you?' I say.

'Actually, I didn't do badly, all told. We agreed to go our separate ways about a year ago.'

I take a sip and clench my jaw as the Scotch burns the back of my tongue. Nina in those days struck me as a thing of ether. I remember her high cheeks and fashionable oversized earrings and the smell of rose that trailed her wherever she went. But she wasn't defined by that as much as she was by how little she revealed. She was impenetrable, to me at any rate.

Seb takes a large mouthful from his glass and clears his throat.

'About Grace,' he says.

My heart leaps at her name. For a moment I argue with myself about it. I want to know about her and how she is and where she got to, but at the same time, I know that my body can't contain the pain of hearing about her. The extent to which she has flown out of my reach. I hold out my hand to cut him off. 'It's okay,' I say. 'You don't have to.'

He shifts on the sofa so that he can turn his body towards me. He sighs and nods.

'Where did you end up, Xander? For all these years?'

I laugh, catching myself by surprise. The idea of trying to sweep up and assemble the shards of my life from thirty years ago seems suddenly absurd.

'Here and there,' I say at last with a smile.

He looks me in the eyes and attempts a smile in return, but it dies on his lips.

'I'm sorry,' he says. 'I should have done more.'

For a second I don't register what he is saying.

'Done more? What do you mean?'

'After Rory. You know. I should have tried harder.'

I turn my body so I can face him more squarely. 'I don't understand.'

He shifts again in his seat. 'I don't know. We should have – I should have tried harder to help you.'

This stills me. 'I didn't need help, Seb,' I say. 'I wasn't your problem.'

'I was supposed to be your mate, Xand,' he says, shaking his head sadly before standing up. He takes a breath and shrugs away the memories. He rubs his eyes and it's clear that he's tired. 'I can lend you some pyjamas if you like. I'll leave them on your bed.'

I consider telling him not to bother but then wonder whether he would prefer it if I didn't sleep on his sheets without clothes on.

'Thanks,' I say, getting up too. 'I'll be out of your hair in the morning.'

Seb stops as I say this and looks at me from the doorway. 'Look, I don't need to know what this is all about if you don't want to say. But you should stay, at least until you get yourself sorted out.'

I laugh again and hope it's not unkindly. 'I don't think getting sorted out is really for me, Seb.'

He hesitates and then finally he says, 'I know you need the Bens and I know it's been a long time. But—' He has run out of words. He exhales loudly, his hands on his hips, and then adds, 'I do worry about you being on the streets where anything could happen to you.'

Bens. I have no idea what he's talking about. Is it me? Has my mind dropped this too or is it Seb? Instead I nod at him and then add a half-smile as if I know what this means. But I have no idea.

15

Saturday

The light as it shines through the room, its angle, its intensity, tells me that it must still be early in the morning. If I am to make any use of the day, I need to get going.

After washing I dress quickly and creep downstairs as quietly as I can. There's no sign of Seb, who must still be asleep or already at work. My, *his*, coat is on the newel post where I left it and I slip it on. It has already begun to mould itself to my contours so that it feels like my own thing. The velvet collar is soft against my skin. The shoes I don't recall removing are there in the hallway. I put them on and leave quietly, pulling the front door softly shut behind me.

Outside the February weather is cold. Something in the air gives a memory from a long-forgotten Guy Fawkes night, even though we are months on from November. There is a hint of fog and the slightest trace of sulphur in the air. I walk to a bus stop and the reality of what happened at the police station on Thursday night marches along with me. A charge of wasting police time. All I had done was to report a crime, a murder, and yet they had referred my case to the CPS to charge me.

I still can't understand how he managed to slip past them like that. I wipe a hand over my face and wait for the bus. When it comes I board it with Seb's pass and find a seat at the back, wrapping my coat around me for comfort. Out of the window I see another bus draw alongside and momentarily I have the sensation of giddiness as our bus appears to slide into reverse. The narrow advertising strip on the side of the other bus pulls away with the bus. *Ariel 3-in-1 pods*. I shut my eyes against the memory but it invades anyway.

The day that I met him.

Grace wanted me to meet him. I think she thought it would make me feel better about him. It didn't.

'Ah, Xander, I've heard such a lot about you,' he said to me when I walked into his yoga workshop. He sandwiched his hands around mine. They were warm and tanned. He was wearing white linen and floated about like a beatified ghost as I stood stiffly next to him in a black herringbone suit.

'Ariel,' I said, lifting my voice. I was there to give him the benefit of the doubt. 'Mabel loves you,' I said, my heart sinking immediately. 'I mean the yoga.'

I switched my gaze to Grace and saw her cheeks flush.

'Mabel?' he said with a half-smile, looking at us both.

'Oh,' I say, irritated with myself. 'Sorry – pet name.'

'Pet name, eh? She's an enigma, that one,' he said smoothly then and stared into her eyes. A second too long.

I became conscious of my smile tightening. The air suspended around us and for a minute we all found ourselves looking at each other with fixed smiles.

'So, Ariel. That's an interesting name. Puts me in mind of—'
I said before he cut me off.

'I know. I know. Ariel, the Lion of God,' he said, dismissively
waving his hands in the air. 'I get that a lot but I prefer—'

'Actually, I was going to say detergent,' I said and then before
he could answer, I stalked out of the hall. A second later Grace
came marching behind me, whispering angrily at me.

'Couldn't you just for once—?'

'What?'

'Not be an idiot?' Grace said, catching and then overtaking
me on the street.

'I came, didn't I?' I said, running behind her.

'Well, if you were planning on sulking like this, you needn't
have bothered.' She stopped in the road to hail a cab.

'In my defence, I wasn't *planning* on it, it just happened.' I
caught hold of her arm but she shrugged it off as a cab came
squeaking to a halt beside us. As the taxi pulled away, she stared
silently out of the window. For the whole journey she said nothing and all I could think was that we were heading in the same
direction but that she was moving further and further away.

I press the bus bell and alight. The air here feels different, condi-
tioned and cleaned, as if in Mayfair the very air is sanitised. I
walk until South Street merges into Farm Street and within a
minute I am standing there at number 42B. I stare at the glossy
black door. Even now, in the bright morning light, the place
gives me a chill. She must be in there somewhere.

I can get the police to believe in me if I get evidence. If I find
more out about him.

But now I'm here, uncertainty bleeds into me. I cross the road so that I can see the house better. The master building is a large red-brick Victorian terrace with the door to 42B tucked away beside the main run of steps. I sweep my eyes upwards and see that the sash windows above the door are shut, curtains drawn against them all. I walk a few doors along on the opposite side until I am at my earlier watch-post.

There's nothing out of place here.

There's still no police presence.

No police tape.

No sign of anything ever having molested the peace of this road.

Just then I see the door to the main house, 42, open, and my heart falters. This is it. A middle-aged woman appears in the doorway, steps out and turns back to lock the door. I watch as she picks her way carefully down the stone steps. Before she has managed the last step, I have crossed the street and reached her. She looks up at me as I near, her face fielding a half-smile. She is used to a world that treats her with care and kindness and she isn't afraid of me. Because nothing in her life was ever allowed to frighten her.

'Excuse me,' I say. I am instinctively self-conscious but her smile reassures me as she takes me in. I am in Seb's clothes and I am neat enough to slot into her reference so that she knows me by archetype.

'Yes?' she says to me, her pale eyes are those of a husky. She is older than I had thought, perhaps seventy rather than fifty.

'I'm sorry to trouble you ...' I say. The words are forming before I have even evaluated them. I don't know how the sentence is going to end.

'Yes?' I notice that she tenses her glossy cream handbag closer in to herself. I have made her anxious now.

'I'm here to meet a friend of mine from 42B, only I can't seem to get an answer at the door.'

'Oh, you mean Mr Ebadi?' she says, her voice glass.

'Erm, yes,' I say. 'That's the chap. You wouldn't happen to know where he is?'

She looks at me blankly.

'At his girlfriend's perhaps?' I offer.

'Oh,' she says then, frowning. 'I wasn't aware he had a girlfriend.'

'Ah,' I say, my heart dropping but my mind racing forwards.

'And you say you've tried his bell?' she says, cocking her head.

I nod in assent.

'Well, you see it can be a bit what I would call sticky. There is a trick to it. If one sort of wiggles the button. Come on, I will show it to you. We used to own that flat too, you see.'

At this I panic. I cannot have her ring the bell but at the same time I can't think of a way to stop her.

'There must be a loose connection,' she says as she bustles over to 42B. My heart beats as I scramble about trying to think of a way out of this. It feels like a ludicrously small thing to panic over but I can't have her ring that bell. Her hand quivers over the button and just as she is about to press it, I take her wrist.

She turns to me in alarm.

'Sorry!' I say, my voice softening in a way that I hope reassures her. 'I just. You see the thing is I don't really know the chap. The truth is, I'm an FI,' I say, scraping at memories from my banking days.

'An FI?'

'Oh. Financial Investigator. I'm just conducting some routine due diligence. It's a tax thing. Look do you mind, Mrs—?'

'Wilbert,' she says clearly.

'Mrs Wilbert. Would you mind if I were to ask you a couple of questions?'

'Oh,' she says, frowning. 'Only' – she inclines her head conspiratorially – 'the police were here just yesterday.'

I feign surprise. 'Really? What about?'

'I'm not sure,' she says, walking back towards the pavement. 'I only caught a glimpse of them as they were leaving. None of those flashing lights or what have you. I didn't think anything of it.'

I walk in step with her as she goes back in the direction I came from.

'Mrs Wilbert, is Mr Ebadi in the habit of entertaining late-night guests?' I say, twisting my language around her upper-class settings.

'Oh,' she says, stopping. 'Let me see. I don't sleep so well these days. You know they always told me that I'd go deaf with age but it hasn't happened yet, unfortunately. And these walls let in all the sound, you see, from down below. Yes, I think it was Tuesday night. I heard a lot of banging about. And definitely voices.'

My heart skips at this. 'Did you hear a woman's voice?'

She stops mid-step and looks in the air as if searching in it for something.

'I couldn't say, my dear, to be perfectly honest. There's always noise coming from there. If it's not a party it's the television set.'

'What about the next day? Did you see him then, Ebadi?'

'No, I don't think so. I've tried to get the environmental people on to it but they don't seem to be interested enough to do anything about it.'

'Okay,' I say, disappointed a little. She doesn't catch my eye but is still groping around in the air for something more.

'Wait. Now you say it, I think I did notice something in the morning. It was very early, mind you, around six or so. I heard some voices outside, and a van. That was what woke me, you see. So I looked out of the window, but it was just some men moving some belongings out of the flat. People have no consideration for others. Fancy. Six in the morning!'

I can't pull my eyes off her as I digest what I have just heard. *He came back.* With *help.*

He must have had her body moved. That's why the police didn't find anything.

'Did you see him?' I say.

'I don't think I did. Just the removal men. I don't believe that he's the kind to get his hands dirty. Young men don't these days, I find. Now my husband, he used happily to—'

Before she can finish the sentence, I have thanked her and run off down the road with this news expanding in my head.

16

Saturday

By the time I reach south-east London, it is around midday. Even though the world is immense and for all intents and purposes boundless, we find ourselves locked into an orbit of just a few miles. Familiarity draws us in, a home for our troubles. I need it, the familiarity, to concentrate without being distracted by my environment. That's why I'm here, in Dulwich Park, with the beginning of a headache but a clear mind, to think.

It was always Grace, this place. A memory crashes around me, or a dream. There's a bench and I'm digging with my hands. The earth gives way and then nothing more.

We could have made it work. I still believe that.

I remember reading to her under the tree there and then reuniting with her after we split up. In a way we grew together in this place, the trees and us, sapling to oak. Once, I took her blindfolded across the park in the middle of summer. Her birthday was in December but she hated the winter. That year we had decided to celebrate it in August when the sun was shining so she could have a birthday photograph in the sun. I had hidden a picnic of sandwiches and champagne by some trees earlier in the morning and then surprised her by having Seb and Nina turn up.

'Oh, my God. Xander!'

'Happy not birthday, Mabe.'

I remember another time, a few weeks after the incident with Ariel. I had tried to convince myself and her that I wasn't jealous, or more accurately that I no longer was, and that I understood my jealousy was a violation of her trust. I walked her casually through the park – a small box burning a hole in my pocket. There was no reason to be nervous, not really – it was just a peace offering but it had the quality of a proposal. Perhaps it was, in a way. We ambled hand in hand towards the boating pond but skirted the edge. There had been a time when Grace pulled me towards boats but eventually she gave up when I'd resisted enough times. I hadn't wanted to dilute the day that we'd taken the boat at midnight. To get on one of these pond boats seemed like a violation of that memory. We passed the parked green pedalos and were a few paces on when I turned her back.

'C'mon then, Mabe,' I said. 'Just this once.'

She raised her eyebrows in surprise and then lit up. After picking her way artfully on to the boat, she sat grinning on the bench seat, while I paid. The sun was shining hard so that by the time I had manoeuvred us out of the mooring, I was already flushed through with heat. I rested a little then as the boat glided under its own momentum. I produced the box. Heart beating.

'It's a conch,' I said as she lifted out the tiny gold shell suspended on a gold chain. 'Fibonacci and all that,' I said, trying to sound careless about it.

She put it straight on and beamed at me as I breathed out relief. She wore it then, every day.

Until she didn't.

And then there were the gifts from Ariel. Little nothings, really. Cheap trinkets from China Town: yin and yang note-paper, joss sticks, badges with Buddhist symbols on them. The truth was that I wouldn't have been so jealous if I hadn't met him. He was sylph-like and moved as if dancing every step. And there was I, cumbersome, big, static. Still, I think I could have got over it had I not seen how he looked at her, like prey. And more than that, how she didn't see it. I couldn't believe that she didn't know about men who preyed.

Our argument came with a smiling face. A small jade Buddha. It had been a Christmas present (Grace didn't even see how facile that was, a Buddhist statue at Christmas). She had unwrapped the tissue in front of me and pulled the little figure into the morning light and gazed at it a second too long. Stroked the smooth head a little too delicately.

'So thoughtful of him,' she'd said and placed it carefully on the mantel.

A day or two later I accidentally knocked it off. It was a common-or-garden dusting accident.

'Xander!' she said when she saw the chip. 'You did that deliberately!'

'It was an accident!' I said, laughing. The laughter went down badly, so in the end to prove it was an accident I agreed that Grace could have it in the bedroom. We only had one bedside table, so there it stayed, in benign splendour, next to me.

The smiling green man made my stomach turn every time I saw it. So one night, as I turned out the light, I winked at the statue and rolled into bed. Later, when it was dark and Grace was fully entombed in sleep, the Lord Buddha suffered another terrible accident. This time, he shattered into a thousand glistening lives.

In the morning, Grace left. Left me.

It was a Saturday and she packed a bag and strode darkly out of the house.

'Where are you going? It was an accident.'

She said nothing except what she signalled by slamming the front door as she left.

I was so angry that she had ruined our only day off together that I spent the time doing the things we'd usually do together on a Saturday. First, a trip to the Horniman grounds. I rooted around before heading to *our* bench and sitting there for a while, gazing out over the views of London. Then I went home for brunch, and ate croissants over the papers. I kept expecting to see her come in through the doors with an apology, but she never did. By the time the phone rang I had swung back and forth so many times between annoyance and rage that I couldn't settle. It was just a bloody cheap toy you could pick up anywhere. Why all this drama? Unless it meant more to her than she'd admitted.

So when the phone rang that night, I answered it with a wash of gratitude and relief. I knew I was always going to forgive her. Of course I was.

'Hi, Mabel,' I said.

'Hi, Xander. It's Seb. Grace is with us.'

'Oh,' I said. 'When is she coming back?'

'That depends on you,' he said and then sighed over the line. The phone changed hands and then Grace was on.

'Meet me at our bench if you want to,' she said plainly and then hung up.

It was here that I came – where I am now – to this very spot, and I apologised to her. The expanse of green and its open air gave me, and gives me now, a sense of freedom. It makes me feel as if there is room for my mind to sift and reason. Back then I reasoned that Grace loved me. She knew me, she knew I loved her. Ariel was nothing, a distraction. And my jealousy was just proof of how much I loved her.

But now the process of thinking makes me quiver. Every cell in my head that is occupied by this murder makes my head throb. I breathe until the facts become clear: this man must have killed the woman. He arranged for people to move the body. There was clear evidence of that: a van and two men booked specifically for the purpose.

I pull my coat more tightly around myself in order to encourage some warmth from it. I need to move. I need to get going on this before time spins away and he escapes again. I stride through the grounds until I am on the main road, and it's not long before I'm back in Paddington – Purple Zone. The headache is now in full flow, but this is too important. I push through the glass doors of Paddington Green Police Station. As I step through the doorway, I make sure my hair is still tied neatly away. Then at the desk I ask for Blake or Conway.

'Just on their way now, sir,' the officer says and indicates a place where I can sit.

He calls me *sir*. It's not lost on me, the power of these clothes. Then a few minutes later a young man comes and ushers me to a room to wait. A second later Conway and Blake enter, their faces cold. I stand.

'I need to speak to you about the murder at 42B.'

The two of them exchange looks.

'Shall we get this done now?' he says to her.

She looks straight at me and nods. 'Come on. Let's get an interview suite.'

I am escorted into a room similar to the one I was interviewed in twice before. Blake and Conway are wearing the faces of strangers and sit me down without looking at me. Once they have settled themselves and the tapes are unsealed, Conway laces his fingers together.

'Xander Shute, we are arresting you on suspicion of wasting police time. I won't repeat the caution but so's you understand, the caution still applies. You don't have to say anything but it could harm your defence if you don't mention something you later say in court.'

I nod. And then, remembering, I say it out loud, 'Yes.'

'On the last occasion you were here, do you recall you made an allegation to me that there had been a murder? And that you witnessed that murder? Of a woman?'

'Yes,' I say slowly.

'First of all, do you agree that that is what you said to me?' Conway says seriously.

'Yes,' I say.

'And you went on to describe the attacker as being a white male in his late twenties–early thirties?'

'Yes.'

'And you gave an address of 42B Farm Street in Mayfair in London?'

'Yes. You know all this.'

'And you gave a description of the interior of the premises where you alleged the murder took place?'

'Yes.'

'And do you stand by those details that you gave?' he says, crossing his arms. I notice one cuff of his blue shirt is frayed on the fold.

'Yes, I do. Where's this going?' I say, confusion growing.

'Then just remind me please how you described the inside of the premises.'

I know I am pulling an expression of puzzlement as I speak but I can't fight it.

'Well, there's a black front door down the side of the main steps. With a number 42B on it.'

'Yeah,' he says, nodding, tugging at an earlobe.

'There's a hallway once you go through,' I say, closing my eyes to let the detail come flooding through. 'Victorian tiles on the floor. Black on white. There's a Tiffany lampshade on the light. A large gilt mirror – ornate. Cream walls I think. And then at the far end of the corridor, there's another door and when you open that there's a kind of double room. As if it's been knocked through. A fireplace ahead and to the left. Two leather chesterfield sofas opposite one another. Bookcases along the walls. A dining table and six chairs in the other half of the room. Mahogany. Silk patterned rug on the floor. Do you need me to go on?'

'No, thank you. That accords roughly with our note of what you said last time,' he says.

'And are you maintaining this account, Xander?' Blake asks.

'Yes, of course I am,' I say, still confused by what is coming. I know something is coming, the questions are setting it up. I just don't know what it can be.

'Two uniformed police officers attended the address on the night that you reported the murder and confirmed that there were no traces of a struggle or any assault, let alone any fatalities.'

'Yes. You told me that last time,' I say. 'And you spoke to the guy that lives there. Ebadi? He had an alibi. I know that. But I have more information about that – information that changes things,' I add.

To my surprise they ignore what I say and continue with their questions as if I haven't spoken. 'Showing the suspect exhibit PJW/2. Mr Shute, would you look at this footage please?'

Blake has opened her laptop and is playing what looks like CCTV film.

'What's that?' I say. 'CCTV?'

Without looking up, she says, 'No. It's the footage from the body-worn camera by the searching officers.' She spins the laptop round so that we can both see it.

'As you can see that is him approaching number 42B. Do you recognise the door?'

'Yes. That's it,' I say.

'Okay and in a minute, you'll see the gentleman opening the door. Mr Ebadi.'

I watch, transfixed. This was almost the scene from this morning. I think of the neighbour, Mrs Wilbert, her hand poised over the doorbell. I shake my head and focus again on the screen. The door opens and I see a face. I recognise him from the still they showed me last time. I look carefully. He looks different now that I see him in motion. Different from the man I saw in the half-light strangling the woman.

The officer wearing the camera and this Ebadi speak for a few seconds. Ebadi is smiling at first, and then there is a look of concern, confusion even. He nods after a moment and waves the police in without hesitation. But I know why that is. He doesn't care about the police coming in because the body has been moved. He will have cleaned the place up so confidently that twenty-four hours later, the police are being ushered in without pause. Either he knows that the police will not find anything, or he's calculated that his chances are better if he lets them in now, so he won't have to see them return with warrants flashing.

The footage runs on until Conway presses pause, and I, too, freeze. My mouth drops. I stop breathing.

This cannot be.

The feeling I have now is of the world coming to a halt on its axis. It seems like the Universe is crashing past me at speed. And I am just standing there, motionless.

It's not the same feeling as the one I had after Rory. That was disbelief. Reality had been exposed simply as mist.

I feel myself mentally leave the room under the pressure of the moment.

Rory.

Pulling at me again.

We didn't really recover from our teenage fighting. We tried, as adults, to relegate the past into insignificance, but instead it began to invade all our spaces and push us apart whenever we tried to draw near. It didn't matter whether it was neutral ground or not, it seemed like neither of us could cross the bridge to reach the other. I wonder now whether I could have tried harder, but when I put myself in that space, I remember that I did try. I went to his new flat soon after he bought it. He never came to me. But I did go to him.

I arrived at his building in Ludgate Circus, bringing with me the heat from the street. It was one of those buildings that had been 'reinvented'. Traces of a former glass-warehouse or coffee-vault or some kind of faded glory were there deep in the brick. And now, crowding and rocketing land prices had polished the rust away and called it new.

An old lift clanked into place and I remember the smell of it as I pulled the concertina gate across and waited as it lurched between floors. My pulse quickened as it always did when I was in a confined space. Then finally, after those slowly ground-out minutes, the doors opened.

For some reason I had expected there to be a party, in full flow. Girls in gold dresses and spiked heels, men with rolled sleeves gesticulating in the air. I expected the balcony looking out on to the street below to be crammed with laughing and smoking. I expected it to live up to my vision of his life as a high-flying hedge fund guy. Instead I walked in to this vale of silence perforated only by muted jazz weeping from a pair of Wharfedale Diamonds.

'Rory,' I said and hugged him awkwardly, a bottle of champagne in one hand. 'Congratulations on the new place.'

'Thanks, Xand,' he said, and waved me in. 'No Grace?'

'Oh, you know Grace, she wanted to come, but double-booked herself as usual. Some Ayurvedic thing.'

'Drink?' he said, slipping away into an open-plan kitchen.

'Go on then,' I said. 'It's still cold.' I held out the bottle.

The flat was just as it should have been for Rory. Polished parquet ran the length and breadth of the place. Rugs were laid artfully here and there. A few had even climbed on to the walls. The windows were impressive: floor to ceiling, with views across London. I stood at one and slid it open.

'I like the windows,' I said. 'Beginning to wish that we'd got something like this. All this light.'

'Yes,' he said, emerging from a glass wall. 'The light's good.'

The champagne he passed me tasted sharp and fresh.

'So, seen much of Dad?' he asked, taking a hand through his copper hair.

'No. Busy house-hunting,' I said and leaned out into the view below.

He nodded and breathed it in with me.

'If you get a chance, you should. He'd like to see you,' he said, turning his face away.

There was an edge to the comment, or I felt one.

'It's you he likes to see,' I said.

The air was warm, summery. Up at this height all the heat and moisture had gone from it, so the breeze when it came, came with a cool undertow.

'Look, Xander, whatever you think about him, now is not the time to hang on to it. He's fading. It won't be that long now.'

I looked across at him and saw the same childhood face. Eyes like smudges. Hair tousled as if fresh from sleep.

'I'll go and see him next week. Take a bottle of that Macallan that he likes,' I said at last.

When I turned I saw that Rory had walked back inside. The atmosphere began slowly to fizz in a familiar but unsettling way. I went in and saw Rory's silhouette behind the glass wall of the open kitchen.

'What?' I said, rounding the partition.

'I didn't say anything.' He busied himself with some dishes that didn't need the attention.

'No, but you meant something,' I said, staring at him.

'Look, if you're pissed off about the drinking, don't take him a bottle. You don't have to be an arse about it.'

I didn't know whether I was still pissed off about the drinking, or something else. They both drank. Mum and Dad. But the words come loose from nowhere.

'You didn't have to put up with him when he was drunk,' I said.

'What do you mean?' he said, looking up at me.

'You didn't have him, reeking of—' and then I stopped, letting the words founder. In the silence that followed, I saw the realisation dawning.

'What are you saying, Xander?' he said after a minute.

'Forget it.' I headed towards the front door.

'No, Xander. This is important,' he said, coming after me. 'If you've got something to say—'

'See you, Rory. I have to go,' I said, harassing the locks to work the latch.

He stood, arms folded, behind me. 'Well? Have you got anything to say?'

'Mr Shute? Have you got anything to say?'

The screen blinks at me, strobing between the paused frames. I am back in the police station. The video plays on in my head. The number 42B, in brass against the black door. My brain is

113

whirring, making and unmaking connections when they don't fit. I am familiar with this process. It is, even in the teeth of this madness, comforting having my mind untangling the puzzle.

I know how this resolves itself. Soon, the solution will crystallise and emerge whole. I know my mind will get there: it's slower than Rory's, but still good.

I stare at the screen which just looks back. I cast my eyes away and shut them tight.

Untangle it.

The dryness in my throat won't be swallowed away. I can't make sense of it. The familiar warmth of resolution doesn't arrive. My head thuds and the room begins to close in on me.

In every solution, time is a constant. So, what is the answer to this? What can the answer be to this? My heart begins to pick up pace as the realisation descends to its perfect end.

I am finished.

I stare at the screen.

The floor – the Victorian tile – is gone. In its place is smooth, pale grey marble, threaded through with darker veins. The walls are no longer painted cream but one side is entirely mirrored in what looks like a single glazed panel. Reflected against it, the opposite wall is decorated in tiny mosaic tiles. Tiny spots of starlight shine from the ceiling.

My mouth is open but there is nothing to say.

Blake lets the video run on. The camera and the other officer follow Ebadi along the hall and into the house. Marble again on the floor, running straight through, its gloss firing light in every direction. As the camera turns I see the fireplace is there, but it too is cased in grey spidery marble. The camera turns briefly again and instead of the chesterfields there is a white sofa in a large L. The lens darts round with the movement of the officer and as it does I see the dining table is gone. Where it once stood, there is a huge, ornate glass coffee table bordered by what look to be cushions. Then I look more carefully and see that it is not a coffee table I am looking at but a sunken *dining* table. It has been dropped about three feet into the ground.

All since Tuesday night.

17

Saturday

'It's impossible,' I say. There's no solution to this formula.

'Is it?' Conway says, but he's not really asking.

My brain continues to whirr and click through the gears. Could the murderer have changed everything? The murder was late Tuesday night. I told the police about it Wednesday night. They claim to have visited the address that night. It couldn't be. Is it a trick of some sort? Is it the wrong address? But even as I am asking myself the questions, I already know it's the right place, but somehow the impossible has happened.

'It's not exactly the way you described it, is it, Mr Shute?' Conway again.

It's not. There is no hiding from that. I don't want to hide from that. It's the truth.

'Well, the layout is the same,' I say in desperation but the words fall from my mouth like pebbles on to sand.

'Nothing is the same, Mr Shute. Nothing that you have described to us, *in detail*, is the same.'

'But—'

'I will ask you a final time, Mr Shute. Did you witness a murder at this address? At number 42B?'

I notice that Blake has curled into herself in pity.

'Yes. I know what I saw.'

'So how do you explain that video?' she asks softly. Her voice pleads.

'I can't. But I saw it.' And then a thought comes to me that I voice straight away. 'There in that room where that sunken table is. Did you check under there?' I say but the question dies in the air. It's not possible.

'Xander. Mr Shute. Can I be really clear?' says Blake. 'If you maintain the lie, we are going to have to charge you with the more serious offence of Perverting the Course of Justice. If you accept it now as a lie, we can consider the lesser charge of wasting police time.'

I shake my head. This feels too fast and – wrong.

'I – I know what I saw. Something's not right.'

The two of them exchange glances. From one, a look of regret. From the other, irritation.

'Fine. Mr Shute,' says Conway. 'We are formally charging you with Perverting the Course of Justice and we are terminating the interview. The time by my watch is fifteen twenty-two.'

The tapes are switched off and I am led out of the room and out towards the front exit.

I turn to Blake and try to catch her eye but fail. In the end I stop and face her.

'There's something you need to know about Ebadi,' I say.

She raises her eyebrows and waits.

'Two men came and removed the body the next morning,' I say. 'The neighbour from the main house, she saw them.'

Conway stops ahead of us and turns around.

'Are you telling us that if we speak to Mrs Wilbert, the neighbour, *again*,' he says, 'she will tell us that on Wednesday morning she saw two men remove a dead body from the house?'

'Well. No,' I say. 'She didn't see the body, but the van. It must have been put into the van,' I say quickly.

'So, she saw a van?'

'Yes. She saw a van and then she saw the men and they were clearly removing things from the house.'

'Okay. I think we're done here, Mr Shute.'

I turn back to Blake but her expression is set. 'You have to check,' I say.

She stares but says nothing. At the barriers the two of them wait and watch me leave.

'We'll be in touch, Mr Shute, if we need you sooner, but until then you're to be back here in two weeks. March 1st,' Conway says.

I push the door and step out. As my foot strikes the step, the world feels improbably solid. But I know it isn't. I've just seen evidence of that on a screen.

My head throbs as I reach the bottom of the steps. None of this makes sense.

My mind needs room to run. There has to be an answer hidden in the facts somewhere. It just needs the right lens. If I stand back or to the side of this problem, I know I will be able to find the answer. And that it will come to me in a burst.

The light is beginning to fade and with it, whatever warmth it had brought. I look up as I leave the station behind and start a path in a loop around the building. It is a desolate place. I know that when the summer arrives, the light will make even these bricks quiver again with life. But at this moment, nothing around me feels capable of life.

As I walk around in a large circle, my mind begins to unfold, tracking the past as I go. The murder happened. Then a phrase that I have liked and stored comes to me. Is it Occam's razor? Sherlock Holmes? Whoever it is, I remember the principle. *Eliminate the impossible and whatever remains, no matter how improbable, must be the truth.* Does that hold true? If it does, then the truth is that the murder took place, because I saw it with my own eyes. I watched the before and the after and I saw her lying on the floor. The red wine blooming across her chest. She had stopped breathing. She was dead. I saw him leave. The following morning, I was in hospital. That night I was interviewed by the police. The same night the police went to the address. It was definitely the right address – I saw the video.

So far, so good.

But then it begins to break down. The door was the same door. The building was the same one. But could I have got the address wrong? Could I? I think about this carefully. No. I couldn't have. The exterior was the same one from my memory. And when I went, this morning and saw it in its flesh, it was that house.

In the footage the interior was the same, in a sense. The dimensions were all the same. The windows hadn't moved. The fireplace was in the same location. The cornicing on the ceiling was the same. It was the same flat. That is now one of the facts. There was a murder. In that flat. I can't distil that any further.

Then as I round the boundary of the police station again, I come to a sobering conclusion. However improbable it seems, someone redecorated the house in the space of one day. It was unlikely, more than that, it was improbable. But not impossible. With enough money what could a team of say ten men do in twenty-four hours?

Unlikely.

But not, I have to conclude again, impossible. I am sure I saw this once on television. A woman leaves her house for a day and returns to find it transformed. A TV crew, an unlimited budget and a team of workers changed the garden, the kitchen, the bathroom, the bedrooms. In a day.

It was unlikely. But not impossible.

Ebadi is a dangerous man. He could arrange a disposal quickly and discreetly with the money he seems to have. A man with these connections, who could call on men in a van to remove a body, could surely make decorative changes to a house. Even make them discreetly, quietly. Although Mrs Wilbert the neighbour heard noises in the night.

I begin to race through the changes in the house. The mirror could be put up quickly enough. And the floor. A tiled Victorian floor couldn't be pulled up and retiled that quickly. But a new floor could be tiled on top. Without any mess. The grout might not dry hard in a day, but unless you touched it, you'd never know. Each day that passed would put it more and more firmly in place. By now it would be setting hard.

The darkness begins to establish itself and I sense something behind me. My body freezes as a shrouded figure comes hurtling towards me. I tense and then relax as he passes. A jogger. I breathe again. I think about settling somewhere nearby for the night and then I think of Seb in his house. Is he wondering whether I'll be coming back tonight? Should I return there to spend another night in the warmth, or should I stay out and allow my mind the space it needs to stop aching? I can't afford to have my bones and skin become used to comfort after everything I have done to season them against the ravage of weather.

The smell. Wouldn't the place smell of work? Damp tile adhesive? But then what do police do when they make what they think is a routine call? Would they feel like they could make comments about strange smells to Arab millionaires in their Mayfair homes because a tramp made a complaint? Or would they have noticed it at all? Would the house have been carefully doused in oud and frankincense to mask the smell?

A chill wind stings my ears as I am thinking this and before I know it, I have decided to make for Seb's house. The beating in my head has dissipated. The thinking is done for the day and I know what I need to do: sleep. A good night's sleep now can help me more than an unbridled mind. Insufficient sleep interferes with the neurons' ability to encode information and translate sensory stimuli into conscious thought. Without sleep the brain's cells can't communicate with each other. If don't get more sleep, the memory lapses will continue to worsen, I am sure.

I take my bearings and head south, tight-roping through the Green Zones.

Although I know what has to be done, I also know there's a limited window in which I can do it. There will be no help from Conway or Blake. I can't see either of them helping me to expose Ebadi. They already feel as if I am dissembling. Lying. They have charged me with this: Perverting the Course of Justice – criminal lying. I have to do this by myself.

18

Saturday

'Eaten?' Seb says without looking up. He is in a soft, pale blue crew-neck. Just the sight of him on the sofa gives me comfort.

I shake my head. The time, blinking at me from the stereo equipment, says 21:10. As soon as the hour registers in my brain, my stomach begins churning. 'No, I'm okay.'

He looks at me with a half-smile and taps at his mobile.

'The local Chinese. They're usually pretty quick,' he says. 'Am I remembering this properly? You like Chinese food? Or you did, back then, I mean.'

In that phrase, I am transported. Chinese food every Friday night – me and Grace. That had become our ritual, a way of creating a line of tradition to give our relationship the appearance of longevity.

'Yes,' I say. 'Well remembered. Mabel's idea,' I say to Seb, who is scrolling through his phone.

'Mabel?' he says, looking up before remembering again. 'Grace. That's right. You called her Mabel.'

The fire snaps in the grate and a pocket of steam hisses from a shifting log.

'What was that all about anyway? *Mabel*?'

It was months after having met her that she told me that Grace wasn't really her name. Not her real name, but her middle name.

'Hate my first name. Why would they give me Grace as a middle name and such an awful first name?' she'd said.

I can't now remember what I said in reply. The details about where we were or what we were doing elude me. In my created memory of it, we were walking somewhere beautiful, kicking autumn leaves into a slip of wind. I would have told her it wasn't such a bad name, but now that I'm made to think about it, I can't pull it out of my memory. It's there on the threshold, waiting to be carried over, but I can't quite grasp her name. How stupid of me. Is this the sleep or the kick in the head?

I called her Mabel, which wasn't her name. It was supposed to be sweet, but she complained that it made her sound like an old dame.

Seb is perched at the edge of his seat, looking at me. Waiting. Interested.

'*Ma belle*,' I say. 'It was supposed to be *ma belle* but then it just became Mabel.'

'Ha,' he says, then laughing softly, 'That's right! I remember now. She hated it.'

'She did,' I say.

There was something else to it too, but I can't remember now what that was. Some clever thing about it. Maybe, some Maupassant, knowing how I am, something literary like that.

Though Seb was the literary one. Somehow, he seemed to have read everything, heard every piece of music, seen every play.

'Do you remember that friend you had? Sri Lankan guy?' I say, snatching it out of the past.

'Thamba? Was he called Thamba?'

'That's him. And do you remember how he thought he knew everything?' I say, smiling at the thought of it.

'Oh, yes! The record shop. I picked up some Beethoven. And that's when he said it.'

I lean against the chair and shut my eyes to savour the sweetness of it before releasing it.

'It's not even Beethoven who's playing on it.'

We sink into silence. I sink into Grace.

'Grace liked him though.'

'Grace liked everyone,' he says, smiling. 'Xand, I'm sorry about, you know,' he says slowly, feeling his way. 'What happened, I mean. I should have been there.'

I wave his apology away with a smile. 'I know, Seb. But I didn't need you to be there. I was okay. People go through break-ups, separations.'

'But you went through more than most people. With the – bereavement.'

I stop him with my palm out. Not Rory, I can't talk about him. All those wheels have turned and ground what they needed to grind.

'I can't pretend none of it happened. But time moves in one direction, Seb. I can't think about this now. It doesn't serve anything.'

He nods sadly.

'You know we went looking for you a couple of weeks after the funeral. A bunch of us. You'd been spotted up near the Horniman.'

This news takes me by surprise.

'Why?' I say.

'Because you went missing, Xander. We were worried,' he says and even now, what must be thirty years on, his brow softens in concern.

'I didn't go *missing*,' I say. 'I just decided I needed a break.'

'A break? You became homeless. No, not home-less. You became a homeless *person*.'

The criticism lying in those words is given life so that I can't ignore it.

'I didn't become a homeless person, you judgemental—' I bring myself up short. There is anger swelling that I have to keep from flowing over.

'I left my house,' I say calmly. 'I left some bricks and mortar. That's all. I didn't need it. Or any of the stuff,' I add, looking around.

'But you need it now, don't you?' he says. His tone isn't unpleasant. It's enquiring. Soft. But my hackles are up.

'Really?' I say. 'I don't think this is a good idea after all.' I get up. Before I have made it fully to my feet, I feel his hand on my arm.

'No. I didn't mean that,' he says, looking up at me. 'I just meant. If anything, I meant to say that I was sorry. And you should stay here. As long as you need to. And I know you'll be wondering about the Bens,' he continues.

That word *Bens* was something he said before and I didn't know then what he meant. 'What are you talking about?' I say. My temples send signals that they are being squeezed in a vice and I groan as the pain washes over me.

He's silent for a while, careful of my distress. When next I look he is staring at me.

'You've forgotten about the trunk?' he says, testing the ground.

'The trunk?' Whatever it is he means by that, I have clearly forgotten it.

He is about to say more when the bell rings. 'Food,' he says brightly and gets up.

I hear him walk down the hallway and click open the door. The exchange there at the door is muted and jovial.

The word softens as I turn it over in my mind. *Bens*? Or is it *Benz*? *Bends*?

My memory has been crumbling for years, like it has for everyone, probably. But the concussion and the lack of sleep must have rubbed away some of the finer details. When they return, the memories come not as you would imagine, in gossamer threads, but in waves. And again, as I remember remembering, I see the madeleines, and Proust. All of that is embedded now, entwined with all remembering. It is enough to exhaust any mind.

The door slams and then Seb is rustling through the corridor with what must be bags of food.

As I enter the kitchen, he says, 'Just grab some plates from that cupboard.' He points with his chin as he lands the bags carefully on the table.

We eat mostly silently. He is avoiding something and I am too. But everything in the air between us is heavy and fecund and wants to be born. We eat until there are only ruins. He flicks his eyes across to me every few seconds, on the verge of saying something. Eventually he can't help himself.

'Can I ask you a question?' he says, squeezing the foil edges of a container together.

I don't look up or speak but he reads it as assent anyway.

'How were you okay out there for so long?'

I stare at him because I can't believe he thinks I was okay. I begin to speak when he adds, 'I mean mentally. Psychologically. Being—' he stops. 'I just. I'm not sure I could have done it and survived like you.'

I think about this while he decants the empty boxes into a bag. 'I don't know,' I say at last. 'I'm not sure I have survived.'

19

Sunday

It is late and the house shrouded in darkness should be enough to help me drift off, but it isn't. There is wine in my veins but not enough to bring on sleep so I go downstairs. In the living room I see that Seb has left the turntable spinning. Then in the back of my head I remember that as a student he'd leave his record player spinning empty – something to do with the mechanics suffering more wear by being switched on and off. The smoothness of the motion throws me back and the memories come. All at once. Sheets of them.

It was after the fight with Grace. We sat on our bench at the Horniman and started again. Something had shifted in our relationship and we began to like each other again. At first we went for walks again in the Horniman grounds. Then later we explored more and more of London. We shopped in markets on cobbles behind Borough. We hung around Soho cafés and Whitechapel bagel shops and on hot summer nights we'd chew through hot salt-beef and rye. We went like tourists to Greenwich to see where Mean Time started. Every weekend gave us another chance to both escape and dive into the world. When I remember it now, I remember it imperfectly, memory filtering out the flies and grit of ordinary happy life. When I remember how we attacked our new lives, I see only the stylised memory. Diving into the waves and always coming up glistening. Camden Market, Portobello Road, St Paul's Cathedral.

It wasn't long before we began to look for a real home. Not the rented extravagance that we'd been living in near work, but something we could bed our roots into. Something that was capable of anchoring us, harbouring us, together.

Money was no object, or no obstacle at least. Work was so good at that time that it's hard to explain to people who weren't there to see it, just how idiotic it was. We had so much spare cash that it was unthinkable that we wouldn't just buy something outright. So, we began to save. At first just a slice of extra cash diverted into a savings account. But then, after the first few thousand pounds, the lunacy of it hit us.

'Well, what else shall we do with it? I'm not sticking it into one of your funds,' Grace said, over takeaway Chinese food one evening. She was sitting cross-legged on the carpet. Ra-ra skirt. Black tights. Her hair shining a clover-honey blonde in the low light. She touched her shell pendant absently.

'Not the stock market. I'm not saying that, but the market's about to become quite volatile. That's what the modelling is telling us at any rate.'

'What, then?' she said, rubbing her chopsticks against each other to remove the splinters.

'Maybe vary the portfolio a bit?' I said. 'We could take a selection of low-risk bonds maybe and you know, let the money work.'

'No way. Inflation risk too high,' she said through a mouthful of rice. 'Not to mention the currency risk. And we'd be tying it up to the maturity date however long in the future.'

Currency was really Grace's thing and I trusted her instincts.

'But we'd get gilts, obviously, so there'd be no currency risk. It's all sterling,' I said.

She nodded and put her sticks down. 'There's still inflation and the lock-in. It's not looking good out there, inflation-wise. We're much better off getting, what, six per cent in our special interest account?'

I nodded. I hadn't expected anything, I was just having the conversation. One of those conversations without any pressure or urgency. We could do it or not, it didn't matter that much – it made a difference of just a point or two. But we were mathematicians still. At heart, we wanted the maths to make sense. It wasn't really about having more money; it was just getting the numbers to chime in a way that felt rhythmic to us.

'Though,' she said finally, 'we could just buy dollars. That's going only one way at the moment.'

It was all just money. If we lost anything or made anything, it wouldn't be life-changing. Solid international currencies were pretty safe.

I skewered some chicken and black bean sauce with a chopstick.

'Yeah, maybe,' I said.

After Grace. After the whole thing. After she left, that final time, I emptied out the account and took it home in hundred-dollar bills. Hard cash. It sat there in the living room – the same room we'd spent so many nights in, curled on the sofa, watching TV into the vanishing night – a quarter of a million dollars. In cash.

Except by then there was no TV and no Grace. Just me and a block of money where the TV used to be and odd scraps she'd left behind in drawers and cupboards.

When we gave notice on the flat, I needed somewhere to put it all. It had been so frustrating getting the money out of the bank that the idea of taking it back there was just too much. The telephone conversation I had with the bank clerk the week before I withdrew it all comes back to me.

'We can't close the account unless we have both signatures. It's a joint account, sir. We'd need Ms Mackintosh to sign her consent.'

'But I added her name. I'm the one operating the account,' I explained.

'Yes, sir. But when you added her name, you agreed that the account could not be closed without both signatures.'

I looked at the phone, wishing that it would become sentient just to witness my frustration.

'But that is stupid.' I thought for a moment, frustrated by everything. 'Can I withdraw as much as I want in cash, at least?'

'Yes, sir, there are no restrictions on withdrawing cash. Except for dollar amounts above ten thousand dollars, you would need to order the cash a week in advance.'

'Fine,' I say. 'I'll have the lot. I'll be round in a week to collect it. I'll bring my own bag.' She stuttered immediately, trying to say something, but I holstered the phone.

I try to sleep again but the bedroom is too warm for me so I come back downstairs, to the kitchen where it is cooler. At the sink I quietly pick up dishes and begin to wash. The window on to the garden reflects the darkness so well that it becomes a mirror. I study my face briefly. There are deep lines there that I don't see when I picture myself. The hair has grey strands that aren't there in my mind either. But the eyes. The eyes seem younger than I feel. When I look into them I'm staring into a memory of a younger person. I catch flashes of myself as a child. There's either innocence still buried in the layers of life or something else. Vulnerability perhaps. I see that boy and I want to hold him.

I need to sleep. The dishes are done and draining on the rack but still I stare at the window. No longer looking at my face but through it into the garden. My hands are pink from soap and hot water but it disappoints me that the dirt has gone. It's as if I have turned my back on myself.

I need to sleep. The peace I felt from the evening with Seb has burned away like morning mist in the sun. The woman is in my head, clamouring, and I desperately need to get away.

From the window I see that the early morning light is still an hour or so away. The dark sky has that tender, wintry quality, so that the approaching light, when it comes, will seem fractured. I get Seb's coat and wrap it round my body and slip into the garden.

Some of the chill of the February weather has gone but it is still cold enough to draw fog from my lungs. I crouch at the edge of the lawn, in the shrubbery to touch the earth. It feels cool and comforting. If I don't sleep I won't be able to think. I feel my way in through the veil of slowly descending light and pat at the bushes. They are thick here. I crouch down and shuffle my way in, cracking joints as I do. Years of cold have damaged me.

As soon as my head touches the soil and the night settles on my skin, I begin to feel free. Seb, Ebadi, the neighbour, the woman, her face suspended in agony – all of it is far away. Unreal. But I am a person trapped with hands and feet in each of those lives. Blake and Conway both drift away, unenclosed by bricks and walls. Rory, he clings for a moment with Grace and the dollars.

I think of that day decades ago, watching Seb staring into bin-liners of dollar bills. I'd needed somewhere to put it all now that the flat was vacant.

Seb was shocked and at first I didn't understand why. I walked over to the bags and tried to inhabit his shock – seeing it for the first time, a quarter of a million, in cash.

'Dollars are a better bet than sterling right now,' I said, to help rationalise it.

'Xander?'

'What?' I said.

'It's not normal,' he said. 'People don't have this much cash in a bin-bag.' His palms out in exasperation.

'I just … I just need to simplify my whole life at this point,' I said and tied away the paper faces staring up at me.

I remember that Nina wasn't there. But I have the sense now looking back that she was about to walk in on the scene. And that we – Seb – were desperate for her not to see this.

'And what do you propose to do with it all? You can't keep it here,' he said, looking around the kitchen as if I was asking him to put it in a cupboard.

'Well, where else do you expect me to put it? I don't have a place yet,' I said.

'Oh, for Christ's sake, Xander. Why not?'

'I don't know,' I said. 'I can't face it yet. And maybe. I don't know. I'm still hoping that we can use it. To buy the house – Grace and I.'

He stopped and considered me for a minute before walking around the box to put an arm on my shoulder.

'Oh, mate. Don't do that to yourself. It's over.'

'It was over before but that didn't mean we couldn't get back—'

'Not over like this,' he said, letting go of me.

'What? How can you know that?'

In the gulf between question and answer, I thought he'd begun to understand but I was wrong.

'Nina told me. It's finished, Xander. It's time to move on,' he said, smiling sadly at me.

And then the memory fades away once again. That life is a dream away, a whole dimension away. I shut my eyes and curl into the thick roots of the shrub. The scent of mulch and wood fill my nose. As I breathe I feel embraced back into the Earth.

I am in the Green Zone. Mayfair. 42B is pulling me into its field again. I feel rested, better. I am ready for this. Only an hour ago my eyes had opened to a sense of morning in the soil, a beautiful dampness rising from dirt that only dawn brings. That smell. Light was shifting and I rolled from under Seb's shrub and stretched my limbs, the embers of a dream bumping in my head. All I remembered about it was my hands plunged deep into mud, searching for something. Uncovering something. An *un*burial. I stopped the thought, reminding myself I had to focus. Ebadi. The name repeated in my head until I knew I had to come back here.

I walk past the house, scanning it for signs of life. There's nothing. The house is cloaked in silence, curtains drawn. I sit on the steps a few houses away on the opposite side of the road and stare. There's no sign of building work. But even as I think it, I have an idea, the truth of which rings through me. If I get closer there will be something. There will be dust on the pavement. Drops of hardened tile cement on the step. A rogue blister of grout crusted to a gate post. A splash of wet plaster. Somewhere there will be a spot missed.

I cross the road and my heart begins to drum, the closer I get. I am on the cusp of understanding. There's bound to be something if I look closely enough. Then I am there at the door itself. I study it for traces of work but the door remains resolutely polished clean. The threshold step is smooth. I run a hand along its surface but there is nothing to give it away. Backing slowly up the path, sweeping every inch, I stoop from time to time and fan my fingers across the surface. But there is nothing here, not a single streak of white or bright.

What has happened? None of it makes sense.

Withdrawing to my step across the road, I turn it around and come to another resolution. Each of these subsequent conclusions is the retreating end of a wedge, each thinner and more fragile than the last.

Ebadi can't alter the chemical properties of the admixtures used in the cement. The rate of cement hydration would remain at a fair constant. That's simply chemistry. If the mixture went down on Wednesday, it would have crystallised to some extent by now, but that process would still be ongoing. In other words, the grout lines and the adhesive would still be hardening. It is still only Sunday. The mix in this relatively cold weather would still be hydrating the cement. I still had some time left, if I could get to the tiles and lay my fingers across them, I could prove that it was recently laid. The grout would come away under my nail. The tiles could be moved without cracking them.

Somehow, I have to get inside.

20

Sunday

For now, all I can do is wait. The hours pass, bearing witness to just a few souls passing by. People arrive occasionally by car, drivers stepping briskly out to open doors and shut them again. But pedestrians – there are only a handful. Nobody notices me. In the anonymity of these clothes, I am absolved from the usual sidelong glances of people that see me as a threat, without looking at me properly.

The afternoon has drawn in and the chill comes. It begins to occur to me that he might not be there. He might have left just before I came. Perhaps he's not even in the country. The curtains are drawn too tightly to discern anything. A spike of cold air prods at my body so I get up to look for some insulation. It only takes a few minutes to find a newspaper on the seat of a nearby bus stop and to stuff balls into my cuffs. A few minutes later and I begin to warm up, swollen with paper.

I rub my hands before putting them into my pockets. My fingers touch the cigarette lighter and I draw it out to examine it in the light. A flash of a memory comes to me. Lighting a cigarette in the heavy rain. Pushing open that door to 42B.

Seb in fact didn't smoke. Or at least he didn't when I knew him and hasn't these last days. Nina and I were the smokers. She, the elegant smoker with thin cigarettes that smelled like Turkish Delight. Me, the needy chain-smoker. Grace didn't like smoking and made a face whenever I lit up. 'Could you try cutting down?' she'd say.

'I could. But then I wouldn't be cool any more.'

And then another memory comes slicing through the fog. I met her for dinner once, after she had left me, and she lit up a cigarette at the table as the waiter brought our menus. I raised an eyebrow at her.

'What? Only you're allowed to smoke?' she'd said.

'No, I just—'

'What?' she said irritably.

'I just thought you were smarter than that.'

She stubbed out the cigarette on a saucer. The top of her chest flushed – red and bare. She caught me looking at the place where her pendant used to sit. 'I lost it somewhere in the move,' she said, fingering the space. 'In the flat.'

Now I see the door to number 42B open. Ebadi steps out and shuts it behind him to an elongated beep. He walks along the street away from me, merrily almost, jangling keys at his side and over to a small silver Porsche. The indicators flash as he opens the door and gets in. Then he is gone, the car growling as it powers up the road and away out of sight.

I look up again at the house. Silent. Locked. *Empty.* Can I get in?

That door opened once before. I try and remember what it was like on the inside and the lock, was it an old Yale?

When we were teenagers at school, there was a craze of trying to pick locks. We had all seen something on TV with the *Man from U.N.C.L.E.* or James Bond or something else implausible. A hairpin would go in, the hero would grin at the girl and a flick of the wrist later there'd be the confident oiled click of an opening lock.

When Rory and I tried it, it didn't work. Not once in hours of trying.

Then, because we were who we were, we took out books and read in encyclopaedias about how locks worked. Some of the words come to mind now: base pins, cylinders, the shear line where all the pins line up. We learned about 'bumping' and how you could force a key through the lock to make the pins jump before quickly turning the lock.

But it never worked. We never managed to pick a single lock, though we pretended to the others at school that we had. That we didn't have the tools on us, but we could do it if we ever needed to.

There was another way, though. Funny, I haven't thought of this for so long I have to close my eyes to lure the memory into light.

In the early days when I squatted, when the street hadn't yet penetrated into me. When I was fresh. I remember how much I hated communal living, the smells, the grating nerves and tensions. But occasionally people shared tips. Where to get soup on Monday, who had a supply of methadone. Which shelters had waiting lists and which ones would never turn you away.

In one of the bigger communes, I remember a man – I don't remember his name – a snake-faced man with no hair and round blue eyes. He grinned all the time as if he knew something nobody else did.

'You can always find a place if you use your nut,' he said. He would say this kind of thing – meaningless leftovers from some other half-digested conversations he'd once had.

I nodded. Sometimes it was better to let the talk exhaust itself.

'Arches. Disused shops. Commercial property. Lock-ups – that's my thing,' he said, taking a gulp of lager from a can. For breakfast.

'So, if it's a lock-up, how do you get in? Isn't it locked up?' an older man next to me said drunkenly.

'Ha! Yeah, mate. But you got to choose your whatsit.'

I looked blankly at him as I turned out my boots to dry them.

'So, certain locks you can open. Like Yales. If they got a Yale or even a small padlock, then you're in, mate.'

'How?' I said, suddenly interested, remembering my picking days.

'Lloyd key,' he said. I looked at him and waited.

'What, you don't know what a Lloyd key is? 'kin' hell, mate.'

Within five minutes he had made me one from an old plastic cider bottle. It was just a strip of plastic around three inches wide and about six inches long.

'It's the curve on the bottle that gets round the door jamb. You just shove it in through the gap and over the lock bit and then push. Most doors will open to that. Design flaw, innit,' he said, before flicking it away on the ground.

How many years ago was that? Ten? Twenty? Longer? There is nothing in my memory of that place that ties it to a time period. No flat-screen TVs. No chintz. No shagpile carpet. Just bare floors and boarded-up windows. The heavy, toxic scent of mould.

A siren blares in the distance and I am jolted out of the reverie. Midday has long gone and from the position of the sun in the sky, I know it must be late afternoon. I walk to a parade of shops near the library and look for a recycling bin outside one of the shops. I find one and scavenge what I need and return to my spot. The Porsche isn't there – Ebadi hasn't returned. Hunger makes a call but I dismiss it to sit and carve out my own Lloyd key from a plastic bottle. The cans these days are flimsy and won't cut so I scout around until I find an empty lager bottle. I tap its neck against the kerb until it breaks. Now I test the edge with my finger – it's sharp and slices easily through the plastic. The key cut, I settle in to wait. I can't do this in the light. It will have to wait until the sun has gone and I have gathered some darkness over me.

I turn the plastic in my hands. An hour passes. With each spent minute I know he is closer to returning home. And now the light has finally dropped, I am here, up against the door to 42B. Those large stone steps up to my left shield me a little from view, but there is nobody around anyway.

I press the edge of the Lloyd between the door and the frame where the Yale is. My heart is beating faster than I want it to, so I have to take a break to give it time to settle. But my head-ache has returned and I'm beginning to think of it as an alarm or a warning. What I am doing here? Breaking into this house seems like the worst thing that I can do. I don't know what I am hoping to achieve except I know there is something going on.

Either that footage was showing the wrong house or something behind this door is a fraud.

My breathing settles somewhat and I grip the plastic hard and shove it into the gap. It bends, too early. I withdraw it, straighten it and put it through again from a different angle where the plastic seems more rigid. Then the edge hits something solid and what must be the edge of the latch.

Suddenly the sound of a siren in the distance sends my heart into my throat. I know that it's not near enough to be a threat but I have pulled the plastic out again. I pause, attuned and ready for the slightest sound now my back is against the street.

Silence again. I put the Lloyd key, this plastic scrap, back into the gap and push hard. Then through the wood I sense that the plastic has caught the smooth curve of the lock. And then it hits me, and I freeze: the beep when he left. That sound – the long beep. There's an alarm. I can't break in. But, more than that, the alarm is new. It wasn't there before. He's just installed this. To hide something? What else could be the reason for the sudden need for security? And then there's my story – he knows having an alarm will interfere with my account. I won't be able to explain how I got inside if there had been an alarm to get past.

21

Sunday

Money. With enough money you can do anything.

There was a time when the money men were Americans. There were a few Brits, but most were Americans whose names still ricochet across the ages: Buffett, Gates, Koch, Rockefeller and Trump. Now the money includes Arabs. I've seen the change. Sports cars tearing up Knightsbridge. Rolls-Royces in Mayfair. Their wealth is so great that it confers anonymity – the ability to move through the world behind privacy glass and high gates. To those that want to flaunt their wealth, the Louis Vuitton, Armani, Rolex, Cartier ensure that if they want they too can be anonymous by all looking the same. You couldn't pick a single one of them out of a line-up. I remember those designers from my days in the City. But I never understood fashion.

Enough money and you could disappear.

Enough money can make whole streets disappear.

Ebadi, whoever he is, has enough to give him access to these roads. To park his car, to hold his parties, here in Mayfair.

Money.

I think about *the* money. Until we had that Chinese it hadn't crossed my mind for years.

1989.

I try to retrace the path but there are wide gaps in my memory of it. It has been almost thirty years since she left London. Thirty years since I have seen her or heard her voice. I don't know where she is. I don't even know where she *might* be. Maybe I should ask Seb about her after all. Maybe even meet her again once more. Nina will know where she is even if Seb has lost touch with her.

One of the last times I saw her was in the house she had been renting north of the river after she left me. Her belongings were still in boxes mostly. A few had been opened and a loose frying pan or a dinner plate had been poached from here or there. A jade Buddha was on the mantel. Even after all this, a jade Buddha smiling vindictively. She seemed surprised to see me but let me in once the hesitation had passed.

'So. It looks pretty permanent. This move,' I said, brushing past her and looking around the living room cum kitchen.

'It is, Xander. For us, I mean,' she said, following me.

'I don't understand why it has to be. What was so wrong that we can't get past it?' I said, and even as the words left my mouth the sound they made me shrink.

'I don't know what you want me to say. We've grown apart,' she said, crossing her arms.

Seeing her things here like this, things I recognised and felt were a part of us, gave me a jolt. 'I just don't understand that, Mabe. *I* haven't grown apart,' I said. I leaned against a wall to give her room to pass.

'Then I have,' she said. 'And I can't go through all that again now. Not here in this stupid house and this ridiculous furniture!'

'But you don't have to be here,' I said, moving on to one of the old leather sofas. She looked at me for a moment and opened her mouth, then shut it again. Her hands were clamped together.

Ma belle. We can get over this. We have to because I can't survive this life without you next to me. Look at me, I'm disintegrating. I've tried to rationalise my way out of it. The act of living is fundamentally solitary and I'm accountable completely for this situation. For all my situations. I am a function of my own choices and I can be happy through some other choice. I know this, intellectually. But look at me, Mabel, I'm fucked.

That's what I wanted to say. Instead I looked at the floor.

She sighed. 'Xander, why are you here?'

'The money. I wanted to know what to do about it,' I said, grasping. 'But not just that. I thought we were friends still and that I could …'

Grace began to pace between boxes as if deciding and then undeciding which to open. She paused. 'I don't think we can be friends. Not yet.'

'That's fine then,' I said, standing up. 'Friends was your idea. Your choice not mine.'

'I didn't choose any of this, Xander. It just *is*.'

'You did choose it. I chose you but you chose this,' I said and waved my arms at the room.

'That's the problem though. I am not one of your choices. I'm independent of you. I exist autonomously.'

The words pelted me. 'I know that. I just – emotionally, I feel tangled up in you.'

She took a breath. 'Look, I know with your dad and every-thing … But that's not an excuse for how you behave towards me. It just isn't.'

'I think that's unfair,' I said and felt my face run hot. 'How I behave? Just me?' When she didn't answer I stood up to leave.

She caught up with me by the door. 'Listen. Xand, let's have dinner. Book somewhere nice. *Do* something nice, for me and maybe we can talk. Because I do love you. I just don't love *this*. This side of you.'

I nodded but I knew everything was sliding away from me. I was being deleted from her life, like the pendant that had gone from her neck.

'I want you to think seriously about it. Whether you can allow me to be my own person, make my own decisions, *see* who I want for coffee, without it being a row.'

She meant Ariel and my heart tumbled at the possibility of them together. I nodded and was through the door when I remembered. 'The money,' I said.

'Keep it for now. Let's see what we decide,' she said.

Keep it for now. I remember now. She said it because she knew that she could trust me. And she trusted me with it because she knew I didn't care about it. I never cared about money. I was never one of those people who *did* things with money. I'd met plenty of those others who could change everything with their money. They'd twist the world to do whatever they wanted it to.

And this guy, Ebadi, he could be one of these people. Men who turned up at his door in the dead of night. Men who turned up at the drop of enough money to rebuild, refurbish and clean up. I look up and I am at the door of 42B. The memories keep drawing me away so that my attention is splintered. I'm aware of it only once I am out of it. But I have to focus harder and harder to remain here. This burglar alarm. This incontrovertible thing. I have to think of a way around it.

22

Sunday

On my way through Hyde Park, I see spare food left on the bench. I carefully smooth the aluminium wrapping out before folding it into my pockets. The clean parts of the sandwiches I eat in a bite or two.

When I pass the children's play area, I feel a thud as I remember that this is where Squire attacked me. I wonder whether the police will have done their investigations by now. And what has Squire told the police? There's no value in him lying to them, but value has multiple meanings when you live as Squire and I do.

I stay in the Green Zone and navigate the whole of Hyde Park, but the way I have carved up London into zones feels too flimsy now. It's always been quite plastic, bending as money changed the character of the places, but now after what has happened, with Squire and with the murdered woman at 42B, I have to reorder these zones.

The grass's damp scent reaches me, but I shrug it off. Memories encourage ghosts. And even as I think it I feel Rory catch my hand as he used to when he was small. He would catch it and run, wanting me to outrun him and pull him along so that he could go faster than his body would allow. Little, beautiful Rory.

And then we grew up.

He called me a few times when he got the job in London but it never worked. When we spoke as adults we became children again. Perhaps that was the problem. Ultimately, we were condemned to live in an imperfectly remembered and therefore imperfect past.

Finally, he persuaded me to meet him for coffee in the same week that Grace moved out. There was a new patisserie on Fleet Street. Doo-wop played through speakers in the wall in a gentle hum.

'How's Grace?' he said, once our coffees arrived in delicate china cups, and I lifted my chin to give him a look but he didn't look back. He looked worn through.

'She's fine,' I said and then stopped. 'Actually, she's not,' I said then. 'Well, she is, but we're not. She's moved out.'

He stopped stirring. 'Oh,' he said. 'I'm sorry to hear that.' He ran a hand through his hair, messy and youthful. His eyes, though, were older. Shadows played beneath them. 'Are you okay?'

'Yes,' I said. He studied me and was about to speak when I cut him off. 'I went to see Dad,' I said.

He nodded as if to himself. 'Yes,' he said. 'That's why I asked you to meet me.' He looked at me then, straight in the eye. 'I know what you said to him.'

I felt my stomach drop.

'I know what you said to him, Xander.'

'What? What did I say to him?' I said, feeling my temper rise.

'You said he'd burn for what he did.'

'I don't know what that means, Rory,' I said, dropping sugar lumps into my cup. 'Because it means nothing. He's got dementia. Even he doesn't know what he means any more.'

'He was lucid. Why would you say that to him?' he said, staring. But there was no anger there, only sadness.

I sipped my coffee and looked at him. 'That can't be the reason you brought me here.'

His coffee remained undrunk.

'He told me, Xander.'

'He doesn't know what he's saying, Rory.'

'He did. And I am sorry,' he said, and I watched as tears began to track down his cheeks.

'I'm not sitting here for this,' I said. I got up to leave. He took me by the sleeve, and then stood himself, pulling me into an embrace.

'I'm so sorry,' he said again. His shoulders heaved and slumped as he sobbed. I returned him to his seat.

'Sit. It's okay,' I said. 'You were seven. It's okay.'

'But I didn't even see it, Xander,' he said. 'I didn't even *notice.*'

'It's okay.'

'He loved me. I knew he loved me. But I thought he loved us both, Xander. Equally. But now?'

'But now what?' I said. 'Nothing's changed. He still loved us. Still loved me.' And then after a pause, I said, 'It was drink. The whisky. When he had that much of it, it took him over. It wasn't him. Not really.' I said it for us both, whether it was true or not.

He wiped his face with his sleeve and as it came away, I saw him for a second as he was when he was a boy. Flushed and enquiring. Innocent.

'I want you to know,' he said then, holding my arms across the table. 'He didn't touch me.'

'I know,' I said.

And then I saw him collapse. From inside the eyes, collapsing all the way down.

23

Sunday

There are tears running down my face. I am in the park still and I am crying, but now there is laughter breaking through. It isn't funny but I can't cling on to the present and I need to. Has my time at Seb's house done something to me, blunted the sharpness that I had and had to have to stay alive outside? The day is ending and the best thing to do now is to wait out the night somewhere close. And then, just like that, those two imperatives chime as one. Tonight, I'll sleep out.

There was a man once who built an underground home here in the park. He collected cement and timber and dug ten feet down into the soil in a copse and made a bunker. The rumour was that he stayed undetected for ten years. It never crossed my mind to do that. The point for me was not to be enclosed – even amongst all this space.

I head out of the park and disassemble the strategy I have decided upon. To bypass the alarm I need a key or I need Ebadi to neglect to set it. I don't have a key and I can't wait for him to forget his alarm. So this is the only thing I can do. The woman died cruelly. My mind wants to hold me responsible for some part of that cruelty and to punish me. But my psyche hasn't understood that about me – that I accept the cruelty. The cruelty was always there and has never been punished.

It was an act of cruelty on my part to make Rory suffer. There are no loose, unguarded comments. I knew what I was doing when I said that to him and what the consequences were. Suffering. It was deliberately inflicted. At some visceral level I wanted him to feel it.

But I misjudged how quickly he would fall.

There are no people left in the park. The wardens have begun their rounds in their little green cars and have shepherded everyone out and are now heading north to the other end of the park.

The cold is like a soaked cloak around my shoulders. I draw my lapels close and hurry out of the park. Once I cross the road I look for somewhere I can spend the night away from people and traffic. There is a lamp post with a white-painted cycle tethered to it and dead flowers in its spokes. Some poor sod died on this grubby road on his or her way somewhere before a whole life and all its arrangements was brutally stamped out.

I think of Rory until a drop of rain brings me to myself. Finding a place to bed down for even just one night requires careful thought. I avoid anywhere within a throw of a pub and I avoid high-traffic areas. And then to escape the worst of the weather, I look for a narrow alleyway or small side street that is sheltered from the rain – and then sit there for a few minutes. Some of these alleys are wind tunnels and it's not always easy to identify them immediately. And then there is the question of supplies. The deep recess of an office block is one thing, but without insulation it's not much use. I start by finding a convenience shop with bedding – sleeves of cardboard waiting to be taken away – and then I search for the right 'room' in which to lay it down.

This shop is ideal. There are long sheets of cardboard propped up against a commercial bin. I select the driest pieces and also grab the end of a large roll of foil – just enough for a few strips. I have been here before, I think. There are large recycling bins at the entrance to the nearest alleyway, which I remember has out-of-date food from the shop. In the alley I lay the sheeting down in layers against a wall before rolling myself into the leaves.

As soon as I shut my eyes, I am back there with Rory. I do feel as though I killed him. That he was pushed, and didn't simply fall. My confession pushed him as he stood teetering over the edge. I feel him now in my arms, crying.

I curl up tighter and try and order my thoughts. Ebadi. How did I let him do what he did? I replay it in my head to understand the moment of my indecision because I need to know when I decided not to act. The thought exhausts me as it tumbles through my head. I'm so tired I'm not certain I know where the house is any more. The wind has picked up and suddenly I am aware of the cold again. How quickly I got used to comfort. Now, I am dreading the onset of night.

24

Monday

Morning comes and I crawl from my cardboard sleeve and pat myself clean of loose debris. At the mouth of the alleyway, in the bins, I find some packaged sliced ham and peel back the film. My thoughts in the cold of the morning feel crusted in ice. I crouch and unwrap the foil strips that I had tied around my wrists and ankles. The flesh underneath is warm and I close my eyes at the comfort. Once I found sheets of foil down the alleyway of a group of buildings in Soho. They'd been perfect large squares – something related to photography or art I decided – and I'd covered my waist and the full length of both arms with the foil. Parts of them had lasted months until, like everything, they finally withered away.

I have to move now that I am breakfasted. I head to Paddington Green Station at a march. Twenty or thirty minutes later I am there and go straight to the bored desk sergeant.

'I have information to give about a crime,' I say.

He looks up as if he is surprised. Then he is appraising me, almost dismissing me. It is only my voice, the undisguisable education feathering each word that keeps him from pushing me out of the door or into a cell. Seb's clothes are losing their power with dirt and usage.

'Is Conway here? Or Rachel Blake?' I say.

He turns to a phone and dials it before mumbling into the mouthpiece. 'DI Blake' – he emphasises the name – 'is on her way. You can wait there.' He nods to some painted blue metal seats behind me.

A second later Blake appears in a polka-dotted dress. She looks different. It's not the dark hair tied into a ponytail or the dress which tries to recast her from severe to softened. It's her face. She has a look that I have seen before: of a person who has walked into the night and kept on walking. She opens the low gate and beckons me through without a word or even a glance. I follow her as she tries one of the rooms we have been in before but it's locked. She keeps pulling door handles until finally one gives way. It looks the same as the other rooms I have been in, featureless and bland.

'I have some information,' I say. 'About number 42B.'

She rubs her face vigorously for a second and when her hands leave, her face looks raw.

'I haven't got time for this, Xander. There's no murder. You're already under charge for perverting, don't make it worse for yourself.'

I nod impatiently, waiting for her to finish.

'I know all that, but I've been back there. There's a new alarm.'

She stands up and makes for the door but then pauses to face me.

'You went back? To 42B? If Simon Conway was here, you'd have had your bail revoked and you'd be lying in one of those cells,' she says, pointing along the corridor. She sits down again and looks at me.

'Look. I don't know how you ended up like this. But you seem to be getting yourself together now,' she says, waving a hand at Seb's clothes. 'Don't ruin it.'

'Me, don't ruin it? There's a whole new alarm system in the house. Don't you find that at all suspicious?' I say.

'No, Xander, it's not. I think it would be more surprising if he hadn't had a new alarm put in after the police turned up at his door, asking about a murder. And so what if he's got an alarm? Why is it suspicious?'

I look at her in exasperation until her face gives way.

'Look, I don't know what you think you saw. I mean, I believe that you think you saw something. And maybe you did. Who knows? But you didn't see it there, if you did. You're mistaken.'

My heart starts racing and I can't tell why. My throat begins to tighten.

'I am not mistaken. It was there. I saw it happen there. A woman has been murdered and you aren't doing anything about it!' I am shouting now. 'But if you won't I will.' I look down and see that I am standing up.

'No, you won't. You're going to go home. And so am I. We're both going to get some sleep, and I'm going to forget you came here. And then next week you're going to answer your bail for a further interview in relation to the assault on Mr Squire. For most people that would be plenty to be getting on with. So please, let's go now.'

I walk out of the room and don't turn back until I am out of the station. Anger pushes blood through my veins at pressure. I don't know what I can do to make them hear me. A woman died, horribly. I watched it happen. I worry about her decomposing somewhere cold. I worry for her family.

The light is brighter outside than it feels it ought to be. I shut my eyes against it as I walk and as I do, an image of that room slams into my head. The scent of woodsmoke from somewhere fills my nose and that forces the room in my head to drop into sharper focus. A fire burning in a grate, the crackle and hiss of the logs. And then that song.

There's trouble on the uptrack
And trouble going back ...
But the vision of a girl on my mind won't go away ...

I have stopped walking and I know that to look at me now, motionless in the middle of the street, I'm one of those people you see shaking their fists at the world. Grizzled, angry, strange. But the memory is coming and I need it to crystallise. I have to keep hold of it, no matter what. So I sit where I am on the street without opening my eyes because I know if I open them, the pull of this memory will go. If there are people walking by, staring at me, I don't care.

The ground is cold and hard. I try desperately to land the memory but it feels wispy and insubstantial. I lean hard against the low wall behind me to feel something solid. There's something my mind has stored and now with synapses firing, it has found some significance to it. What is it?

But the image dissolves, and in its place is Ebadi's home as it was on the police video. I scream for the memory devoured now, roughly, rudely, by the vulgar new one. The footage is eating my memory, contaminating it and invading the peace of my mind like an earworm.

I have to think of something else to destroy the memory worm: Seb, the house, the dollars, Grace, Rory. I slide one image after another into my head to shake my head back into order, but it's no good. I can feel the invasive thoughts knocking. The resilience of them.

And now that word, *resilience* is setting its own hares racing. I wasn't resilient enough. That was the problem. That's what she thought. Grace.

When I saw her in her new flat, surrounded by boxes, she said she'd wanted me to do something nice for her. I chose dinner at a Café Rouge. It had been a student hang-out and now that we were fully grown, being there was dizzying, as if I was looking down at us from a height.

We ate solemnly. The meal had a biblical quality to it and by the end of it, I was more certain than ever that it was over. Finally, to break the gloom I reached into my pocket and presented her with the small box that was waiting there.

'It's your conch,' I said as she took in the tiny gold pendant. 'I found it in a drawer.'

She peered into the box and smiled sadly before taking it and closing the lid. We ate the rest of our meal in silence.

'I think it's time for me to go,' I said.

She nodded. 'I'll run you home.'

Grace pulled up outside what had been our house. I looked at her face and was shocked by how unfamiliar she had become, and how quickly.

'I can come in for a coffee,' she said, looking at her watch, 'but only for fifteen minutes or so.'

'No need,' I said and got out of the car. I walked up to the front door and put a key into the lock. I looked round to watch her leave but then stopped. She'd switched off the ignition and was now climbing out of the car.

'I can stay for longer,' she said evenly, walking towards me.

'It's okay,' I said. 'There's no need.' I removed the key from the lock and waited for her to leave.

'Well, I'm coming in anyway,' she said. 'Just for a minute.'

I sighed then and put the keys away into my pocket. 'You can't come in. I can't even go in. I've given the place up.'

Her mouth dropped into a small O. 'Why didn't you say?'

I shrugged.

'Well, get back in then,' she said, indicating the car. 'I'll take you to your new place.' She was halfway to the car before she realised I wasn't following.

'There is no new place,' I said.

'What then? Where are you staying?'

'Seb and Nina's,' I said, lying.

Grace took a step towards me, hooking a stray golden curl over her ear. 'Nina never said.'

I shrugged again. 'Maybe she doesn't know yet.'

'You mean you haven't moved in yet? Where have you been staying?'

I walked towards the car and opened the driver's door for her to get in. 'Here and there. Don't worry. I'm not as fragile as you think,' I said, and shut her in with a soft thud. She looked dolefully at me through the glass and then wound down the window.

'I know,' she said. 'It's me. I'm too fragile, I think. To help.'

'But if you knew that just seeing you, what it does for me,' I said before stopping myself. 'Forget I said that.'

She shivered in the damp air and then fussed around her collar for a minute. I saw the shell there glinting under her chin.

The window rose smoothly up and then, with a small smile, she drove away.

That was almost the last time I saw her, I think. We met in the street once. And then, that was it.

I have to walk. I have to walk my thoughts into the pavement. Grind them into the concrete and stub them out. When I focus my eyes again, I see that I am at the library. I look up at the building. It is a cathedral. I begin to walk around it. Each step I take feeds a stream of invasive thoughts into the ground. I can feel myself shedding them as I circumambulate the building, until dozens or more circuits later, I am nothing but a pilgrim.

Me on one side and the universe once again on the other. In perfect balance.

25

Monday

By the time I walk inside the library, the day has begun to cool. I shiver and make straight for the armchairs.

I shut my eyes to summon the memory of that room, and before long I am there again, the flames licking long shadows on to the walls. I am on the floor, squinting at the scene at the far end of the room, and she is there, bent backwards over the table. There's something about this scene that I'm missing. My head knows it but my heart stalls each time it draws near. What is it? The music drifts in waves over me.

> *There's trouble on the uptrack*
> *And trouble going back*
> *I've had trouble with my memory*
> *And trouble with my back ...*

For a second, I fall asleep and I have the sensation of remembering something important. I am caught between sleep and wakefulness and in that twilight some memory has hardened but just as soon as I wake, it evaporates.

'Xander.'

My eyes open and I see a face that I know. Long black hair hanging down over brown eyes. The smile is soft.

I take a moment to put the world the right way up.

'Amit,' I say.

'Xander. Where have you been?' he asks with concern. 'I was, I don't know, worried about you? Looked for you a bit on the streets.'

'Worried why?' I say, sitting up.

'Just,' he says and then after a pause, 'you didn't seem right. Like you'd forgotten – stuff. I asked some guys about you. They told me I should stay away from you.'

'Oh,' I say, touched. 'Just had a bit of concussion. But you shouldn't go looking for me, Amit. It's not safe.'

'You're telling me,' he says with a grin.

I think about why I am here. 'You couldn't help me out, could you?' I say conspiratorially.

'Of course, Xander. I'll never forget, you know. What you did.'

I stare at him in confusion and then in a panic because of what that means for my head.

'When I was being robbed. By those lads?' he says.

And now, with that nudge, the memory comes back. It wasn't far from here, just around the back of this library. I remember seeing two young men – early twenties, maybe a bit older – bothering a schoolkid I had seen earlier in the magazine section. When I got near it was obvious that they were mugging him.

'Oi, you, piss off,' I had said, walking up to them. They were skinny, more mouth than muscle.

They turned and one instantly shoved a knife in my direction. I took a quick look and saw that he was holding it like you would hold a wand, with the blade pointing down. I slapped his hand away and watched the knife fly into the road.

'You're fucking dead,' he said and started to hit me in the face and body. The punches stung but I could feel the pain was soft. Even as I put my hands up, all I could think was they hurt, but not as much as the one I'm about to hit him with. And then I squeezed my fist tight, drew my arm back and punched him hard. His face burst like a plum and he went down. The other one looked at me for a second, took in my size, and then ran.

'Oh, that? Anyone would have done the same,' I say.

He pulls a wallet from his blazer pocket. 'No way would they.'

'No, not money,' I say, waving it away. 'I need to find someone.'

'Okay,' he says, stretching the word. He smooths his school uniform after returning his wallet to his blazer pocket. Everything is neat on him. The tie is tightly tied, the blazer looks as if it has been brushed. Only his hair is free, long, tousled.

'How do I find a person? On that?' I say, taking him to the computers off to the left.

He looks at me as if I have gone mad. I haven't used a computer since I used to code. Of course, I've seen them, but I don't know how to use them without drawing attention to myself. I don't want a librarian fussing around me with passcodes or whatever I need to access the web.

'I need to access the World Wide Web.'

'You mean Google?' he says.

Of course, *Google*. 'Can you just show me the basics?' I say.

'I can get you to their homepage,' he says and then sits at one of the screens and types quickly on the keys. Within a couple of seconds, the computer has shifted to a white page. Under the Google name is the search box.

'Christ, that was quick,' I say. 'Is the modem always connected?'

'The what?'

'The modem,' I say, to a continuing blank expression. 'Never mind. Am I online?'

He nods. 'What are you looking for?'

'A missing person. Is there a way of getting to a missing persons list somewhere?'

'I don't really know,' he says, pulling a chair over for me. 'Who are you looking for? You could just type the name into the box here,' he says, pointing the cursor to the search space.

'I don't know her name,' I say.

'Erm. Well, that's going to make it hard to find her,' he says. There is a smile on his lips as if this is some kind of playful diversion.

'Girlfriend?' he laughs.

'No. Look, is there a missing persons page?' I say seriously, wishing I could do this by myself.

He types *missing persons list UK* and hits return. Immediately a list of sites appears at the top of which is one that says 'UK Missing Persons Unit'. He clicks it and we are taken to a page with a kind of form on it.

'Gender female,' he says to himself as he fills in the lines. 'Age when last seen?'

'I don't know, late twenties,' I say, watching him type.

'I'll put twenty-five to thirty,' he says. 'Ethnicity?'

'White?' I say, not sure what the form wants to know exactly.

'White European,' he says, and then presses a button that says *search*. I hold my breath without knowing why.

A moment later the results are displayed.

'Only one,' he says. 'Do you want case details?'

I nod as he presses the button.

'Oh. She's been found. Found at the roadside. Eyes: blue. Clothes: waterproof jacket. Possessions: an Oyster card and some cash. And jewellery.'

I stare at the photofit that appears on the screen and realise that I don't actually know what the woman looks like. All I can see is her dark hair and her body as it is bent back over the table. I remember her bloodstained shirt. No, wine-stained.

'Not her,' I say to Amit. 'Thanks anyway.'

'We'd have more luck with a name,' he says then. 'I know you don't know it but we might be able to find it.'

This shocks me a little.

'What? How?' I say.

'Well. Who is she, this woman? Where do you know her from? Where does she work?'

I shake my head at every question.

'Where does she live?' he says, running a hand through his hair.

'I don't know,' I say. 'Wait – if you know the address, can you find out on the computer who lives there?'

'Probably,' he says nonchalantly.

'How?'

'Just,' he says, and then looks at me as I wait for more. Finally, he waves his hands in the air and says, 'World Wide Web magic.'

'42B Farm Street, Mayfair,' I say. 'Type that.'

We sit at the computer for the next few minutes as Amit slips effortlessly from one website to the next. He has the ability to flick back and forth between lists and sites before I've even registered what is on them.

Finally, he looks up and says, 'I can tell you when it was bought. But that's all I've got.'

'The flat? Really?' I say, surprised.

'Yep. It was bought in May 2017 for – wow, 7.2 million pounds.'

The number makes me blink. 'Does it say who by?'

'No. But you could find out by looking at the electoral register, apparently,' he says after a few more clicks.

'Can I do that online?'

He taps away for a moment before turning to me. 'You can either go to Westminster Council and look at it. Or you can buy it.'

'Buy it?'

'Yep. But it looks expensive,' he says. 'I think it's for companies, really. Credit cards or whatever.' He taps away some more and then looks up, his face brighter. 'Or the Land Registry has a thing, look. You can buy a title register for three pounds. Not sure what that is though.'

There aren't three pounds on my person but I need the information. 'The title register will tell us who owns it. Amit, I can pay you back, do you think you could?' I say, but before I can finish the request, he has already completed the form and typed a bank card number into it. Within seconds the title information comes back.

'Summary of title, address,' he says, scrolling down. 'There it is, owner: Arathorn Industries Limited.'

I sigh but muster the energy to thank him.

'No probs,' he says but continues to tap away. 'Yeah. No good. Can't get any details of the directors or anything.'

The screen shows that the company is registered offshore. 'Don't worry,' I say. 'I'm really sorry, Amit. I think I've wasted about an hour and a half at least of your study time.'

'It's fine,' he says. 'I was going to do French. Can't stand it. Who is she, by the way – the woman?'

'I don't know. But something happened to her and I need her name so I can ask the police if she's missing.' Even as I am saying it, I realise I'm not making much sense. 'I have to go,' I say. 'What time is it?'

He points the cursor at the screen again. '18:58.'

'Thanks for your help.'

He nods, and I get up and leave.

Once outside I weigh up what I know. An expensive flat. No more than that. A spectacularly expensive flat. A place for a millionaire, even a millionaire tied up in enough illicit wealth that he can call on fixers to fix his mistakes. Maybe this wasn't even his first murder. A person like that who can click his fingers and have people emerge from the shadows to clean away his messes could develop a taste for mess.

The cold makes me huddle into myself and then from nowhere, the side of her face blooms into view, framed by dark mahogany curls. I couldn't save her. I correct myself: I could have saved her but I *didn't*. And now I can't even find her. How many people might be looking for her? How long could she go before being missed? That website that Amit happened upon, documenting the thousands of people who go missing, showed me that most people go missing *quietly*. A person or two notices. The police don't have time to devote much effort to them. And then, months later, they are found – dead in a field, by a road. Just dead. Is this what will happen to her? Will she die without a body or a funeral?

I can't let that be what happens.

At Rory's funeral there was nobody from home. Everybody, except me and Grace, was from his new life – work colleagues, mainly. A few friends from Cambridge who went on, like him, to live and work in London. All these young men and women stood at the graveside, their faces in ruin but their clothes immaculate. Funeral chic. The women cried, the men nodded quietly. Afterwards a few came to pay their respects, and offered me their hands to shake.

'They didn't know him,' I said to Grace.

'But they loved him anyway,' she replied. She looked into the sky as it began to spit. I looked at her and saw that she was like them. Her face was blanched with grief but her dress was new and looked fashionable. Her golden hair, frivolous against the funeral blacks.

'Thanks for coming,' I said to her. 'Even though we're not—'

She held my arm in both hands. 'Of course,' she said. 'I loved him. And you too.' She gazed into the sky as if searching for a speck of light in the steel clouds.

'Just not enough,' I said and she released my arm.

'Xander. Not here. Please.' Her face pleaded with me.

'I'm sorry about your loss.' I looked up to see a young woman with a short black bob, her fringe brushing her eyes. 'I'm Taz. I worked with Rory.'

Nodding away her condolences, I waited for her to leave. But she lingered.

'I – um. How did it happen? He seemed such a calm person,' she said then, pulling her scarf closer to her body against the weather.

I looked at her hard. 'I killed him,' I said. My mouth filled with something metallic from the air. I'd had a lifetime to absorb, reconstitute, *reinvent* whatever had happened to me. The pain had turned my cells inside out, but I'd adapted over time. Rory, though, was too old when he found out, too brittle, for the onslaught of pain. And above all, I'd known it.

If I could have stopped him, or spoken to him in the moments before he jumped, I might have told him that. I might have told him how proud he'd be of himself if he could see himself as I'd done.

'He's – he doesn't know what he's saying,' Grace said quickly, turning me around and leading me back towards her car. She clicked along on her heels, pulling me, glancing occasionally into the sky. The threatening rain would ruin her hair.

It is only when Amit taps me on the shoulder that I realise that I have been crying. I look up and wipe my face with the back of a hand. His breath comes out misty in the cold air.

'Amit?' I say.

He sits next to me for a moment but his legs dance so much that he has to stand up. 'Listen,' he says, then thinks better of it whatever it might have been. 'Are you okay?'

'I'm fine,' I say. 'Really.'

'Okay,' he says, weighing up whether to say what is on his mind. 'That woman.'

'Yes?' I say, wondering whether he might have carried on searching after I left.

'You know that Farm Street is just around the corner. I saw it on Maps.'

'Yes. I know it is.'

'Well, if she lives there, can't you just knock on the door?'

I consider what he has said and try to assemble into some order what I can say to him in reply. I don't want to alarm him unnecessarily.

'She doesn't live there exactly. That's where she went missing from.'

'I don't get it. So, did she live there and now she's gone?' he says confused.

'Kind of.'

'Does anyone live there now?'

'Yes,' I say.

'Can't you speak to them? Or have you already?'

'I can't.'

'Why?'

'Because I think *he's* the reason she's missing,' I say, and then realise what I have said too late.

'Shit. Do you think he killed her?'

I say nothing but have an urge to confide in him, this boy, who won't find it hard to believe me.

'Yes,' I say at last.

He looks at me wide-eyed. 'Shit. That's dark.'

'Yes,' I say, and then I tell him what happened, in desperation, glad to have someone to share it.

He stares at me the whole time as if he cannot believe his luck at being included in my confidence. I have to keep reminding myself that he is still a child but I can't help seeing him as I see Rory at that age. Fully grown. Almost.

As soon as I have finished telling him, the remorse sets in.

'Amit,' I say, shaking my head. 'I'm sorry. I should not be telling you this. Look, I am obviously just a crazy homeless guy. You know that, right? Just forget it all.'

'So, she could still be there? It's not even a week ago,' he says, bouncing a little on his heels.

'This was a mistake.' I get up and begin to walk down the road.

'No, wait. We should go round there.'

'Really, should we?' I say. 'Does that sound like something we should do?' The tone in my voice isn't one I recognise. I've never liked sarcasm.

'Yes. We should. If she's dead we could definitely find out whether she's still there.'

'How?' I say, stopping.

'The smell,' he says. 'Six days rotting – we did this in biology. That place will be stinking.' He scrunches his nose.

'She's not in there. I think some men came by and took the body.'

'Then at least let's see if we can find her name out,' he says.

'How?' I say. 'I can't go anywhere near the place.'

'Trust me,' he says. 'I'll do it. You wouldn't even have to be there.'

'No. It's too dangerous,' I say, and hold him by the shoulders to underline the point.

He turns on his heel and faces the other way. 'I'm going anyway,' he says. '42B, isn't it?'

Before I can answer, he has jogged away.

When I catch up with him he is already on Farm Street, scanning the doors for numbers. I reach him just as he is about to walk through the gate to the main house.

'Amit, no,' I say to him in a heavy whisper. The darkness bathing the house disguises his expression so I don't know how he has reacted.

'Okay,' he says at last, and follows me back to the pavement.

'Xander?' he says after a moment.

'Yes?'

'If I were you …'

'If you were me what?'

'I'd hide.' Before I can stop him he has run back to the house and has pointed a finger at the bell. He turns towards me in the darkness and waves me away with his other hand. Then before I can react, he presses.

I have time only to notice that there is a second new lock on the door. A legacy from hearing about my second attempted visit from the police, no doubt. Amit has now turned to the door, and panic grips me as I scramble for a place to hide. I hurry across the road and find a car I can crouch behind. I reach it and quickly duck out of view. My heart is racing. I peek my head up over the bonnet and make out Amit still waiting at the door. I hope nobody is in.

My heart counts the seconds as they thud by. With each passing one, I begin to relax. Ebadi must be out. Then I see a crack of light outline the doorway, growing until it has turned Amit into silhouette.

I cannot make out at this distance what is being said, but Amit is gesticulating with his hands to a figure in the doorway.

It must be Ebadi. After a minute Amit seems to turn to go but is stopped by something Ebadi has said. Ebadi steps back into the house and just as I think that the door is going to shut safely between them, Amit follows him inside.

26

Monday

As I wait here in the growing darkness, panic begins to overtake me. Amit has just walked into the house of a murderer and I let him. I don't even know what he'd planned to say to him. If he went over there and started talking about a dead woman or a missing woman, what was Ebadi likely to do?

I cannot sit here, hiding behind a car, and let him come to harm. Not this time around.

I get up from my position and march towards the house but an unformulated thought stops me. My brain begins to click and shift through the gears and once it has, I stop and turn back. I can't break the door down. So, then I have to ring the bell. What if he refuses to open the door? What if he opens the door and refuses to let me past? Calls the police? What if, having heard the doorbell and seeing me, he panics and does something to Amit? I can hardly call the police. They wouldn't come after all the fuss I have created and laid at his door. Or if they did they would arrest *me*. My heart begins to pump and suddenly I feel light-headed. I don't feel in control of events and I know now why I have laboured so hard to avoid having to care for another person. My life on the streets doesn't allow any room for that. I have tried so hard to stay alone and yet here I am.

The safest thing is to wait. He has no reason to kill a boy. An identifiable boy, with long hair, in a school uniform. A boy who would be missed, by hundreds of people. An image of Amit comes into my mind. In it he is being strangled. I shake my head to rattle the picture free. It disappears.

But there are others waiting to take its place. I try to think of something else. Someone else. Rory. Grace. Seb. I screw my eyes shut and see Amit in a box, being buried.

Rory. Grace. I will myself to think of anything but this, so that I can contain this panic of Amit being buried.

It was harder to bury Grace than to bury Rory. The physical interment was one thing. Rory went into the ground with all the rituals of goodbye. The rites signal that it's time to move away, to move on. When that lid closes, when the box is lowered, when the earth is scattered and the words are said, when the belongings are tidied away, the message is inscribed: move away now. There is nothing left. These goodbyes have been extended too long already.

I breathe in deep draughts.

Grace was different. She didn't stay in one place to be put under soil. She kept living in my head, in a hundred different incarnations. There were no rituals. One day we were there spinning in one another's orbits, like twinned planets, the next she had moved out. *Ma belle.* Gone. And with her everything that she had accumulated, then later absorbed into our lives, was gone too. The debris she left was minimal: a hairclip in the bathroom, a forgotten mug with a work logo on one side, that pendant, some possessions of equivocal ownership like records and books. But there had been no rituals so she, though alive, was harder to mourn.

I've held on to the memory of the last time I saw her and how I looked up when I saw the shoes.

'Xander,' she said, and crouched down on to the pavement to speak to me as if I were a child. She was dressed for work, her hair like pale honey, shining in places. Newly cut. Newly bright. Her perfume was light, like breath on my face. The shell nestled in a dip in her chest.

The shame I felt when I saw her looking at my hands comes back now.

'Come on,' she said, and stood. 'There's a café over there. Let's have some breakfast.'

Though I hesitated, the need to be with her was too strong.

'Not that one,' I said. 'They won't have me. There's a place around the corner.'

I'd known the owner of the café before I took to the streets. He was Iraqi and had been a physicist before he had sought asylum in the UK. 'Saddam's bombs. I make them work not so well. So of course, he want to kill me now,' he'd said. 'And family.'

'Mr Xander,' he said as I walked in. 'Same as usual for you?' He stopped then and looked at Grace. Pristine.

'Please,' he said, taking a tea towel and wiping down a table in the window. 'Please to sit.'

Grace smiled and we sat at a Formica table.

'Very intelligent man. Very intelligent,' he said pointedly to her about me before withdrawing.

Grace took a breath and then forced a smile. 'Nina told me about, you know, *this*,' she said, opening a hand in my direction. 'I hadn't realised it was this bad. Are you okay? I mean I know you're not okay but—'

'I *am* okay,' I said.

'You're not,' she said. 'Nina and Seb have both said they'll have you for as long as you need.'

'As long as I need? For what?'

'To get yourself together.'

'I am together, Mabe. I am together.'

'Then what's all this about?' She dropped her voice to a whisper as a pair of plastic menus were brought to us.

'Thanks, Udhey,' I said. He smiled sadly before shuffling away again.

'Well?' she said.

'Well, what?'

'You're a highly qualified, intelligent man. You owe it to yourself to do more than this.'

'I am doing something,' I said, picking up the menu.

She forced it down with the palm of her hand and looked into my eyes.

'I know that with Rory ...'

I held up a hand to stop her.

'Okay. I'm sorry, Xander. I know you're mourning him still and I know it's going to take time for you to find your way out. But this isn't the way.'

I traced circles in the menu with my thumb before looking up. 'But you know the way, I'm guessing.'

She sighed and straightened in her seat. 'There are a thousand ways to the truth, Xander.'

'Truth? You think his death had truth? Do you think it was just? That it had its own morality somewhere? Really?'

'Well, whatever this is,' she said, 'it's not moral.'

The words stung. They always stung when she said them.

'What? What am I doing that's immoral?'

'This! The begging, Xander! You have everything going for you. Some people don't. Some people are reduced to this because of circumstance. What's your excuse?'

'I don't need an excuse, Grace. It's called free will,' I say. 'You would have understood that a year ago. Before you *changed*.'

She humphed. The sound and smell of the cooking together squeezed my stomach a little.

'You tell me what's so good about your life. If you had twenty-four hours to live, would you spend ten of them working? No, you wouldn't. You'd be here. You'd be out. Living.'

She sighed then and looked at me, resigned.

'Let's just order,' she said.

When the bill came, I instinctively reached for my back pocket and then stopped in embarrassment. Grace pretended not to see and left a twenty-pound note, telling Udhey to keep the change.

'You know there are still all those dollars,' I said. 'They're at Seb's so – just take them when you want.'

'Yes, he told me. I still can't believe you took it all out in cash!'

She got up to leave and then changed her mind and sat back down again and took the purse out again. I held my hand over it quickly.

'No. I'm not taking your money.'

She looked at me in surprise. 'I wasn't going to give you money, Xander. Why are you in so much trouble? You've got a quarter of a million dollars. You don't need my money. That is my whole point!'

'Then what?'

She sighed. 'I just wanted to tell you that we're ... I'm going away for a few weeks in December.'

I tried to master the muscles in my face as I took in the news. *We.*

'Why are you telling me this?' I said.

'Just – here,' she said, getting something out of her purse and sliding it across the table.

'What's that?'

'The spare key. To my place. I just thought, if you needed somewhere, it's going to be empty over Christmas and – well, you'd be doing me a favour, actually. Have someone watching the place.'

I slid the key back over to her. 'I don't need it. Thanks,' I said, and stood up. She picked it up and moved it nearer to me.

'Take it. If you don't use it, don't worry. You can post it back through the letter box when you get a chance. Just in case you're – I don't know. Desperate.'

Reluctantly I took the key and put it in my pocket. We stepped out into the street and stood not knowing what to say next. Eventually she just touched my arm and walked away.

That might have been the last time that I saw her.

A chill wind rips through my clothes and I am shaken back into the street. Amit is still in that house. It has been too long. I have to act soon, otherwise ...

I look around on the street for something to hold. Something heavy like a brick is what I need. I can knock on the door and when he opens it, I can clump him with it. Force myself in. Or, better, smash an upstairs window with it and lure him outside to investigate, and maybe that will get him or Mrs Wilbert from the main house to call the police.

After a hurried search I quickly learn that there are no spare bricks in Mayfair. I begin to pace in small circles as desperation takes hold of me. I don't have a mobile so I can't make a call even if I wanted to. And the phone boxes, once on every street corner, have vanished over the years.

I take a breath and cross the street towards the house. There are no windows on the ground floor that I can look through. The windows at this level must look out on to the high-walled garden at the back. But there is a letter box.

Through the flap my vision is blocked by a fringe of bristles. I put my ear to it and listen. Nothing. Until I hear the noise of a door being unlatched and the faint drift of voices being chased by their makers. They are coming back. He's safe. I drop the flap and run back to the car and crouch.

A minute later the door opens and to my relief there is Amit, framed in light. He is shaking the man's hand. Ebadi. He waves as Amit turns to leave, and slowly the door shuts.

I breathe again.

On my feet I beckon to Amit, who is twisting his neck, looking for me. He catches sight of me at last and runs over. I scrutinise his face for signs of harm or alarm until, at last, he reaches me. Smiling.

'Amit. Are you okay?' I say, staring into his expression.

'What? I'm fine,' he says, putting a hand through his hair.

'What the hell happened? When you went inside I thought you might have been killed!' I am losing control over my voice.

'It's fine, Xander,' he says, laughing. I find myself relaxing a little but my throat is still tight.

'So how did you get in?'

'Oh. I told him I used to live here when I was a kid and if it was okay could I see my old room again,' he says, straightening up.

'You did what?' I can't quite believe how brazen he had been.

'I found something out you're definitely going to be interested in,' he said and nodded at me to follow him down the road.

27

Tuesday

I'm back in Hyde Park. Alone again. I have found a dry patch in a dense clump of bushes on the outer edges even though I shouldn't be here in the dark after the Squire thing. What if he ends up back here again and starts bothering me? Could that get me into trouble? I beat the thought away. Squire's playground patch is at the other end of the park, and I need to be near number 42B – that is the most important thing right now.

The bushes are thick enough to shelter me from wind and rain, and from other people. In the deep blue of the night, I venture out to forage for food and packing material. I get dry boxes from the front gardens of houses I pass. The world has become a place where everything is delivered to the door and there is no shortage of boxes. Food is harder to come by. In the end, because I am desperate, I simply walk into the supermarket and ask for any expired sandwiches. The young woman at the till tells me that they aren't allowed to give me any for health and safety reasons but that if I happened to take them, she wouldn't stop me. I thank her, and take three packets and a wrapped slice of currant cake.

Then I think about Amit and the danger I led him into. For what? And at what price to me? I am unsettled now by this responsibility I seem to have for him and the uncomplicated way in which I completely failed him.

As I walked with him he replayed the encounter. He told me how he'd been allowed to wander freely through the house as Ebadi, interested only in ensuring he didn't steal anything, lazily followed him. But Ebadi could tell from Amit's voice, his uniform, his kind of school, that he was safe. I imagined how Ebadi would have relaxed when he was sure there was no threat from Amit. This genuine young man with eyes brimming with life.

'But then I got talking to him,' Amit said, those same eyes flashing now. 'I asked him how long he'd been at the house.'

'And?'

'He's only been there a few months, he said. He has a family in Yemen – a wife and two children.'

'Okay.'

'And I tell you what. That place is immaculate. There's no dead body smell in there at all.' He was eyeing me to measure my reaction.

'The hall. The floor. Did you notice it?'

'What do you mean?' he said.

'The grouting. Was it new? Did it look like it could have been recently done?'

He looked up as if searching. 'The floor?'

'I think it's a new floor. It's a long story but I think he's just had it laid,' I say.

'Oh. I don't think so.'

'Did it smell damp or of cement?' I said, pressing him.

'No,' he said. 'It was normal. Clean. And there was one other thing,' he continued, excited.

'What?'

'He was really nice.'

'Amit ...'

'No, wait. He was. He asked me what I was studying and I told him English and History and French.'

'So?'

'So, he went over to a bookcase and gave me this.' He pulled a small hardback from his pocket. I took it from his hand. It was similar to the school copies I'd had once: *L'Étranger*.

'He gave you a cheap Camus, that doesn't change anything,' I said.

'Xander,' he said, looking around. 'I don't think it was him. He even told me I could pop round tomorrow and he's going to dig out some more books for me. For free!'

My heart dropped. 'No – Amit. You can't go back there. You don't know what I know,' I said. 'You don't know what he's capable of. Sure, he can act nice. Just as he must have done with the police. He might even *be* nice, most days. But he killed a person, Amit. Stood over her and strangled her.' I snatched the book from his hand and flung it high into a neighbouring garden.

Amit's face hardened and he ran quickly in the direction I had thrown it. He returned empty-handed. 'I don't want to talk to you,' he said and stormed off.

The cold night passes slowly and I fall asleep not long before dawn. When I wake it's with the terrifying idea that someone has killed Amit. Of Amit being rolled up in a curl of turf.

When I reach out with my hand and touch the hard, icy ground, I am pulled back into wakefulness. I need to move. I gather up the flattened boxes. I don't want to leave them here. If I leave the den whole, it will become cuckooed, and places like this one, safe and dry and obscure, are hard to find. I fold the cardboard before pushing it deep into the bush, out of sight.

It is still too early for there to be many people around. I get up and walk into the lifting sun. My thoughts cycle back again and again to this question: where is she? I need to find out where he has dumped her body. She can't have just vanished. She is somewhere. For now. Until she surrenders to disintegration.

After some minutes of walking, the blood has warmed my muscles through. By the time I get near, the traffic on Park Lane is in full commuter flow. A right down South Street and I am on the road heading straight towards Farm Street. The building is washed in golden morning light and it makes a fraud of what happened in that house. There is only one thing to do now and that is to confront him. If I challenge him, what can he do? I will present him with what I know. That I was in the house at the time he killed her. That it was I who made the noise that startled him. That it was my strange smell that caused them to comment. And that I watched as he strangled the life out of that poor woman.

Some twigs cling to me and I brush them from my clothes, marching straight to his front door. The brass numbers shine in the morning light as I approach. Now I am here, in touching distance of the bell, I hesitate. How will he react? Will he let me in or will he just shut the door on my accusations? In the end it doesn't matter. I have to do it. But then, just as I am about to knock, there is the sound of movement coming from within.

I back down the front path and walk a little way up the road. When I am at the next house along, I stop and look. My heart is beating. I don't understand this sudden skittishness that has overcome me. Am I afraid of him, or of what I might do? Ebadi emerges between next door's laurel hedge and the wall. I watch as he leaves, taking care to double-lock his door. The Yale and then the deadbolt. And then he is out of his paved area and on to the street, walking away from me.

I turn and follow him. Initially I convince myself that I am still settled on confronting him but then as I get closer, I find I'm curious about where he is going. Before long we have reached Park Lane. The traffic has begun now to slow to a drip as he turns right and carries on towards Marble Arch.

I am ten or fifteen feet behind him, unnoticed. The other pedestrians are dressed for work. Suits and polished shoes join ranks with smart dark jeans and pea coats. The weather is still cold enough to bring plumes of vapour from their mouths. Ebadi is wearing dark jeans and an olive suede bomber jacket. From the edge of a cuff, I can see a heavy silver watch. As he walks I see flashes of red from the soles of his basketball shoes. I expect him to start threading through Edgware Road but instead he stops at the Tube and descends into the station.

Should I turn back? His house is empty now, and maybe there is a way of getting in that I haven't had time to properly consider. But then – two locks. The crowd carries me forward so that in seconds I find myself in the guts of London, pushing in behind an alarmed elderly man as he goes through the barriers. They open automatically at the swipe of his card and I manage to squeeze through with him. I apologise when he tuts at me and then I glare at the barriers as if they're at fault. I turn around to find that I have lost Ebadi.

I plough on through the crowds on to the escalator, and then see the flash of his red soles on the Central Line platform heading west. It is crammed full. This platform lined with people under its curved walls makes me dizzy.

Please stand behind the yellow line.

A gust of hot, oily air passes so close that I wonder that they are not drawn into the track by the pressure differential. The Bernoulli principle. I shake that thought off. I still have my eye on Ebadi who is on his phone, sandwiched between commuters. A train screeches along the platform and stops. We all bundle on, squeezing into every available space. In the crush I lose sight of him for a moment until I see him through the glass in the doors dividing the carriages. He seems carefree. He checks his expensive watch and then lets his arm dangle by his side.

It's when we approach North Acton that I see Ebadi patting himself down unconsciously, waiting for the doors to open. I hang back until the last possible moment and then I jump off too. I pick up a *Metro* newspaper from a bench and hold it close to my face as I follow him. I don't want him to get a good enough look at me to risk him causing me a problem. If l look down at my newspaper, he won't see me. He presses an expensive wallet against the pad and walks through the barriers.

The daylight is disconcerting. I need to push through the gates behind somebody else but I am exposed by all the light. As I approach them my heart begins to kick up a beat. I can't easily shadow someone through here. There is a member of staff by the front exit. Ebadi will see immediately if there is a commotion. I shuffle forward slowly, eyes searching out the best option. Then, with relief, I remember the Oyster card Seb gave me is in my pocket.

Outside the sun has vanished from the sky, leaving it steel grey. A few seconds later, as if to confirm the change, it begins to spit out a fine drizzle. Up ahead I see Ebadi, red soles lighting each step. His head is down against the wind. I follow until he reaches a fork in the road – Park Royal Road. Along the left side are some pitiful-looking houses, broken and unloved. To the right there is what seems to be a large park edged by a low brick wall topped with iron railings. He crosses over towards the park and stops at the entrance.

What is he doing here? In a park, miles away from his home? I approach the curve in the pavement, announcing the brick pillars of the park gates. There is a sign affixed to the left pillar which reads MAIN ENTRANCE. And then I see in green letters two words immediately above them and my heart stops.

ACTON CEMETERY.

28

Tuesday

I don't get on with cemeteries. The ghost of Rory lingers around every hallowed space. He is hard enough to escape on good days when I am busy surviving. Even on those days he comes through, snaking in through cracked veins. And when he does it takes all my effort to shut him out.

But here, he flies straight at me from every corner. He is everywhere. Smiling. Reproachful.

The ghosts press hard against the shell of my skull but I push myself ahead. Ebadi is hunched uncertainly against the cold, but there's no uncertainty in his route. He skirts the old chapel at the foot of the path and then makes straight for the field of graves. He weaves through the headstones, picking over the uneven ground. The wind bites as I go, forcing my face down.

Ebadi is heavier-set than I remember, but he moves smoothly despite his weight. I pause to watch where he goes and as soon as I do, he stops too.

As the wind cuts through me, he plunges his hands into his pockets to bring out fistfuls of petals. The wind carries them away to land on broken ground. As he releases the last of his confetti and touches his hand to chest, I realise something with a jolt. Maybe he has buried *her* here. Maybe he's managed to remove her body to this graveyard. What better place for a decomposing dead body? A sanctified space for a woman he no doubt loved. Of course, when I think of it now, in this cold light, he couldn't have, wouldn't have simply dumped her in a river or some waste ground. He would have wanted to be able to commune with her. He would have needed a place to exorcise his grief and beg for redemption. Or at least to hide her in plain sight.

I fix my eyes on the gravestone. From this distance it looks smooth like marble, similar to the marble that now paves his hallway. The coincidence begins a furious sadness in my chest. Even in death she couldn't avoid being *possessed* by him. Ebadi looks up to the sky and then makes his way back to the path. I look past him, feigning a casual glance before heading off at a tangent. I circle round behind him so I can watch his back receding towards the exit. I keep looking until he is just a dot and has passed through the gates. Then I make immediately for the smooth gravestone.

What am I expecting to see engraved there? Her name? Would he be that bold? And then other questions begin to rain down around me. How did he get a space here? Would there have been a death certificate? What about a ceremony? A service of some kind? Immediately behind me I feel the weight of a person, not quite pressing, but following. There is no sense in turning around.

I know it's Rory.

I stand before the stone and stare.

It has started to drizzle again and the mist feathers my face as the wind blows. Droplets trickle down the lettering and the engraved dates:

MISHAL ALI

1971–2019

I remember. The name he called out at her as she lay there, dead – was that Mishal? There is something below it in what looks like Arabic lettering but could just as easily be South Asian. But it's that name, Mishal, that stills me. She has a name. Whatever else he might have done to her, he didn't bury that.

When I crouch to touch the stone, I notice how clean the grave itself is. There is a slab on the ground matching the head-stone. But where the other graves are fringed in grass, this one isn't. There is only bare soil, darkening in patches as the rain continues to fall. This grave is newly dug.

My head is spinning as I walk towards the path. There are gaps in my understanding of what has happened. I don't know how exactly he has managed to bring her, Mishal, here. I don't know whether it was money or influence or subterfuge. At least I know she is here, and I know who she is. I just don't know what to do about it.

I make my way back to the Tube. In less than an hour I am walking up the road to Seb's house. I have to do something about this but to understand what, I need to talk to someone about it. Opening up to Amit feels as though it has opened a sluice gate.

I haven't told Seb about any of this and he has just let me be when I have been there with him, politely, as if to ask would have been an intrusion. He's stayed out of my way, even though I have been living under his roof and in his clothes.

As soon as I knock on the door, I realise he won't be home. It's midday. He won't be home for another two or three hours. But just as I turn away, I see shadows behind the glass of the front door. A beat later, the door opens.

'Seb,' I begin to say, 'I didn't think you'd be home.'

He is still in his work clothes, pink silk tie knotted tight. He hasn't been home long. He gives me a serious look and puts a finger to his lips. I widen my eyes at him for an explanation.

He calls out to somewhere behind his shoulder. 'Whoever it is, they've gone, Detective.' He gives me a look that says *go*.

He is trying to help me evade the police, but I need to speak to them about what I have just learned.

'It's okay,' I say to him, and push past him towards the kitchen. 'Detective Conway,' I say, rushing in. He turns to face me with a cup of tea in his hand. His suit looks cheap next to Seb's and pouches under his eyes tell me he is tired.

'Mr Shute,' he says gravely.

'What's happened?' I feel suddenly as if I can't breathe.

'Happened?' he says. 'Nothing's happened as such. We wanted to talk to you about Mr Squire, as you know.'

'Oh,' I say, suddenly remembering. 'Okay.'

'But there's one other thing.'

I look at him expectantly. He puts his cup down and strides towards me.

'Xander Shute. I am arresting you on suspicion of murder. You do not have to say anything. But it could harm your defence if you fail to mention when questioned anything you later rely on in court.'

'Murder?' Suddenly the air around me has become thin. Too thin. 'He's dead?' I say, steadying myself on the door frame. He says nothing but takes out handcuffs from his pocket and methodically tightens them on my wrists. Seb follows me as I am led to an unmarked car.

'A solicitor – can I get you a solicitor?' he says breathlessly.

'No,' I say. 'But—'

'What is it?'

'Thank you,' I say. 'I just wanted to say that. For being here when I needed you.' He stands there by my side, helpless as I am put into the back seat of the car. He takes out his phone as we are waiting to leave and dials a number but then hesitates and replaces the phone in his pocket. He stares at me through the glass as if he is trying to tell me something.

The car smells of new plastic and makes me feel ill. Conway climbs into the driver's seat and starts the engine with a button. He looks over his shoulder at me before he pulls away but says nothing.

My heart thumps in my chest. As the car races, so too does my pulse. All of this space is shrinking, pressing down on me. I don't want to be in a cell. I can't be in a cell again. There is no way of connecting to myself under this pressure of space. My hands become cold and clammy and then my face. The blood is redirecting itself. I know that's all it is but knowing doesn't help the crushing sensation that I am having a heart attack. And now I wonder whether that is what is happening.

'I'm having a heart attack,' I say too quietly to be heard. I focus on something outside myself to reboot my system. To stop the panic, if that's what it is.

Murder?

Squire?

I have been arrested on suspicion of murder. That must mean Squire has died. If there was ever a chance of him confirming to police that it wasn't me who stabbed him, it has gone.

Conway accelerates along the road in silence until I see the sign above the building once again. PADDINGTON GREEN POLICE STATION.

He parks then unclips his seat belt. When he turns to face me, he gives me an arch look.

'You've really done it now, haven't you, Einstein?' he says, and then steps out of the car. I wait, desperate for him to open my door. But he doesn't. He skips up the steps to the front entrance and disappears behind the glass doors. I can't breathe.

29

Tuesday

My throat is tightening still, but I lid the panic by focusing on something concrete. I dredge up as much of the details of the allegation as I can as I sit in the police car. I breathe slowly and evenly. Details. I need to be prepared this time. But there's so much dust on the memory now.

It's no good. The heat is stifling and the breaths I take feel hot and laboured. I prod at the window buttons but I know already that they're not going to work. Panic rises in my chest, and within moments I am wishing that Conway was back here to let me out. I look around and then see a police officer on the steps, in uniform, and I tap against the window uselessly. He lights a cigarette and smokes it unhurriedly. I am maddened by his slowness and insouciance.

'Help!' I shout at him but he doesn't see me or hear me, trapped in this glass and metal padded box.

And then Conway appears at the front door. He saunters towards me. My breath quickens as he inches closer. Finally, he is at my door and opens it.

'Thank God,' I say, panting. 'You can't do that! I have a condition. I'm claustrophobic.' My voice rises and I am suddenly embarrassed by the weakness in it.

'It was two minutes,' he says, and then nods at me to follow him into the station.

I am processed exactly as before. Rights carefully explained to me again and I am left to read the same forms. But this time I am taken to the interview room much more quickly. It's as if time has suddenly sped up.

Conway and Blake are there. She looks much less fried than the last time I saw her. I shut my eyes through the caution and wait for the first questions. I am still, even now, debating whether I should tell them the truth or just go 'no comment' as they do on TV.

'You do not have to say anything but it may harm your defence if you fail to mention when questioned anything you later rely on,' Conway says.

It may harm your defence if you fail to mention. I don't remember this from TV. It is new.

Their eyes flit between one another and me. They are telegraphing something to each other but I don't know what. The tension gets too much and I find myself speaking before I can stop myself.

'Okay then. Say it. He's dead. I know what murder means.'

They look at me, their brows creased. They exchange looks once again.

'So why am I here? Is there new evidence?' I say, searching them both.

Blake looks at Conway with realisation. It's just the slightest of looks. A millimetre by which she raises her green eyes at him. His face, weighed down by age and *this* no doubt, doesn't move.

Blake is the one who speaks. 'Xander. Mr Shute. About Mr Squire. We got the blood results back from the lab. It's not his blood on the knife.'

'What?' I say. I don't believe it.

'We conducted a video ID procedure and he was unable to pick out his assailant. That's not to say it wasn't you. It's just, well. We're going to NFA it,' Conway says.

'NFA?' I hear myself say, but I am flooded with relief.

'It means "no further action". But, as DI Conway has said, if further evidence comes to light, you could be rearrested for it,' Blake says.

'Okay,' I say. 'Then why am I here?'

'*Murder*, Mr Shute.'

'What?' I say, confused. 'I don't understand. You said he's fine.' I look wildly between the two. 'Unless. There's another murd—' The rest of the word catches in my throat. My heart begins to pound in my chest.

'Mr Shute. Are you okay? You look a bit pale,' Blake says.

Although I am shaking, I nod.

'I'm going to remind you of your right to a solicitor,' she says. I think of the solicitor from last time. The one I kicked out. What was her name? My heart races.

'No. Don't need a solicitor,' I say.

'Okay. Following investigations into the allegations you made—'

Allegations *I* made? I don't understand what she means.

'We have uncovered certain further evidence. And we have to hand it to you, Mr Shute.'

'Hand what to me? And what allegations?'

'Number 42B,' Conway says, stabbing a pen in my direction. 'The murder you told us about.'

My heart is banging. I am not sure what is happening but it is happening at a speed I cannot match.

'You – found the body?'

'Not exactly, Mr Shute. The body was never lost,' Conway says. 'It was recovered immediately after the murder.'

'I don't understand,' I say. 'Immediately? Where is it, then? What's happening? And why haven't you caught him? You know where he is. You know who he is.'

My voice is too loud but I cannot calm it or the convulsions in my head.

'Xander, listen to me.' Blake leans over and stares at me, somehow managing to slow the thudding in my chest. 'We weren't aware of a body when you came to report this to us.' She pauses. 'Xander ... the person you described to us? The one who you said was killed in front of you seven days ago?'

I nod, desperate for her to continue.

'That person has been dead for thirty years.'

30

Tuesday

My head spins.

Thirty years.

The words land and keep landing around me in deep thuds. My palms begin to itch. 'I don't understand,' I say. 'There were two murders? In the same place?'

'No, Xander – Mr Shute. Only one,' Blake says flatly.

I'm lost. 'What do you want from me?' I have to pull my voice down from the ceiling, where it has risen.

Blake shuffles some pages in a file and then picks out a glossy image. 'Do you recognise the person in this photograph?' she says, sliding it over to me.

I stare at it. It is an enlarged picture of a woman with dark curls. I can make out the side of her face and the top half of her body. I look harder and as I do my breath begins to come in snatches. It's her. It's the woman from that night. The room comes then into my mind, cascading into place inch by inch. She's lying down. Her face is turned, covered by hair spilled across her face.

'When was this taken?' I say, breathing hard.

She takes another photograph out and then another. They're pictures of the room. Just as I remember it. The walls. That silk carpet. The chesterfields. The one I lay behind is there clear as day, in one photograph. The picture catches the light just as it was. It's that room. Just as it was.

'When were these taken?' I am shouting now.

My heart drums, quickening with my breath.

'December 1989,' Blake says.

Everything stops.

Again, I look at the pictures. They do have the quality of pictures from the eighties: the colours are washed-out in places and over-bright in others. I can feel my brain filling with a rush of blood. I don't know what has happened.

'I …' I shake my head at the table, confused, unable to piece the fragments of time together. 'What? *How*?'

'I began to dig into this case, Xander, after you came back. You seemed so *certain*. My superior officer recognised the address. He worked on the original case.'

'Original case?'

Each new statement confounds me further. I am on the precipice of an abyss.

'It's kind of a cold case, Mr Shute,' Conway says. 'It was put down as an accidental death in 1989. Is this the woman you saw being murdered?'

I look again at the picture. It is unmistakeably her. I nod.

'For the tape please,' he says.

'Yes, it's her,' I say, swallowing hard.

'Who is she, Xander?' Blake asks softly.

'Who is she? How am I supposed to know who she is? *You* should know. That's *your* job.'

'We do, Mr Shute. But we were hoping you might tell us something more about her.'

'I can't tell you anything.'

I look at the photograph again. It's her but I can't understand how she can be in a photograph from thirty years ago. 'This is all wrong,' I say.

'Wrong how?'

'Wrong. Just wrong. This – this was days ago. Not thirty years.'

'I assure you, Mr Shute, these photographs were taken from files that have been in storage for all this time. So, tell us how you saw her being killed a week ago when she's been dead for nearly three decades?'

'I don't know. It doesn't make sense.'

'Funny, Mr Shute. We were thinking that too. Doesn't make sense, does it?'

I push the chair back from the table to stand up. The floor seems to be moving. 'It was less than a week. Not years,' I say.

'Here's what we think, Mr Shute. You did see that poor woman being strangled. As you tried to tell us. But you must have had some kind of breakdown and suppressed the memory. Did you have a breakdown, Mr Shute?'

'Breakdown? No!' I say, sitting back down.

'I mean, we've been looking into you, Mr Shute. You used to have a very different life, didn't you?'

'So?' I say.

'So, Mr Shute. How does a respected, highly qualified computer scientist with a degree from a top university, with a highly paid job, become … you?'

'What do you mean?'

'I mean, look at you. I don't mean to be rude, but you're not exactly a well man, are you?'

'*Well*? I am well. I'm well. Just because I have an alternative lifestyle doesn't make me *unwell*.'

'Alternative?' He pauses. 'What I think is that years of being out on the streets broke you.'

'I don't have to listen to this,' I say.

'Actually, you do. So, tell us. What's your version of this?'

'I – I've told you. Again and again. I saw her being killed. Last week,' I say and as I hear the words, the certainty I feel begins to drift and fall to my feet.

'Okay, let me tell you what we think. We think that you killed her, Mr Shute.'

'*I* killed her? What? Why would I kill her? I reported this to you!'

'Yes, you did. And I, *we*, believe you thought you could distract us by reporting it. But it was you all along.'

'What? This is ridiculous. Why would I have come to you?'

Blake hands another picture to Conway.

'Who was she, Mr Shute?' he says.

'I don't know. I told you. I don't know her.'

'Well, that's not a clear picture, is it? Take a look at this one,' he says and places a Polaroid flat on the table as if he is dealing a card. It snaps as he lays it down. 'This one was taken when she was still alive.'

I look at Blake. There is a wash of emotion over her face that I can't place. Something like regret or guilt. I push the picture back at Conway, without looking at it.

'I said I don't know who she is.'

'Look at it, Xander. She was called Michelle. Who was Michelle, Xander?' Blake asks.

The name. Just the utterance of it pricks a memory from somewhere. Then I remember. Mishal. *Michelle*? At the cemetery. The new headstone. And then I recall him in the room itself as he stood over her. He called her that. Didn't he? *Chelle*. I try to unhook my mind from what I can see, from this room and these two police officers, and try to let my mind spring back to that day.

'He might have called her Michelle, I think. But there's mo—'

'Michelle?' Conway cuts me off, looking at Blake.

'Who did?' she asks.

'The killer, Ebadi.'

'Did he? You're sure?' Conway says.

'Sure? No. Not sure. I was hiding behind a sofa. I'm not sure. But the name. I've seen it. But not Michelle, like you're saying it. *Mishal*,' I say, inflecting the word.

'So, you don't know Michelle, but Mish*al* rings a bell, you say? Tell me more about that,' he says.

Mishal rings a bell. Something in that phrase he used sends a current through me. My eyes begin to water in the expectation of a realisation that is just there at the edges of my grasp.

'I saw the name in a cemetery. Ebadi. I followed him. I think I know where he buried her,' I say.

'Actually, Mr Shute, we know exactly where she is and it isn't buried. She was cremated. Scattered over a park.'

'But, Mishal,' I say. 'It *has* to be her. Just – you have to look. Mishal. Acton cemetery. M. I. S. H. A. L.,' I spell it out.

They ignore me, and then at a nudge from Blake, Conway flicks the photograph over to me once again. I look down at the picture, knowing that it is fruitless. And then my heart stops.

'The name we have for her is Michelle Mackintosh. Not *Mishal*. We have identified her and that's her,' he says, placing a finger on her face. 'And with her is a man you might recognise. The police investigating this case at the time haven't made a record of who that man was. Isn't even a great picture to be fair, but you know him, don't you, Mr Shute?'

I look down at the man in the picture again and rub my eyes. I don't understand.

'Can you help us with who he is?'

I stare at the woman standing next to the man. She does ring a bell. *Belle*. Michelle. Ma Belle.

Ma Belle. *Mabel*.

The woman in the picture is Grace.

And that man beside her is me.

31

Tuesday

I am back in the police cell. There, in the hot space of the inter-view room, with everything collapsing around me, I managed to do just one thing right: I asked for a solicitor. And so here I am, waiting for them.

The idea that the killing happened so long ago is sitting in my head, immiscible, like oil on water. I can't absorb the information. I do know one thing, however. The problem – all problems – are mathematical in nature. The solutions are there in the analysis and I have been through the possibilities.

1 The police were lying to me in the interview to get me to confess to something. I've ruled this out. To make it work there would have to be illegality, not to mention effort on a monolithic scale, and I don't think Conway is capable of either.

2 The police are telling the truth and there was a murder thirty years ago, but not the one that I saw. That means there were two murders. But it's highly unlikely that there were two murders of two young women in one place. There's a probability factor here that I have

tried to calculate on too little data, but whichever way I unpack it and whatever the variables are, the probabilities are too remote. Then there is the simple fact of the picture – that was me, without a doubt.

And that picture of Grace, Michelle Grace Mackintosh. *Ma belle*. My Michelle. Our joke. That name she hated. *Common*. And now to see her, to see us, in that Polaroid from all that time ago, it feels like a heavy piece of machinery inside me has slipped its gearings and is shuddering to a halt. I can't work out what she has to do with it. It can't be her who was killed. It's not possible. And yet from the list of what seems possible, it suddenly has shifted from possibility to likelihood. I have to accept that my memory of what I saw isn't true.

I slide to the floor. Looking around this cell, I know that I have to get out. I need to shed some of this debris that has gathered around me and get out into the air and walk. The concrete is cold against my legs. I lean back into the wall and then begin to rock. With every point of contact, flesh against stone, a tiny fraction of this buzz is earthed into the ground. It can't be her. I tell myself this over and over. I'd have known it. Surely, I'd have known it. Known her anywhere. But then what was it about that night that I remembered if not the name? Didn't I have a sense of knowing? Could Conway be right? Could I have supressed the memory?

And then the realisation punches home: Grace is dead.

When the door opens I am not certain how much time has passed. I look up from my place on the floor and meet the hazel eyes of a young woman. She looks down at me and nods at the officer who leaves.

She comes and sits next to me. Her suit seems used to these conditions and hangs from her slight frame. It's the same solicitor from before. Her hair, pulled off her face with clips, shines bronze in this light.

'Feeling okay?' she says – the vowels are long – *ohkay*. Northern. I look at her face. A sprinkle of freckles across the bridge of her nose makes her look young.

'Yes. I just have to ground myself. You came back?'

She nods. There is a breeze of something fresh coming her clothes. Lemon?

'Look, I have just had a look at your disclosure. And I had a word with custody already.'

'And?'

'And it seems that you're not ...' she says, and points a finger at her temple and makes small circles. 'You've been tested apparently.'

'Nice,' I say, mustering a small smile.

'The bad news is that you are an idiot. The good news, however,' she says, getting to her feet and helping me up, 'is that there's not enough evidence here to hold you.'

Standing, I turn to face her. 'What? But I was there.'

'Were you, though?' Hazel eyes blink at me.

'Yes. I described the whole place to them. They know I was there.'

'I've had a listen to your interview. You weren't there in 1989. You were there last week.'

'But – it was *her*. That's the same woman I saw being killed. And it turns out I knew her. Grace was my girlfriend.'

She digs around in a small brown leather bag for a pen. 'Don't know about no Grace. Michelle Mackintosh is who they have. Anyway, if they had enough evidence they'd have charged you by now. They've got nothing.'

'It's the same woman, Miss —'

'Janine. Jan.'

'Jan. It's the same person. She just called herself Grace. It was her middle name. I knew her.'

'It weren't her middle name, though. I've seen the birth certificate. There is no middle name. Anyway, we go back in, you go "no comment". We get out of here and talk properly later. Understood?'

I take her forearm in my hand so that she faces me when I speak to her. I have to make her understand. 'It's her. I'm telling you. I'm not mad. I'm not stupid. It was her.'

'Look. We are about to go into a police interview. Unless you are in the mood to confess to a murder, I suggest you take my advice. No comment. Got it?'

'But—'

'Okay. Let me ask you. Did you kill her? This Grace or Michelle or whatever her name is?'

'No!'

'Okay then,' she says, staring straight at me. 'No comment.'

We are back in the interview room and Conway has now got a sheet of what look like questions in front of him. Blake is next to him and is corralling papers from a file. They look like they are going into battle.

Conway cautions me again and then introduces my solicitor Janine Cullen, 'for the tape'.

'I have advised my client to answer "no comment" to all questions asked,' she says, as soon as her name is mentioned.

'Well, Mr Shute, that is your prerogative. But we can still ask the questions. And it is your choice at the end of the day whether to answer any questions. It's just advice. You're the one that has to explain in court why you didn't answer questions.'

'I understand,' I say, and immediately Jan gives me a look. 'No comment.'

'Mr Shute, would you agree that you reported a murder to us on the 13th of February this year?'

Janine jumps in immediately. 'That evidence is not admissible. He wasn't cautioned before he made those comments.'

'We can let the courts decide admissibility. I'm still going to ask the questions. You reported a murder to us and you gave an address of number 42B Farm Street in Mayfair. Yes?'

'No comment.'

'And you described in what I would say is a fair amount of detail the inside of that property. Do you agree?'

'No comment.'

'Were you telling the truth when you were describing the property?'

'No comment.'

'You described the property right down to the tiles on the floor.'

'Is that a question?' says Janine, coming alive.

'Do you agree you described the tiles in the hallway?'

'No comment.'

'In fact, you described it to us on two separate occasions. Do you agree that these police photographs of number 42B Farm Street exactly match your description? For the tape the suspect is being shown exhibit RG/2.'

'No comment.'

'The question we have to ask is how you managed to describe the location of a murder from almost thirty years ago?'

'No comment.'

'Because if there is an innocent explanation, we'd like to hear it. Do you have one?'

'No comment.'

'Do you think you might have, say, read a news story about the murder?'

'No comment.'

The questions, each of them, make me cringe. But I expect them – all of them. I am a fish in a barrel being machine-gunned.

They continue like this for almost an hour. I can't look at Blake. It is as if I have disappointed her.

Eventually the questions lose their power. The repetition becomes bland. I begin to fade in and out of concentration. *No comment* I say to everything. It becomes so much of a rhythm that I almost miss it when it happens.

'This photograph of the deceased. For the tape exhibit RG/5. Is that you in the picture?'

'No comment.'

'Is there an innocent explanation for you being in a picture with the deceased?'

I want to scream the answer. *We were lovers!* I look at Jan for permission but she doesn't give it. The questions grind on.

Were you in a relationship with Michelle? Did you live together? Did you two split up? What was the reason for that if you did? Did she find someone else? Or did you? Did you have any reason to feel jealous about her?

'We believe that you were both in a relationship before she died. We also believe that you disappeared soon after her death. What was the reason for you disappearing?'

'That's not a proper suggestion, Officer. There is no evidence that Mr Shute disappeared,' Jan snaps, cutting in again briskly.

'Well, if you didn't disappear, where did you go?' Conway continues.

'Again, Officer, there is no evidence that he went anywhere.'

'Well, that is for you to answer, Mr Shute. Where did you go? There's no record of you on any electoral roll.'

'No comment.'

'We did some digging into the file and we found that Michelle had a number of bank accounts. Were you aware that she was earning a considerable salary at the time of her murder?'

'No comment.' I say the words but alarms are going off in my head.

'We found some bank account statements in the file. There is this one statement for a dollar account that we found. And we found something quite interesting. And I think you know what that is, Mr Shute.'

Jan looks appalled. Her expression changes as if she is making a decision of some kind.

'This bank statement, exhibit RG/6 for the tape, shows a dollar account in the name of Mackintosh and Shute. Is the Shute on that account you, Mr Shute?'

The room begins to press in on me. I look to Jan but her face has set hard. Whatever she is deciding has begun to take shape.

'No comment,' I say in a whisper.

'There's an interesting entry there on that sheet, Mr Shute. It shows that you cleared the entire account, in cash, just a matter of weeks before her murder. Is that the reason she was killed, Mr Shute? That's a sizeable sum. Just over a quarter of a million dollars. Where is the money?'

'We are ending this interview now, Officer. This is outrageous. I haven't been given any disclosure about this. It's unethical and you know it.' Jan stands up. 'Are you charging him or not?'

'Actually, those are all the questions we have for you at the moment, Mr Shute. We are terminating this interview. The time by my watch is 21:17.' He switches the tapes off, and turns his attention to Jan.

'We are still at an early stage with regards to investigating the offence. Obviously, this a serious charge. It'll be for the custody sergeant now to deal with bail.'

'But you're the OIC,' Jan says. 'You know he's going to do what you want him to.'

Blake gets up from her seat and puts her file together. 'I'm the officer in the case actually. And since we haven't charged him yet and since he seems to turn up here wanted or not, I'm taking the view that he's going to surrender. I'm recommending bail to return in four weeks. That's the 19th of March,' she says, looking into her phone. 'Make sure you come back. It's a long wait in custody for a murder trial.'

Jan looks shocked but manages a curt thank you.

Twenty minutes later I am standing on the pavement, shaking Jan's hand. She doesn't react or flinch at having to touch my skin. I can hardly believe they have released me after all those questions. All that insinuation.

'Thank you,' I say.

'Don't thank me. It's that OIC. She's got the hots for you,' she says, looking up at me. There is a foot in height between us.

I take a deep breath and screw my eyes shut. Did that just happen? 'What now?' I say.

'Now? You make an appointment to see me on Thursday,' she says, picking up her case from the ground. 'And when you do, you need a better explanation for what happened to the money than you gave me in the cells after the interview.'

'But I told you, I don't know where it is.'

I left it with Seb. But that was years ago. I have no idea whether he still has it. He might have given it back to Grace, I think, and then the reality of it hits again. She has been dead for thirty years.

'It's not often money can buy your freedom, Mr Shute. But when it can, you take the chance. The money or your life.'

32

Tuesday

Can Grace be dead? How could I have seen it and not remembered – not remembered that it was *her*? My Grace. Who I loved. *Love.*

I know that people do repress painful and traumatic memories. But this doesn't feel like a repression. For instance, I know that I have suppressed what happened with Dad. I have buried it deep into the folds of my past. It is there, still. I sense it all the time, as a kind of grotesque in a room that I walk around every morning and evening. It's always there, but there are days when it's so well camouflaged that I can pretend it doesn't exist. I know that it does and I know that if I could steel myself I could face it down if I had to.

But this isn't like that. I haven't buried Grace. I haven't erased the memory or airbrushed it out of existence. I have a memory of that night – a clear one.

It's her with me in that Polaroid. It is. I remember her as she was. But the dead woman, when I see her, is older, and less vibrant. The side of her face was flatter – it didn't reflect the light like Grace's did. And the hair was a different colour. But when I saw the picture of her in the interview, I was less sure. In that police picture, with her face captured from the side, as if in sleep, it could be her. I can't be sure that it's not.

I am back at Seb's house. The sight of the old house gives me a warm feeling. It takes me to a time that was more – binary. I need to speak to him and tell him everything. I also need the money, it seems. Murder in jealousy or murder for money: the oldest and most hackneyed of motives. I'm sure Seb will have it still. Or maybe he banked it, or I don't know what. I can't know exactly but there will be a trail, at least, that he can verify. I bring to mind the look on his face when I turned up with the money and how we had packed it into a trunk in his loft with other things that I couldn't bear to throw out – letters, photographs, trinkets.

I knock on the door, bathed in street-light. I hadn't realised how long I had been in the police station. They keep you there, deprived of light and any sense of the day. They strip out all the day's signposts so that when you are released you have the sensation of being in a time-slip.

Seb opens the door with a look that I haven't seen before. Is he worried or annoyed? He is in pyjamas but he hasn't been to sleep – his hair's still in place. I walk through to the kitchen. Every drawer has been taken out and laid either on the floor or some other surface.

'What's going on?' I say uncertainly.

He looks at me briefly before turning away again.

'What is it, Seb?'

He remains with his back to me for a minute before simply throwing his hands up. 'Police, Xander. After they took you, some more turned up with a warrant for a search.'

'To do with me?' I say, puzzled.

'Yes, to do with you.'

I walk up to him and touch him lightly on the arm.

'But, I mean – you told them I don't live here?'

He faces me and I can see the effort he is making to control his emotions.

'I managed to send them away eventually, when I pointed out that the warrant was to do with your premises, not mine, but they'd already started searching through everything. I explained that the house wasn't yours, but they'll be back. I think it's time you told me what's going on, Xander.'

I nod. I don't think I can put this off any longer. 'Maybe we should sit,' I say and take a seat at the breakfast table.

As I tell him about it all, he sits worrying the edges of a wicker place mat and says nothing. Once I have finished telling him about Squire, the drunk in the park, he gets up and finds two glass beakers, silently pouring an inch of expensive cognac into each. He hands me one, and still he says nothing. Then I tell him about number 42B. I describe it all in detail to him. I tell him about what I saw, about the woman being strangled, how I froze and then how I ran. How I told the police it all and how now it seems as though the place has transformed in just a few days.

And then I slow down, hesitant. I am coming to a precipice in the story and I feel the vertigo of it pulling us into a chasm.

'Then they tell me there *was* a murder there after all. But it happened thirty years ago.'

'What?' he says finally. 'You lost time?'

I stare at him in shock. 'No. I didn't *lose* time.'

'Is it so surprising?' He puts the place mat down. 'You were in a pretty bad way back then, Xander. I remember the first time I saw you, after, you know, you disappeared. What was it, a year later? You were a mess. God knows what had happened to you.'

'I don't really remember that period very well.' I feel my head filling with heat. The nerves in my face fizz momentarily and then, without notice, I begin to cry. It's a flood and I can't stop it. I bury my head in my arms unable to do anything but surrender to it.

'It's okay,' he says, and I feel him rubbing my back. This touch, the first in years – it breaks my heart.

In time the tears trickle dry. I look up and see Seb, still here, calm and serene. He sits back in his seat and looks at me kindly.

'Seb,' I say, wiping my face with the back of a hand. 'I don't remember any of it. I don't remember those first months at all.'

I track back through the years, picking out what I can. The day I left. The day I saw Grace on the streets. How she bought me breakfast. Those days are like stones rubbed smooth from years of worrying at them. But they are like relics on a hill – whole but broken off. Even the good ones are fragments of something visual, pulled and glued together with my own brush. I can't distinguish the truth from the patches I manufacture. This must be true of all memory. There is no way of knowing its truth. We can only know what we have spun, and then we are left to believe it is real enough to anchor ourselves to our memories of who we are.

But I am wrong. I do remember some things beyond that day in the café. The odd memory stands out, lit with pain. I remember one night when I slept in the carriage of a train at

Waterloo. The last trains had run their journeys for the night. The carriages were there, lying empty, warm, or at least warmer than outside. I had jumped a barrier and none of the skeleton staff had seen me do it. It had been one of those old-fashioned carriages with the slam-doors. A window slid down with only the slightest of persuasion and I was able to climb through. The carriage was warm still from the bodies and the heat of the track, or the heat pumped through by the engine. I stretched out on a faded seat, the softness of the fabric against my cheek like an embrace. In minutes, seconds even, I was asleep on the narrow bench. And then a crack of light and a sound from the corner of sleep woke me. All I saw was a fist coming into my face. I was dragged off the seat and thrown bodily on to the platform. The indigo of night had just given way to dawn. It was still too early for commuters. Just a few orange-jacketed staff, and these people who were dragging me along the platform. Kicking me until I heard parts of me snap.

Then I really did snap.

When I hobbled away, my attackers were on the ground, broken and bloody. It had taken just a few seconds and when it was done I hurried away. My shoulder was throbbing. My face was pouring with blood. The back of my head felt as if it might have cracked. The dull sick feeling still clung from when my head had hit the platform.

But if you were to ask me what I did for the rest of the day, I couldn't say. I can't tell you what happened for the rest of the year. Or where the year lay in relation to the others. Looking back now, I cannot place very much into any certain time-frame. I think you need people to do that. People are a frame of reference, letting you plot where you are and where you are heading. And to remind you, in words, what each of you did. I didn't have people. I could have, but I never craved it the way that some of the other people I crossed on the street did.

I blink to see Seb staring at me in concern.

'They're saying they know who she is,' I say, collecting myself.

He leans forward, lacing his fingers together.

I take a deep breath. 'They're saying it's Grace. That she's dead.'

He takes a gulp from his glass. I am expecting a tirade, anger. Something. He opens his mouth as if to say something and then closes it. Finally, he decides what to say and speaks.

'Grace? Our Grace. That's who it was?'

'Yes. They're saying it was her. They're saying that she's dead.'

He runs a hand through his hair.

'They think she was murdered? Not an accident?' he says. 'And they're saying it was you?'

It takes a moment for the realisation to hit.

'Seb. You don't sound surprised that she's dead.'

'I know,' he says simply.

'What do you mean?'

'I knew she was dead.'

Hearing this makes the room reverberate. 'What do you mean, you knew she was dead?'

I am standing now and see that I have picked up my glass and I am holding it as if I am about to launch it at him. I am watching myself but don't seem to be able to control what I'm doing.

Seb remains rooted. 'We all knew she was dead, Xander.'

I hear the words but they are so disembodied that it takes time for them to register.

'And you didn't think to tell me about it?' A rage rises from somewhere I cannot identify. As it rises it drags a red veil across my eyes.

'Sit down, Xander,' Seb says to me. His tone is even, as if he is used to this from me.

'No! I will not sit down. Did you? Were you there, Seb?'

'Sit down,' he says again.

'Thirty years, Seb. All this time I have been – been searching for her in some way. How could you have known and not said?'

'Because,' he says and then sighs and relaxes back into his chair again. 'Because you already knew.'

33

Wednesday

I am lying on the floor of the bedroom. The bed has been upturned and all the covers have been removed in the police search. But I would have slept on the floor anyway. My mind feels as dirty and stained as my body.

I knew. When he said that, I looked into his eyes and searched for the slightest flicker or hesitation, but there was none. I knew. I must have known. If he says it to me I have to trust him. I can't trust my battered recollection over his, over anybody's, recollection any longer. I'm not sure what to do with my anger. It's ricocheting around my mind searching for a home, a target. I breathe to try and ground the rage.

To be without memory is to be cut away from yourself. I feel adrift, and the realisation that in those wiped-out days and months, I did things – *could* have done things – terrifies me. I can't move under the weight of the possibility.

My throat tightens, and I gasp for air. Slowly, as if through straws, it comes. It whistles into my lungs and after a few minutes of thin, meagre air, I can stand. I make my way along the landing and find a door and push. The darkness is oppressive so I switch on the light.

'Oh—'

'I'm sorry, Seb. I can't sleep,' I say.

'It's okay,' he says, and pulls himself up against the pillows. He looks at me and waits for me to speak. There is the scent of wood and cologne in the air here, soothing.

'Tell me about it again.'

He sighs sadly. 'Grace?'

I nod. 'What happened to her.'

He collects himself first. 'It was awful,' he says, rubbing his eyes. 'Nina raised the alarm when she didn't hear from her after Christmas. I mean, we all thought she'd decided to stay in the Philippines for a couple of extra weeks.'

'What made you think that?' I say.

'I don't know, Xander. The new boyfriend maybe. And you know how she could be when it came to all that spiritualism stuff she was always into. So we thought she was still there.' He stops and pauses for breath. 'Anyway, it was a shock when they discovered her, in that state.'

I sink to my knees. I know what state that was. I was there. I must have been there. It was Grace I was looking at, the wine creeping up her blouse.

'We tried to find you, Xand, but you'd gone. Nobody knew where you were. After Rory went, you just, I don't know, you weren't right. We could see it. But nobody knew that you'd fall so quickly. It felt like you had vaporised. We didn't see you for a year. And then one day you just turned up. Here. Looking for your stuff. You needed money.'

Dollars? Did I take the dollars, I think, my heart sinking. I can't remember turning up. 'And?' I say.

'I gave you some money and you left. You really don't remember?' he says, cocking his head.

I shake my head. Some of this feels like a memory I had once but whatever strands there were have long since gone.

'Did you really tell me about Grace? I can't believe I would have forgotten that.'

'Yes, well, we tried to tell you, but you wouldn't hear it. No matter what I said, it didn't seem to sink in. You just nodded and left. You took a bag of books with you and went.'

His words are beginning to rekindle memories. I remember the books – I think I remember. Two carrier bags filled with books I had left here. I remember the red creases that the handles ripped into my palms. I remember walking the streets with those bags until one morning I woke to find they had gone. The memory is a haze in that the feeling around it is stronger than the seeing of it. I remember a sadness with it, like a stone flung into a pool.

'Didn't the police want to talk to me?'

'The police? No. Why would they?' He pauses, assembling what I told him last night. 'No. They didn't suspect foul play at the time. They investigated, said it was an accident. She'd banged her head on a table and had a drunken fall. Just bad luck, they said.'

'So, they weren't treating it as a murder? Not ever?'

'No. Not as far as I knew.'

'And then?'

'Well. There was the service. We expected you, of course, but weren't shocked when you didn't show. And then, slowly, we just got on with life. Well, we tried. Nina took it badly.'

I let the news seep through my skin and into my bones. Funeral.

'There was a funeral,' I said. More statement than question.

'Yes. Well, cremation. Nina scattered the ashes.'

I remember now Conway saying this about a cremation. I drop my face into my hands. There is so much of my life that has scattered through my fingers. I am disgusted by my hands suddenly in this clean space and I get to my feet.

'I need a bath,' I say, and then hover for a second because I know saying it like that must seem like a non sequitur to Seb but he just nods.

My body is red with heat and soap. Clean. The water has somehow woken it so that to look at it, it seems bound with energy. But my head remains muddy. Back in my room Seb has righted the upturned bed and laid out some fresh clothes. I pull on the chinos and checked shirt and get into bed. The cool sheets and warm duvet surprise me with their touch. At this moment it is all I can do to stop heaving as the tears roll down my face.

I see Mum in my dreams and even though I know it isn't and it can't be, it feels like an omen. She is young, as she was when I was ten or eleven. She's perhaps thirty, her skin is wrinkle-free and her eyes shine. She is standing at the foot of my bed and smiling. Her hand is out as if she is begging for alms or food. Or absolution. There's a shawl that she has never worn over her head. *I'm hungry*, she says and as I reach out to take her hand, she vanishes. In a blaze of sunlight.

My eyes are open. The angle of the sun says that I have missed most of the morning. I go downstairs feeling groggy. There is coffee on the table. Seb is there, wearing a navy wool suit and a cornflower tie. He smells clean. His hair has been combed smartly into place. A pink square of silk peeps out from his top pocket. I sit and pour out some coffee and take a deep draught. The caffeine stings my blood.

'Okay?' he says.

The sorrow that had infected his voice and manner has gone. I nod and watch as he drinks a mouthful of coffee and then lights a cigarette and hands it to me. I put it to my mouth. It soothes and invigorates me at the same time. I stare at my cup through wisps of smoke and see it beginning to blur. I try to speak but I find my voice has dried out and whatever words I had become lost in a cough. He stands and comes to place a hand on my shoulder.

'I'm really scared, Seb,' I say through tears. 'I think it was me. That I killed her. *What if I killed her?*'

The weight of his hand speaks for him and it remains until the tears finally end. I think about what I said. It is true. I can't tell where the edges of my sanity lie any more.

At last he goes back to his chair.

'If there's one thing I know about you with certainty,' he says, 'it's that you are not capable of that. You loved her. You did not kill her.'

'How can you be certain?' I say. 'When I can't?'

'You said it yourself. There was someone else there. You saw him do it. You just have to convince the police of it. I'll speak to them. I can tell them how much she meant to you, Xander.'

'Thanks, Seb,' I say. 'But I think we're way past that now.'

We spend the rest of the day in quiet distraction. Seb makes some calls and cancels appointments he had lined up for the day. He changes out of his suit and into jeans and a bottle-green cashmere sweater. Then, as the day begins to darken, Seb finally says what I know he's been holding back.

'Can I ask you a question?'

'Of course.'

'What do the police have on you? I mean they had it down as accidental death. What's changed?'

Even though I know it's been coming, I don't know what the answer is. 'I was there. I told them that I had witnessed a murder. Her murder.'

He thinks about this. 'But I'm sure people admit murders all the time that they haven't done. I've seen those crazy people on TV who—' He stops. 'There must be something more?'

'My solicitor thought the same thing. Until—'

'Until?'

'The dollars. They found the dollar account. They know I emptied it, not long before Grace—' I say. I can't bear to finish the sentence.

'What?' he says, stopping to push the sleeves of his sweater back. His face is locked in consternation.

'I remembered, Seb. I remembered I brought them here.'

'Oh.' He frowns. 'The Bens.'

I look at him, confused by that word again.

'Bens. We called them the Bens. Benjamin Franklin. It's his face on the hundred-dollar bills.'

Now it comes back to me and how whenever we made reference to it, we did it as if we were 1930s mobsters. I reach out with my eyes to join Seb in a shared look but he turns away. For a second or two, I hold on to the look I'm giving him until the moment putters out. A thought rolls in my head before I dismiss it. It's uncharitable that I'm wondering if he is deliberately avoiding my eye.

'Seb, I need the money,' I say finally.

He nods. 'Of course. But, why does it matter so much? It's not evidence of murder, surely?' he says, shifting in his seat.

'They think I killed her for the money. That's why I need it,' I say.

'*Your* money, Xand. You can't have killed her for your own money.'

'Half was mine Seb. Half.' I look around the room so that I don't have to look him in the eye. I am embarrassed to have to ask. 'What happened to the money, Seb?'

He moves in his seat, blinking rapidly. 'Nothing. It's all upstairs in the loft still.'

A rush runs through me. 'The dollars are still here?'

'Yes.'

'You didn't bank them or, I don't know, give them to Grace or her family?'

He looks at me. 'As far as I was aware, the money was yours. I was holding it for you. As it happens she didn't ever ask me for it and even if she had, I'm not sure I would have given it to her.'

I take a breath and try and process what I am being told. The money is still here. Improbably, after all these years. A flood of warmth towards Seb for his friendship, for his reliability, fills me.

'Where is it? Can I see it?'

'It's in the loft. See it whenever you like.'

'Can we go now?'

'Now? Really?' he says and waits. He reads my expression. 'Okay. Come on then.'

We walk along the corridor and up the stairs. At the top flight he pauses, looking for something. I do not know what until he emerges from a room with it in his hand: a fishing pole for pulling down the hatch. He looks up to spear the catch, and then a ladder slides smoothly down.

'I'll go first and stick the lights on,' he says, and climbs up. I follow him. The loft is boarded with plywood and is neat and tidy, as lofts go. There is dust, but there are patches where it has been unsettled recently. I watch as he ducks his way across and under the beams. When he stops he looks around and beckons me over.

'Here,' he says.

As I trace his path on my way to him, I see something that catches at a memory. There is a small cardboard box, like a gift box. The memory of it pierces me. I hold it up to Seb.

'This yours?' I ask.

He squints at the box and says, 'No, that's one of yours, isn't it? One of the bits you left. Police took a couple in the search until I got them out. I'm sorry. I couldn't stop them. Shit, look at the mess they've left.' He looks around at the upturned boxes and sticks of broken furniture.

I look at the box in my hand and see trinkets in there from a past life. A miniature doll with the head of a cat. A polished green stone that Grace gave me. A ticket for a concert. Some plastic gold coins. And beneath it all, a small volume of Proust. I pick it out and stare at this thing of mine from a third of a century ago.

'Xand?' Seb calls then. He is waiting for me.

I stop and put the book into my pocket and pick my way towards Seb until I'm next to him, staring down where he is.

There is the trunk. I had forgotten it until now. There'd been an old pine trunk outside the house when I'd come by with the cash. It was Seb and Nina's coffee table. One of the sides had developed a crack which was enough for Nina to throw it out. When we took the money into the loft, I remembered it.

'Sure,' Seb had said when I suggested using it to put the money in. I'd dragged it up the ladder and we'd put the bags into it. Seb had locked it with a padlock he had found and given me the key.

Now looking at it I see there's a layer of dust over the top, thinner than I expected. I bend to open it just before reminding myself again that it is locked and I don't have the key. Did I keep the key? Have it once? There's a memory there, but it's too muddy to reach.

Immediately my brain begins to filter what I know about picking locks once again. This lock is a simple one. The principles are similar, I think, and I rummage around in my head for what I need. Something thin and metal like a pen clip. I hold the lock to examine the mechanism and see something that confuses me. It's in the open position. Unlocked.

I look for Seb to show him the lock but he's busy picking up things that have been knocked over in the search. 'Seb,' I say, showing him the lock.

He stops scrabbling around on the boards and sees the lock. He frowns momentarily before turning a little pale.

'What the—' he says.

I lift the lid slowly and stand up.

Seb and I stare at each other. The trunk is empty.

34

Wednesday

'The police,' I say. 'The police have been up there. They must have taken it.'

Seb stops to consider this. 'No. They were here but they didn't take the cash. Whatever they took they put into clear bags and made me sign for.'

We make our way down the ladder. I turn over the possibilities.

'Unless the police came back,' he says, pushing the loft hatch shut, 'and took it.'

I unpack this as he clicks the latch into place. 'Wouldn't they have to leave something to say they'd been? A notice or something?'

'Yes, I suppose.' He makes his way to the kitchen.

'Who else had access to it?' I follow him into the kitchen and catch my reflection in the black of the windows.

Seb puts the kettle on to boil but then stalls. 'Nina. Could be her. Can't be anyone else in fact. Nobody else has been up there.'

'You think Nina stole it?' I say, shocked. I think of the fine dust layer on the top.

'I know. It doesn't really sound like her. You know how she was even back then – she always had money. I can't see her stealing it. But there aren't any other candidates. Unless – no, I don't think I've even had a plumber up there for longer than ten minutes,' he says. 'I don't know who else it could be.'

'Seb, I need to get it back, or at least find out what happened to it.'

'Well, you better let me speak to her first and try to iron this out. She might have a reasonable explanation.'

'Seb. If I don't have the money, they'll charge me with murder.'

'Okay. I'll call her in the morning,' he says.

I think about this but tomorrow is too late. 'I've got to meet the solicitor tomorrow. She wants an answer about the money. I really need to know where it is. You don't understand. I can't go through a criminal trial. I can't.'

He is in the middle of pouring out coffee but stops. 'Fine.' He takes his phone out and takes a breath. 'Okay,' he says and presses a number on the screen.

I hear the number ring. It rings and rings until I'm sure it's going to ring out. And then at last it's answered.

'Nina. It's Seb. Hi,' he says, and pauses. 'Yes. Sorry. I know it's late. Look, I need to see you. It's important.' Her voice is tinny through the handset. 'No. I mean now. I can come to you or— No,' he says, looking across at me. 'It can't wait.' He pauses for Nina to say what she has to. 'It's better if we do this in person, trust me, I wouldn't ask if it wasn't important.' He waits as she speaks and then shrugs at me. 'Well, it kind of *is* life or death, Nina. Okay,' he says and puts the phone on the table.

'She's coming now.'

My stomach lurches. Now? I haven't seen her for over thirty years. I remember seeing her briefly a few months before Grace and I split up. Grace went to stay with her to think things through but when I went to pick her up, I got the feeling that she thought that Grace would be better off if we simply ended it there and then.

Nina had always been overprotective of Grace. I didn't know whether that was because Grace gave off something that signalled a need for protection or whether Nina just didn't like me.

Once I told Grace that Nina made me feel as if she'd found me under her shoe. She hates me, I said to her.

'That's not true! She just prefers women to men.'

'Or some women to some men,' I said. 'She seems to like Seb well enough.'

'I don't know about that. Not sure she likes him much at the moment either.' I think we were in the kitchen. I have a half-memory of her picking up a tea towel and drying some dishes. 'She's got a thing about controlling men,' she said then, almost casually.

'What?'

A beat passed before she answered. 'She thinks you try to control me with your jealousy.' Then, seeing my expression, added, 'That's her – not me.'

I couldn't believe what I was hearing. 'What? She thinks I'm controlling?'

'I know,' she said, agreeing, wide-eyed.

'Well, she got the idea from somewhere,' I muttered under my breath and then left the room.

233

Later I'd apologised. 'It's okay. I know what Nina's like.' I'd seen Nina just a couple of times since then. Once was on the day I'd brought the dollars. She had been out so Seb and I had taken the cash from the bin-bags and bundled them tightly into carrier bags, the better to fit the coffee table-trunk in the loft. I was passing the last bundle of notes to him when I heard the front door open. It was Nina. We froze. We heard her going through the house and then suddenly Seb dropped the bag that was in his hand and there were dollars everywhere. I still remember how we scrabbled about on hands and knees, picking up cash by the fistful before she came up. Then when she did we feigned innocence.

'What?' we said on the landing as she came up.

She said nothing but knew something was up. And when she stalked out, we both laughed.

The bell rings and Seb gets up to answer it. He pauses by the kitchen door. 'Let me do the talking.'

I wait.

The front door opens in a clatter of locks and chains, then the sound of heels on wood and later the scent of rose. It's a smell I remember. Another madeleine bringing a rush of memory. That rose. Turkish delight.

When Nina comes into the kitchen, she is mid-sentence with Seb and then stalls. She sees me and we lock eyes. Mine see a woman with the same cut-glass cheekbones and bright blue-green eyes that I remember. The effect is as arresting as ever in her pale face. Her fringe is still dark. Only a few fine lines around the eyes give away the time that has passed.

'Xander,' she says. There is no warmth in it at all. She turns her back to me and faces Seb, arms crossed. 'What's he doing here?'

'He's the reason I called you. Have a seat. Coffee?'

She sits but does it by perching at the edge. She makes no move to remove her blood-red coat. It remains draped across her sharp shoulders. I pull my chair back to make room for her but she's not looking at me at all.

'Well?' she says, taking her coffee from Seb.

'Well,' he says, drawing breath. 'It's to do with Xander really.' They both look at me. 'How to begin?' he says. 'Some years back, Xander left some cash here for safe-keeping. After he and Grace—' He coughs when he sees her face. 'Anyway. It's missing.'

She absorbs the information but says nothing. She takes a slow sip and puts her cup down softly. Then she raises her eyebrows, waiting.

'Nina?' I say irritably.

'What?' she says without looking up.

'Did you take the money?' I say.

'What money?' She moves in her seat.

Whatever coldness or indifference she once felt for me has deepened over the years.

'There were two hundred and fifty thousand dollars. In the house. It's gone. All of it.' Seb is getting irate.

Nina blinks at him and pulls out a packet of thin cigarettes from her bag and lights one. The scent of her hangs in the air.

'I don't know what you're talking about. I haven't even seen *him*,' she says, pointing her cigarette at me, 'for thirty years. And I think I'd remember a quarter of a million pounds in cash.'

'Dollars,' I say but she looks away, saying nothing.

'Nina?' Seb says, bristling.

'What?'

'The money. Where is it? It's important.'

A sense of dread grows in me. I worry that if she doesn't have it, then there'll be no way of finding it again. And that could be the end for me.

'You knew I had the money. I know Grace spoke to you about it,' Seb says. 'We had an argument about it. You wanted to give it straight to Grace.'

She wriggles in her seat and then suddenly stands, pushing her chair back with a screech. 'What's this all about, Sebastian? You can't have called me all the way here for this.'

Seb stands and then sits back down again. He looks at me for permission but I haven't caught up with him. 'We need it, Nina. Xand needs it. Now,' he says, pulling his sleeves back.

'Well, I'm sorry you've wasted your time. I don't know anything about the money. I never even laid eyes on it. And then I left you – and this house. And you know exactly what I took with me,' she says and draws her coat together as if to leave.

Before she can get to her feet, Seb puts a hand out. 'Nina,' he says, and then I see that he is holding up an earring. It swings in his fingers.

'What's that?' she says, and we both look at Seb.

'It was by the trunk that had the money in it.' Seb calmly places it into her hand. I stare at her and then him. I didn't see it by the trunk.

'So, I lost an earring.'

'It was by the trunk, Nina.'

'What trunk?'

'The one that used to be our coffee table. The one with all the money in it,' he says, raising his voice.

'I've never even been in your goddamned loft,' Nina says, her voice piercing the air. And as soon as she says it, she stops, and then sighs.

'I didn't say it was in the loft,' Seb says.

'Oh, where else was it going to be?' she says and sits back down. 'Get me a proper drink.'

'You stole it?' I ask.

'Don't be so sanctimonious, Xander. You stole it in the first place. It was Grace's money. You dropped her and then emptied her account.'

'Dropped her?' I say, incredulous at the accusation. And even as I say it, I realise that of all the things Nina is saying to me, this is the thing that hurts most. 'She left *me*. You know that, Nina. You do know that?' My voice now is the one inflected with anger. The earth is shifting beneath me. I don't know who I am if I am not the person who was left broken by Grace. I can't be misremembering this.

'I know what I know,' she says, her tone flat.

'Is that what she told you?' I say. 'That I left her?'

'No. She didn't tell me that, Xander. She wouldn't tell me that – she didn't have to. She was destroyed when you left.'

My head reels and I can't seem to grasp a still moment. I need something to anchor me, a thought, a reliable thought that is beyond shifting. I find nothing. And so, on I spin. In the background, I hear Seb questioning Nina urgently about the money and her responding in slow, liquid tones. I catch splinters of conversation as I spin on and on.

Where is it now? Xander needs it. The police. Police? POLICE? *Murder investigation. It could be evidence. We need the money back, Nina.* It's gone.

Xander.

'Xander,' she says.

'Nina! Don't.'

And then I am here, my face stinging from her hand. The room has become still. Nina and Seb flushed as if they have stepped off a fairground ride. They have been talking but to me they've done it all as if behind glass. All I can think of is this – that Grace said that I'd left her, destroyed her when I did. I can't make any sense of this. Through the fog I see Seb gesticulating at Nina, as if calming her. She is close. Too close to me. And now she is pushing against me as Seb restrains her. Everything is imbued with a muffled, dream-like quality.

'You *murdered* her?' she shrieks, piercing the spongy atmosphere, before chasing her voice with another slap.

'Stop it! He didn't murder Grace,' Seb says, pulling her arm back.

'The police don't investigate people for murder without evidence.'

'They do exactly that, Nina. He didn't kill her.' I hear the words but I am still consumed by this information. Why would Grace have been destroyed by me if she had left me, if she didn't love me any longer?

'She didn't love me any more. That's why she left,' I say quietly to myself.

Nina swings her fringe out of her eyes. 'Even you can't believe that.'

238

'I do believe that. That's what she told me,' I say, and as I do I feel my eyes stinging.

'You want to know what she told me? She told me that you didn't love her. That all you ever loved was a version of her that you had created. You didn't love anything about the real her,' Nina says.

'How can you say that?' I cry.

'Because it's true, Xander. You always thought you were better than her. Cleverer.'

'I did not.'

'You sneered at the things she loved. The yoga, the Buddhism, all of it. You even sneered at her taste in music.'

'Her music?'

'Yes, you hated her music. You made her feel worthless, Xander, at every turn.'

The words ring in my ears and now there is no room in my head for everything else I have been told in the last twenty-four hours.

I am aware of getting up and of following myself along the hall. Seb calls me back and then I am outside in the night. Wading through the air.

I walk hoping for a sliver of calm but for the longest time it doesn't come. And then, at last, it begins. Every step rinses a drop of something from inside my head. Each stride cleanses, but only by fractions. I can't walk quickly enough to stop the thoughts from multiplying, just for a second, so that I can get a proper handle on them. For some minutes I walk in a direction that I've walked before, and then I am at the Horniman grounds again. Something brings me back here time and again. It is as if the ghost of Grace is stronger here.

Once over the low wall I sit with my back against the other side of it. It is hallowed, the space here; I don't need to go further. The wind collects in pockets and then blusters into my clothes, carrying off with it every bubble of warm air. I shiver. A shard of that memory pricks me whenever I am here.

A bench.

My hands in the soil.

There is something in what Nina has said, but I can't for the moment grasp it firmly. The Buddhism – she was right about that – and the yoga. But was I supposed to indulge her in it as she indulged herself? We both knew that it wasn't real, this spiritual odyssey of hers. She wore it obviously and mischievously.

But the music was real. At first, I didn't get it. Pop, maybe – she was young. We all were. But eighties music? The worst of the musical decades, proved by posterity. But later I did get it, when it was too late. She wasn't interested in the artistry or the symmetry or the poetry of the music. She didn't care about the lyrics either. It was the mood she loved, how the music made her feel. It reminded her of things that she'd never experienced and of places she'd never seen. It had the power to alter her emotionally.

I have a memory of leaving her a gift. But her reaction to it escapes me. Maybe I wasn't there when she received it or opened it. But I remember the things before it. I remember Tower Records in Piccadilly. I remember picking out the record and wrapping it and then carrying it to her house in the cold weather. Did I leave it at the door? It was too big surely to go through the letter box. In any case when I bought it, it was so I could tell her that, at last, I understood. It was an LP with her favourite song in it, 'Fils de la Terre' by Jack T. She'd originally played it on a cassette over and over again until one day the tape ran thin and just snapped. She was devastated. Resolved never to replace it. It's not the same if I get another one, she'd said, it could never be the same.

When I bought the record, I wanted her to know that it didn't have to be the same. It could be better instead. Vinyl not tape. Music to listen to in one place, not on the move. A song to be played at home, in confined space so that it could liberate you.

The cold is biting my back against this wall and my instinct knows I must move and keep the blood flowing. I see the boarded café ahead of me and though it is shut, I make for it at a run. By the time I reach it, I know that I will be warmer. The ground beneath my feet is hard and shocks my bones into life. I start slowly and build the pace gradually, then before I know what is happening, I am running full tilt into the night. Running like a schoolboy, freely, urgently and without any thoughts of conserving energy. I pass the café and keep running.

I run until I can run no more. My lungs are burning hot and screaming for air. Then in my mind Grace appears and she is opening the gift. She unwraps the badly taped and papered package and pulls out the sleeve. She is smiling as she takes the record out of the cover and out of the paper slip, handling it by the edges, and drifts over to the record player. The stylus is up with a gentle microphoned thud and then down once more.

Silence.

A hiss.

Then a rhythmic beat until finally the vocal kicks in.

There's trouble on the uptrack
And trouble going back
I've had trouble with my memory
And less with my back ...

And there is her face once again. Her eyes are shut and she is swaying to the music, lost in the mood.

35

Thursday

I need a fire. I jump back over the wall and follow a routine I once knew well. I stoop to the pavement, scrabble around for cigarette ends. When I've collected a dozen or so butts, I put aside the largest one and deposit the remainder in my pocket. Now I need paper. Newspaper is best but now with smartphones you can only find them stacked in metal bins outside tube stations. Eventually I find a discarded half by a bus stop. The edges are damp with something but the main body is still dry. Next, fuel. Wood is really the only thing you can use. Paper or cardboard burns too quickly and smokes heavily. I climb back over the wall again and hunt around for dead branches and twigs. After about an hour of foraging, I have the makings of a decent fire. I drop them in a small heap behind a hedgerow that carves out space for the rose garden. Here at least the orange glow won't be visible to passers-by or to passing traffic.

I light it with the lighter in my pocket and soon it becomes a fire that crackles, taking hold and settling in. The ashes from the paper blow away finally and then I relax. I sit on the ground and warm my hands against the icy night.

The flames make me feel as I always feel when looking into flames. I'm a child after a bath on a cold November night, sitting on a towel being dried by my father. Rory is next to me. The smell of hot coals is in the air. The nostalgia here – at this precise spot in the historical reel – is safe. Mum is nearby making notes for an academic paper. Dad hasn't begun to mutate yet. I'm not old enough yet to poke those fires in him. I lie back and listen to the snap of burning twigs. The randomised patterns settle me. My eyes flicker open and shut.

Then I am in that room, lying behind the sofa. The flames are sending their shadows high up the walls. There's music playing. The argument begins. She has darted to the other end of the room; the man follows, trailing his voice behind him.

If you sorted out your issues, she says. *With your dad.*

My heart thuds like dropped iron.

Her hair isn't the same as Grace's honeyed blonde. But now that I know it is her – *must* be her – it is so simple. She has coloured it, as people do. People change themselves. And then there is the song that is playing. Have I remembered it faithfully or has my memory been reverse engineered? I drop into a slippery sleep. Then the gloaming.

Morning arrives and I sit up to see that the fire has completely burned out. There are only ashes left. I stand and rub my arms down for warmth and then kick away the fire-dust. The night seems to have swept my head clean and now I am purposeful once again. I hurry over the wall and start walking steadily down the road towards the bus stop. I need to cross the river again and head for Mayfair. The bus comes and within moments I am sitting in its manufactured warmth, grinding across the city.

There are commuters heading in rivulets to stations and bus stops, faces muffled against the cold. One is wearing shoes with red soles and for a second, I'm reminded of Ebadi and I think about how only a day or so ago, I was in a cemetery convinced that he had buried the girl there. Mishal. A part of me remains convinced of this even though it now cannot be true. Thirty years ago she died. Grace. *Michelle.*

I reach the library and find that it is just opening up. I make my way over to the computer terminals and fight off the sense of bafflement that creeps over me. I push a button or two to try and get the Google going but I am doing something wrong. There are laminated instructions and I try to follow them but they too are confusing. I'm wary of being seen to be floundering before these screens. I don't want to feel like a child, not now.

I prod around at the machine for the next twenty minutes, coaxing it without luck. I am about to get up and just find a person to ask.

'Xander.'

I see a face I know.

'Amit?' Then I remember something with a feeling like dread.

'Hazel called. I asked her to call me when you come,' he says, but keeps his distance. He is hesitant around me, wary after our last exchange. His tie is loose for a change and with his long hair, it has the effect of making him look rebellious.

'Hey, look. About last time. I was worried about you. And, well – I'm sorry. I shouldn't have behaved like that.'

'It's fine,' he says, looking down.

'Here.' I hand him the Proust that is still in my pocket. 'To make up for the one I took from you.'

He looks uncertainly at it, but then takes it.

'Thanks,' he says. 'I didn't go back there in the end. You were right, it was dangerous.' He smiles at me but there is sadness in it. 'So, how are you?' he says, brightening.

'I've been better.'

He stands in the pause, his arms at his sides, not knowing what to do. I don't know what to do either so we hang there awkwardly until I say, 'Can you help me with this?' I indicate the terminal.

He smiles and sits at the screen, completely at home. His fingers dance across the keys with no effort.

'I need to send an email to my solicitors, but I don't know where to start.'

'Solicitors? What happened?' he says, turning his head round to face me in concern.

'Long story,' I say in a way that shuts off any more questions.

He pauses. 'What's the name of the company?'

'I'm not sure – I know her name – Janine Cullen,' I say, without much hope.

He taps around for a second or two before looking meaningfully at the screen again. Every now and then he *hmms* and nods to himself, absorbed in what he is doing.

'Okay, got it. Here, you can send her an email from my account. Or I can do it.'

I'm dazzled by the speed at which he navigates this world. 'Can you just say that I'm coming in to see her? Today? Like maybe now?'

He gives me a look of amusement. 'I'm not sure that's exactly how it works but okay – sent,' he says.

'Thanks, Amit,' I say.

'It's fine.'

As I get up to leave he calls after me, holding up the Proust in one hand, 'Hope it all works out.'

Her office is a twenty- or thirty-minute walk from the library, up near Paddington Green Police Station. I push open the doors and see the receptionist stiffen as I do. My hands go up to signal peace.

'It's okay,' I say to calm her nerves, 'I have an appointment.'

I recognise that my voice and appearance are a clash. Seb's clothes haven't survived the night very well and when I look down, I notice for the first time that there are smears of ash down my front and charcoal under my nails and over my hands. I wonder if I've touched my face so that I now look camouflaged and ready for battle. I brush my clothes down self-consciously but when I do, debris drops from my back on to the carpet. Twigs, grass and other clinging things.

'With?' The woman folds her arms.

'Janine,' I say. 'Cullen.'

At this she checks her computer, then becomes a little less tense. 'She'll be in in a few minutes. Take a seat, Mr —?'

'Shute,' I say. 'More like the slide than the gun.'

She looks at me unimpressed and then indicates a row of battered chairs covered in blue cloth, spilling stuffing from their corners. 'You can sit.'

There are magazines stacked in a neat pile on a coffee table. I sit and flick through them. *Solicitors Journal. Law Society Gazette. The Lawyer. Counsel* magazine. *Legal Action Group.* There is nothing here that I can imagine any visitor wanting to read. I flick through some back issues of the *Gazette* and start reading an article written by a barrister complaining about legal aid fees. *Half a Shirt Anyone?* is the strapline and it is the most interesting thing about it.

Twenty minutes pass in slow motion before Jan appears at the door.

'Xander. I didn't think you were going to come, if I'm honest,' she says, dragging a wheelie case in behind her with one hand and some carrier bags stuffed with files in the other. Her hair is in a short bronzed plait. The freckles are still a surprise in her face.

'Neither did I,' I reply. I stand to shake her hand before remembering that mine is grubby. Her own are occupied and this thankfully goes unnoticed.

'Come through,' she says, and leads the way behind the reception desk through a glazed door. The lights come on automatically as we walk through. I think about helping her with the bags she is struggling with but I'm not sure what the etiquette is any more. The office is remarkable only for its clutter. There are files of papers everywhere, on the floor, on shelves, on the two desks at either end of the room.

'Take a seat if you can find an empty one.'

I sit and wait for her to do the same.

'So that copper, Conway, is it? He's got a right hard-on for you, hasn't he? What did you ever do to him?'

'I don't know,' I say. 'I get on better with Blake.'

'Yeah. Anyway, your upcoming interview. They've given us a bit more disclosure so this time we might have to actually go full-comment on this one, depending, obviously.'

'Depending on what?' I say, puzzled.

'On what your version is.'

I look at her, waiting to say more but she seems to be doing the same. Finally, she brushes a stray hair over an ear and unsheaths a Bic.

'Well then?'

'Well what?' I say.

'What's your version?'

'My version is that I didn't do it.'

'That's a start,' she says, looking up. 'What's the rest? Why were you in the house? When were you in the house? Are you still going with that whole last-week story or have we reflected a bit since last time?'

I am shocked by how direct she is, but I suppose she has to be. 'I'm beginning to think it was when they're saying. Thirty years ago,' I say.

'Okay. And are you saying you did see her being killed then?'

'I think so.'

'You think?'

'Look, this isn't easy for me. My memory isn't – these last years haven't exactly been what you might call ideal,' I say, feeling my temper unravelling.

'I understand that, I do, but still I need to know. Why are you telling me you *think*?'

'Because I'm not sure if I imagined it. But then I remember the details so vividly. I saw her being killed. I am sure of it. I just don't know if—'

'But maybe you'd have seen some of the police pictures at the time, if you knew her that well?'

'No,' I say. 'I didn't know she was dead. Or at least I don't remember knowing. Could it have been me?'

'What?' she says.

'It might have been me.'

She puts the pen down and looks at me seriously.

'If you're saying that, then you're saying "no comment". Simple as. But, take it from me: with what they have now, it's not going to look good if you go "no comment" again. We can get away with it once, play the disclosure card. But this is one of those cases where you are going to want to get your defence in now. Nice and early. So, let me ask you again. Are you certain that it was someone else?'

I think about this. What Seb said to me yesterday still rings true. I couldn't have done that to her if I loved her, could I? Now, when my back is against the wall, I will fight, but back then I wasn't a man of violence. I hated it. I had always believed that violence was a car swerving out of control: when you lose your temper, you're just a passenger in your own body.

And yet my memory is dashed or repressed or whatever the word is for what has happened to it. It feels not exactly wiped-out, but collaged. Some parts are bright and daring, others dark and patchy. It's the juxtaposition that is unsettling. The memories don't flow from one to another; they lurch around like dreams.

'I'm certain,' I say.

'Good,' she says. 'Why were you in the house? Were you invited in by the deceased?' The *deceased*. The word jars. She was a person.

'I'm not sure.'

'Well, do you want to have a think?' she says. 'Why might you have been there?'

I do have an answer but I'm not sure how it's going to sound.

'I was living *out* at the time. It was cold – I needed a day or two to put myself together. And Grace had seen me on the streets and gave me her spare key. She was going away for a while. Said I could use her place to clean up. That must have been why I was there.' I think of the key I had on me when I was arrested. I don't know what's happened to it.

Janine raises her eyebrows at me. 'So, then what? Did she not go away in the end?'

'I don't know. I don't remember it the way I'm telling it. In my head, it wasn't her place, it was just an empty house that I used as a squat because I had nowhere to stay. I didn't even expect it to be empty, it just was. I mean I think the door was unlocked.'

She had been taking down what I had said but now she has stopped. 'I don't know what to do with what you're telling me, Xander. Did you have a key or was it unlocked?'

'I don't know,' I say. I feel the blood gather into my cheeks, flushing.

She sighs. 'Okay, Xander. My advice is that you go "no comment". We might need to go down the psych route here. I know the police thought you were fit to be interviewed but this doesn't feel right to me.'

'Psych? You as well? I'm not mad. And I'm not seeing a psychiatrist.'

'It's up to you, but this is serious. They're going to be charging you with murder. You can't dick around here, you're looking at life.'

'Charging? They're charging me?' I say, shocked. 'I thought they might decide there wasn't enough to charge me.'

'We have to be prepared for the possibility.'

'But I thought you said they had nothing.'

'That was before they searched Sebastian's house. Now they've got something. And it's not looking good.'

'But Seb stopped them. He said that the warrant wasn't right.'

'Well, whatever time they had was all they needed.'

36

Thursday

By the time my consultation with Jan is over, it is noon. I watch her finishing up her notes and marking certain passages with a yellow highlighter. I feel as if I am in competent hands, but I know that even competent hands can't produce magic.

'Thanks, Jan,' I say, standing to leave. 'It's a lot to think about, but I'll have better answers in a day or two once I have thought it through.'

There's too much for me to process right now. I know myself. I need to go somewhere, cast away whatever of the world has stuck to me, so I can think clearly. I can get there, given time. I turn at the doorway to find Jan looking at me quizzically.

'Where are you going?' she says.

'Back. Home. Or Seb's.'

'We have an interview.'

'We've finished, haven't we?'

'Not with me. The police.'

'What? Now?'

'Yes, now, Xander. Are you feeling okay?' she says, getting up.

'Sorry. I didn't … Did I know this?' I say. The room seems to be tilting.

'They want to interview you again this afternoon about the new evidence. That's why you're here. They made an appointment.'

My heart stops for a second.

'Interview? I'm not ready for an interview. What new evidence? What are they going to ask me?' I say, the panic climbing.

'Stop,' she says. 'We've already been through this. It's "no comment". I don't know what the new evidence is, something from the search, but it doesn't matter. You're way too hazy about the details to give them answers.'

'I'm not hazy,' I say, following her into the reception area. 'You have to understand that I remember what I remember really clearly. I just – I just can't be sure I'm remembering what I saw or if I'm remembering what I think I saw.'

'Or when you're remembering it from.'

'But I think I saw her being killed. Surely that's something I should be saying? If I say nothing, you yourself said it would look terrible.' I track her to the pavement and stand there as she hails a passing cab.

'Paddington Green Police Station,' she says, getting in. The driver tuts at the pointless fare and then scowls when he sees me getting in too.

'Look, Xander. You can't say on tape, *I'm not sure if it might have been me.* You can't even really say it to me. I'm borderline being professionally embarrassed here. If you say that in the interview, you may as well not even have a trial.'

The taxi lurches off.

'But I changed my mind about that. I told you. I'm certain it wasn't me. I couldn't have done it.'

She turns her face and forces her eyes into mine.

'When a murder suspect is asked whether he murdered a person, an innocent one says, "No, I didn't", not "No, I couldn't." Do you see what I'm saying?'

I know she's right, but there is life between the blacks and whites in my non-lawyer's world. There's a part of me that feels with conviction that if I explained it properly, with context, I could make them see what I mean. I have at least this in my arsenal. I have the ability to speak logically and clearly and sincerely.

'No comment then,' I say.

The taxi screeches to a halt and we scramble out. Jan hands over what seems like too much money for such a short journey and then slams the door shut. She carries on speaking to me as we walk.

'Xander, trust me. Whatever is going on in that head, you need to focus. You bring every bit of attention you can. You're going to need it.'

I nod as we walk through the doors and watch with admiration as Jan negotiates our way in with calm assurance. We are shown politely to a room and as we wait Jan rehearses with me the two words I need to say.

'Look, they're bastards, these guys. They'll pretend to be all pally but they are not your friends. They are there to nail you. They will keep telling you it's your choice to follow my advice or not. That you're the one who's going to be on trial. And *Don't you want to get on tape your version of events?* They'll try all that. And what they're doing is making you feel stupid for saying "no comment". But – and listen to me carefully – if you want any hope of seeing life outside four walls this side of the next twenty or thirty years, you'll do as I say. No. Fucking. Comment. Got it?'

I nod.

'I need to hear the words, Xander.'

'No fucking comment,' I say. She reacts. Just enough of a movement of the mouth to be recognised as a smile.

When he comes to collect us, Conway is skittish. Something about having Jan here has put him on edge.

'Come on through, Xander,' he says. *Pally.* Jan looks at me as if to say 'I told you.'

We follow him to an interview suite and Blake is already there. She stands and shakes our hands.

'Can I get you some water?' she asks.

We shake our heads and the tape starts as soon as we sit. Blake does the introductions and then repeats the caution. This time the words clang in my ears. *You don't have to say anything but if you fail to mention when questioned … harm your defence …*

'My client will be exercising his right to silence throughout this interview,' Jan says in a way that makes her sound bored, but really is signalling confidence.

'Obviously that is your right,' says Conway. 'You can follow your solicitor's advice but at the end of the day it is just advice. She isn't the one who's going to be going to trial—'

Jan sees something and quickly leans forward in her seat.

'To trial, Officer? Are you charging Mr Shute?'

'Well, we don't know that yet, do we? Depends on what happens in this interview.'

'Does it?' she says. 'You know that if you have enough evidence to charge my client, then this interview shouldn't be happening at all.'

Conway shifts about, loosens his collar. This dance isn't one he is good at.

'I'm well aware of that, Ms Cullen. Now, as we were saying, there are a few questions we would like your comments on.'

I wait as Blake looks down at a file of papers. She seems less than pleased but I can't precisely describe how she seems. Embarrassed? Irritated?

'Picking up from the last interview we had, I wanted to clarify whether you have now had a chance to consider whether you did know the victim, Michelle Mackintosh?' asks Conway.

That word 'victim' lies heavy in the air. I look across at Jan and she shakes her head almost imperceptibly.

'I did know her,' I say.

'I just want to remind you of my advice, Mr Shute,' Jan says, her voice brittle.

'And were the two of you in a relationship?'

I take a breath. I badly want to explain this part. There is no harm in this part of my story. Jan's eyes are steel.

'No comment,' I say. She relaxes slightly in her seat.

'Actually, there's not much point denying it. At the time of your last interview, officers carried out a search of your bail address and found some interesting things. For the tape I am showing the suspect exhibit RG/9, a selection of photographs. Have a look at these, Mr Shute. These are pictures of you and the deceased. And just so you're aware, these are just a few of the ones we have.'

I didn't know that Seb had photographs. Of course, he must have had some. I think of the one on the mantel.

'Is that a question, Officer?' Jan says.

'No, the question is just whether you are prepared to accept there was a relationship between you both?' he says, flaring.

I don't know how it can *harm my defence* if I accept this but I follow the advice. 'No comment.'

'Okay then. Let's do this the hard way,' he says.

'Exhibit RG/10 is a letter written by hand on light blue note-paper.' I stare at it and remember it immediately. There are yin and yang signs on each corner. This was Grace's trademark paper. She always wrote to me on that paper.

'Do you recognise this letter?'

My letter. How do they have my letter? And then I remember: the belongings that Seb stored in his loft. This must have been part of the stuff that was taken. And then I think of the money and the thought passes through my mind that they might have taken the dollars. But Seb was sure they didn't.

'Officer, I gather this was taken in the course of a search without a proper warrant,' Jan says.

'We can argue about that later, Miss Cullen. For now, let me just ask you, Mr Shute, if you recognise the letter?'

'No comment,' I say, fighting against the urge to explain.

'I'm just going to read it out. It's got a date written on it: November 2nd 1989. *My dear Xander*, it says. *I am not sure whether I am going to send this letter to you or whether it's going to join the others I've started and crushed into balls. I want you to know I never meant to hurt you even though all we seem to end up doing is hurting each other over and over again. This time—*'

I am whipped back three decades. I don't remember the letter and what it said but I remember everything else. What I wore then – an old tweed jacket from a second-hand shop. Which brand of cigarettes I smoked – Consulate. I remember the colour of the walls in the room in which I read it – apple-white. I remember the twisting feeling in my gut. The hopelessness.

'Stop,' I say. 'Yes. I knew her. We were in a relationship.'

Jan is angry but more at Conway than me.

'By the looks of this letter, your relationship ended at her choice, so to speak,' he says.

'Yes,' I say, my jaw tightening.

'How did you feel about that?' he asks.

'I'm going to repeat my advice, Mr Shute.'

'It's okay, Jan. I felt how anyone would feel. I loved her. I didn't want it to end. But it was beyond my control.' I am articulating something I haven't had a chance to become familiar with yet.

'That's an interesting phase you've used though, Mr Shute, isn't it?'

'Is that a question?' Jan says. She is shifting in her seat. Coiled.

'It will be, Miss. You see we also found these at your bail address, Mr Shute. At the bottom of a cardboard box we lifted from the loft. Is that your handwriting? For the benefit of the tape, I am showing the suspect exhibit RG/11, a letter without a date on it.'

I look at what he is showing me. It is still in a plastic police bag but I can make out the writing easily enough. It is my writing, or was.

'No comment,' I say.

'It's easy enough to get a handwriting expert in, Mr Shute, if you're denying it as your writing but it has your name at the bottom. In it you use that same expression you've just used to me now. *It's beyond my control,* you say in a letter you have written to the deceased.'

I am straining my memory to remember this but it is a fog. I look across to Jan who is incensed. Thankfully, she speaks for me as I grope around in my head for memories.

'First of all, Officer, looking at the letter, it's not addressed to the deceased, it seems to be addressed to a *Mabel*. And secondly, if the letter was found at his address, it obviously wasn't sent to Mabel, whoever she was, so I don't see the relevance of this.'

Conway isn't fazed and seeing his face turn smug begins to worry me.

'Actually, Miss Cullen, in the letter that your client has already agreed he was sent by the deceased, she signed it *Mabel.* Was that a pet name you used for her?'

'It was,' I say, and although Jan shoots me a scolding look, I don't have a choice. I'm going to have to accept it.

'We believe that you meant to send this letter but didn't, for whatever reason. In it you say that you can't let her go. You say, it's beyond your control. And you say it one, two – *five* times – *it's beyond your control.* What did you mean by that?'

The memory of that letter flashes in my mind in a burst of colour. There was something in that phrase that I remembered. It meant more or less than it seemed to at the time, but I can't remember now which: was it more or less? It feels like it might have been a joke. But there is sentimentality there that doesn't fit a joke.

'It was a joke,' I say.

'Doesn't sound like a joke.' Blake speaks for the first time. Conway looks across at her with reproach.

'Not a joke, joke. An inside joke but I can't remember now what it is,' I say.

Jan begins to wriggle as though she is climbing out of her body.

'I'm going to remind you of my advice, Mr Shute.'

'No comment,' I say.

'Okay. Just so's you understand I'm going to still ask the questions.'

What was just warmth in the room is now squeezing me tight. The air begins to cloy at my throat and the urge to leave the room becomes desperate. I look over at Blake who hasn't broken a sweat. Conway too sits as if in complete comfort. But still the room wraps itself around me.

'Okay. Maybe to just change gear a bit. I want to ask you about the money. For the tape I am showing the suspect RTG/6, a copy of a bank statement for an account in US dollars. You would agree that this statement shows your name and the name of the deceased, Michelle Mackintosh?'

Jan's eyes begin to widen but I can't read why.

'No comment,' I say, gasping for air.

'Well, it's there anyway on the document. And as we pointed out in the last interview, we can see there that two hundred and fifty-three thousand dollars and twenty cents vanishes out of that account a couple of weeks before her death. Can you tell us who withdrew that sum in cash?'

'No comment.'

'It must have been her or you, since it's a joint account. Was it her?'

'No comment.'

'Was it you?'

'No comment.'

'We have done some investigating since our last interview and according to the bank's microfiche records, the person that withdrew this money was you. What was the reason for that? Did she agree to you withdrawing it?'

'No comment.'

'Actually, we know that she didn't countersign the withdrawal. So, my question is, why did you take this money out before she died?'

My mouth has dried and I have a desperate urge to swallow. But the sheer cliché of it, gulping like a cartoon character, stops me.

'Did you have money problems, Mr Shute?'

'No comment.'

'If you don't mind me saying, you look as if you have money problems.'

'That's not a question,' Jan says before I can say my two words.

'Okay, well, here's a question. What did you do with it?'

'Enough. I am requesting a break in the interview at this point.'

I'm not sure why Jan is so edgy about these questions but I am myself desperate to stop. I need to get out of the room, even for a few minutes. I pull my shirt away from my neck and take a deep lungful of sticky air.

'Certainly,' says Conway with a sneer. 'We are pausing this interview to allow you to have a consultation with your solicitor, Mr Shute. The time by my watch is fourteen thirty-nine.'

37

Thursday

'Why did you stop the interview?' I say.

I think I know why – I am just too embarrassed to accept it. I was foundering. Every question was another rock, every answer a lurch into peril. This bland room we're in makes me queasy. My breathing is still a toil.

'I need to make sure about this,' she says seriously. 'The money. What happened to it?'

'What?'

'The money. What did you do with it? Where did it go?' she says. Whatever patience there was in her voice is hanging on by a fingernail.

'I haven't got it,' I say in the end.

'No shit,' she says, looking me up and down. 'I know you haven't got two hundred and fifty thousand dollars on you. But what happened to it? Where did it go? Speedboat? Renoir? Casino?'

'You don't understand. I kept it.'

Jan squints at me as if I have started speaking code.

'Xander,' she says, tilting her head. 'What are you talking about? Kept it where, in an account?'

'No. In a trunk. At Seb's.'

She hears this and slowly sinks into a seat along the wall. 'Xander. What are you doing to me? Please tell me it's still there.'

'I can't. It's gone.'

'For crying out – okay. We don't have time for this right now. You need to find that money before your trial or that guy in there is going to crucify you.'

'I'm trying,' I say. I think of Nina but have no confidence that she is going to help me. 'But is it that important, really?'

She stands up again and looks at me. 'You're saying, why would I kill someone I love. They're saying, a quarter of a million reasons.'

'No, I get that,' I say. 'But what real difference does it make?'

'Okay. Look. Did you take the money?'

'You know I did.'

'How do we know that you didn't kill her for it? I mean how can we prove that?'

'I didn't kill her,' I say, tumbling at the accusation. The words *kill* and *murder* are being slipped at me blandly like playing cards. Each time I hear them I see her face, frozen in the photo.

'I know. Just humour me. How can we prove that you wouldn't kill her for money?'

'Because, look at me, money is the last thing that drives me. You couldn't find anyone who cares less about money than I do,' I say. I feel the heat rising up my neck. I look at her and she suddenly doesn't seem like the ally I had expected her to be.

'So how do we prove that money doesn't interest you?'

'Jan? Look at me. I've got a degree from Cambridge. I could earn money. I could have more money than I need. But it doesn't interest me. I was walking *away* from all that. That's what *this* is about,' I say, showing her my stained hands.

Her gaze remains level.

'And if you had a boatload of money, how would we prove that you have no interest in it?'

Finally, with that question, a glow perforates the darkness. 'By showing it to them untouched after thirty years,' I say with a sigh.

'So, are we going to be able to do that? Or are we going no comment?'

'I don't know where it is. I know that sounds unbelievable, but it's true. It's gone.'

'No comment it is then, Xander.' She stands up and makes for the door. 'And, Xander, for Christ's sake, say no comment to every question. Not just the ones you don't like.'

I nod rapidly. 'I know. I'm sorry.'

The interview resumes. The formalities are rehearsed all over again. I study Conway for any hint of a change in his demeanour but his face gives nothing away. Blake, however, seems to have hardened. There are no more half-smiles. I am not sure whether that is to deny me or to appease Conway.

'So, to pick up from before we stopped the interview, Mr Shute, to allow you to consult with your solicitor, are you satisfied you have had enough time to speak with her?'

'Yes,' I say. Jan glares at me and immediately I try and correct the mistake. 'No comment.'

'So, what did you do with the money, Mr Shute?'

'No comment.'

'As you know we became aware of this matter because of you reporting the murder of a young woman. Do you recall telling us that there had been a murder at 42B Farm Street?'

'No comment.'

'Would you agree that since there has been a young woman murdered at number 42B, that it stands to reason you were there?'

'No comment.'

'What were you doing there?'

'No comment.'

'How did you get into the house? Were you invited in?'

'No comment.'

'Or did you break in?'

'I did not break in,' I say, unable to resist.

'So how did you get in?'

'No comment,' I say, despite the tug to say something in my defence.

'Actually, we don't believe you did break in. There was no record of a break-in. Police at the time couldn't be sure there was a murder. The coroner recorded an accidental death. But, Mr Shute, it wasn't accidental, was it?'

'No,' I say. Jan slaps the desk in frustration at me. 'I saw her being killed,' I say. I can't deny this. I have said this much already to police.

'Yes. You told us that when you were being interviewed about the Squire murder. So, who do you say murdered her if it wasn't you?'

'I don't know,' I say, anger building from nowhere.

Blake stirs and then says, 'That's not strictly true is it, Xander? What you told us in the interview was.' She pulls up a sheet of paper from a folder in front of her and reads from it: '*The woman. In the house. I saw her being strangled. By her boyfriend.* That's what you told us.'

Conway raises his eyebrows at me. Waiting.

'No comment.'

'We think we agree with you, Mr Shute. She was strangled by her boyfriend. But you were her boyfriend, weren't you?'

'I didn't strangle her,' I say, and as I do I am conscious that my voice betrays my own uncertainty.

'It is interesting, Mr Shute, how you use that word "strangle". Because although the post-mortem records that she died from a blunt force trauma injury to the head, it also shows that she had bruises on her neck. The post-mortem report says this: "Present on the neck, four sites of cutaneous bruising and a further five sites displaying fingernail abrasions. It has not been possible to date the contusions using any back-calculation but a reasonable conclusion is that somewhere up to forty-eight hours before her death, pressure had been applied to the deceased's neck in a throttling action." So, my question is, Mr Shute, did you strangle her?'

'No comment.'

'Is that how you knew she had been strangled? Because you were the one who did it?'

'No comment.'

'Was it beyond your control?'

When he says the words this time, the memory comes in a wave back to me. It was from a film we had seen together at the cinema, *Dangerous Liaisons*. John Malkovich kept saying the line over and over again. I don't remember why, but I remember he did and she, the girl, cried harder each time. I cannot tell them this in a way that sounds good.

'No comment.'

'Okay. The thing that we are concerned about is that it doesn't look that good for you at the moment. By your own admission, you were in her house. We believe she must have invited you in because there were no signs of forced entry. By your own admission, you saw her being strangled. She in fact had been strangled. You were the last person to see her alive and the first person to see her dead. Now unless another person broke into the house while you were there and killed her in front of you and then repaired the door and left, we can only see one way this murder happened. It was you.'

There's no way out of this. 'No comment.'

'You were in love with her. You were writing her letters telling her you would never let her go.'

Jan interrupts, throwing her hands back in high dudgeon. 'It doesn't say that! It says that he *can't* let her go. And, as we have already established, he didn't send the letter.'

'Okay, then that you *can't* let her go. And then we have this money that you empty out in cash from her account. We think that you used that money to help you disappear after the murder. And it did help you disappear for a very long time, didn't it?'

'What's your evidence that he used that money?' says Jan, bridling.

'Well, you tell us, Mr Shute. Did you use the money? Is it lying safely in a suitcase somewhere collecting dust?'

Jan and I look at each other and then flick our eyes away before it can be noticed. My eyes land on Blake's. She noticed.

'No comment,' I say.

'So, you tell us if we have it wrong. If someone else did this murder, tell us who. Tell us how he got in. This is your chance to put your side of the story.'

I don't know what to do for the best. This interview is a mess. Whenever I say something it makes things worse. But I know each time I say *no comment* that a jury hearing it will think I am guilty, that I have no answers to give.

'Okay, Mr Shute. Before we terminate this interview is there anything else you'd like to say to us?'

'No. Just. I didn't kill her. I didn't do it,' I say in desperation.

'Then tell us what you know. Help us catch the killer. Surely you'd want to help catch the person who did this?'

'Yes,' I say.

'So, come on, because at the moment we have no reason not to charge you with this. And there's no reason for me to recommend bail on what little you have given us.'

Jan leaps out of her seat. 'Officer Conway, that is improper and you know it. It's a breach of PACE to offer any inducement for an interview comment,' she says, leaning over the desk, stabbing her finger at Conway. The ferocity of her objection puts my eyes on stalks.

'Wait. Hang on right there, you know that was not meant as an inducement—' he starts, going pale.

Blake cuts in. 'What DI Conway is saying is that it is your right to answer no comment. It is an ongoing right. And to be clear you are not being pressured to answer any questions. But this is your chance. He is right, we cannot recommend police bail in your case. The evidence is strong, Xander. Really strong. And you haven't helped us with your defence. You show us why we have got it wrong and that could change whether we even charge you. But on what you have given us, you're being charged with murder.'

Jan nudges me and I turn to see her shaking her head firmly.

I turn to look at Blake and although I know that she is not my friend, I sense that she is trying to give me a chance. I don't know whether I can survive the walls of a prison when even the walls of Seb's beautiful house feel like a prison. I take a breath and try to slow down the thoughts in my head.

'No comment,' I say.

38

Thursday

They charged me with murder. Jan left. Now I'm here in a police cell, knowing only that there's an emergency bail hearing tomorrow, Friday, at Southwark Crown Court.

I have only been here for a few hours and already the cell is crushing me. If I sit down too long, the walls begin to reverberate, and there is a humming from the lights, or from something else, that I can't shake. It buzzes deep into my skin and under my flesh so that I have to stand every few seconds to shrug it off. Thankfully there is other noise. I can hear men and women talking, their jocularity slamming hard against this doom that I am in. *Murder.*

When they processed me, they gave me a form asking me whether I felt suicidal. 'Of course I do. I'm also highly claustrophobic,' I wrote. Now, when I look back, I don't know why I did that. I thought, idiotically, that they would take pity on me and think again about their bail decision. As if they might just say, we can't keep him here, he's claustrophobic. Let him, the murderer, go.

Somebody brings me a meal boated in plastic. I eat even though I'm not hungry because I always eat whenever there is food. I eat as much of it as I can and save whatever is dry in my pockets. The food is hot and smells plasticky, like Wotsits.

A vision comes to me of Rory and me tracking through an overgrown patch of scrub grass somewhere, a packet of Wotsits each in our hands. I remember it had been sunny after a morning full of showers. We were walking slowly through a park, picking a path through long grass. I began to wade on ahead, running slightly, cutting swathes through the damp grass. I was an explorer, preparing the way for the others in the expedition. But when I looked around, Rory was gone. My heart dipped for a second and I marched back again, retracing the flattened grass. At first, I thought he'd vanished and so I began to panic. But then I saw him right there on the grass, crouched down and sobbing. I went and knelt next to him. I remember the feel of the long, wet grass on my knees, the impressions they made afterwards. There were tracks down his cheeks.

'What's wrong?'

'Wotsits,' he said through shudders of breath. And there they were, scattered along the grass, wet, soggy. There was orange stain on his hands. 'They're all ruined,' he said. Rory, so bright for his age, so old for his years, was at that moment no more and no less than he was. Six.

I took his empty packet and tipped half of mine into his.

'But they're yours,' he said between gulps.

'I'm not that hungry,' I said, pulling him up to his feet.

The lights go low when the night sets in. Ten-thirty, the information sheet said. A signifier of the end of a day in a room without windows. I lie down eventually on the bench and pull the blanket over my head. The mattress is thin but this isn't the worst bed I have had in my life. The bed isn't the problem. When I am out, even when my clothes are wet and stuffed full of newspaper and there is ice under my head, I can still manage some sleep. All I need is the knowledge that the baggage of my life is scattered behind me in tiny mounds, as if from holes in my pockets.

But here, there is nowhere to cast the debris away. If I don't get bail tomorrow, I could be in prison for a year before my trial. The idea of being in a gaol with bars and guards makes me feel faint. My palms are clammy and my heart pounds in my chest. I think for the fourth time this evening that I am going to have a heart attack. It's the same feeling I had when I was locked in the police car. My breath is shallow and is coming out too fast.

It passes. And as soon as it does and my breathing becomes level again, desperation gives way to relief, which itself gives way to a different desperation. I know I can survive the night, but I can't do a year without giving up something of my head. But more than that, if it was twenty years? I'd be dead in two. Less.

They have taken away my belt (Seb's belt) and my laces (Seb's brogues). They think that I can string myself up by my shoe-laces. I laugh at the thought of that but then I begin to choke because I know that if it could be done, I might consider it. And if it could be done, I would find the way.

I lay my head back on the mattress and begin to breathe as rhythmically as I can, counting the *in* breath and the *out*. It helps. I feel as if I am putting a blanket over the mouth of my thoughts, muffling them, snuffing them out like sputtering candles.

I shut my eyes and take myself to Grace and that night. The flames are licking the walls and a record plays. The music is warm, cossetting, unless that is the fire inflecting the music with heat. The crescendo begins its journey, meandering and climbing through the first minutes of introduction. And then.

My eyes snap open.

An officer is at the door. He's checking to see if I am alive because of what I put on that stupid form.

'I'm fine!' I say. 'Just let me sleep, for God's sake.'

'Can't, mate. Have to check you every hour,' he says, and leaves.

And that is how it is for the next eight hours.

By the time I am being shaken out of my cell, I have had an hour's sleep at most. I rinse my face in a small steel sink and then I am in a van off to court. When I arrive, I am put into another cell from where I can hear other prisoners shouting and banging on the doors. If you believe what they're saying, we are in a place where all the staff are cunts.

At nine-thirty I'm cuffed to a guard who walks me down the corridor. I see Jan's face before she sees mine and even though it has been only a few hours, I am so grateful to see her that tears collect in my eyes.

'Jan,' I say, and sit while the cuffs are unlocked. She is wearing another tired black suit but the sky-blue shirt underneath it lifts her.

'Xander,' she says, waiting till the guard leaves. 'Okay, we might not have long, so let me say what I need to. We are dealing with your bail position today. Because you have been charged with murder, your bail is not like normal bail. You don't have a *right* to bail. It's kind of the other way around. The burden is on us to show that there is no significant risk that you would cause injury to anyone.'

'Okay,' I say. 'That's good, isn't it?'

'Not really, Xander. They don't often bail people in murder cases because the fact of the murder is a good basis for saying there is a risk you could cause harm on the logic that if you did it once—'

'But I didn't do it once!' I say, hearing my voice become sharp. 'I can't be locked up, Jan. I haven't got the head for it. I can't.'

'I know, Xander. But the fact is that the prosecution are objecting to bail on those grounds. They say you are a risk.'

I feel defeated.

'Look,' she continues. 'I will do my best, but what I wanted to know was whether there was any way you could offer a surety or security?'

Some of the words she is saying filter into my consciousness but others do not. I can't believe I am going to prison. *I won't be able to do this* is all that I can think right now, and that thought preoccupies me, forcing everything else out.

'Sorry, what?' I say, sensing that there is some information that she wants from me.

'Money. Can you offer any money to help with bail, or maybe you know anyone who can?'

I think of Seb, but I can't ask him for more than he's already done. I shake my head.

It is nearly three o'clock before my case is called. I am brought in through some underground passages, cuffed again to a guard. I walk with her as she chirps brightly to me about something in the news and it hits me that my face is going to be in the papers. My blood begins to run cold in my veins and my palms begin to dampen. We emerge in the well of the court in the dock. I look around for the press but there is nothing happening in the court that feels urgent. Some people in wigs and gowns are chatting casually to one another. The judge's bench is empty. I catch Jan's eye and she waves at me.

A woman in a crumpled gown stands and announces the judge, and people rise and fall as he enters from the back and sits in the red chair. The courtroom is bland and tired and everyone in here seems the same. The atmosphere is more municipal than I expected.

By the time I manage to master my anxiety well enough to hear what is being said, we are midway into my hearing. The prosecutor is on her feet addressing the judge casually, almost bored.

'The Crown oppose bail, Your Honour. This is a serious charge. The Crown say that Mr Shute is likely to fail to answer his bail. He is of no fixed abode and due to the nature and seriousness of the offence, he is likely to abscond.'

When she sits down, Jan gets straight to her feet. She attacks the room with confidence, her northern vowels softening in the process.

'In my submission, Your Honour, there is no significant risk that he would cause injury to another person. Firstly, Mr Shute has no previous convictions for violence at all. Secondly, he denies this offence completely and cannot be considered violent on account of the allegation alone. Thirdly, Mr Shute has been bailed by the police on a number of occasions pre-charge, and answered his police bail every time. We argue that he can be considered as having a satisfactory bail address if the police have allowed him to be bailed there before.' She sits down.

The conviction with which she has spoken fills me suddenly with hope. But it seems so minimal, what she has said. Should there be more to my freedom than these few words?

The prosecutor gets slowly to her feet and consults someone behind her. I look and see that it's Conway. He's here in court. My heart sinks.

'The officer informs me, Your Honour, that Mr Shute, although not convicted of any offences of violence in the past, has been recently arrested in connection with an offence of serious violence. A middle-aged man was stabbed in the neck and left for dead, essentially.'

Jan looks round to me with her eyebrows raised high. There is anger and confusion on her face. She mutters something to the judge about further instructions and comes to the back of the court where I am gesticulating at her.

'What is this, Xander?' she says in a heavy whisper.

'The stabbing. Squire. They can't use that, can they?' I say.

'Why not? And why didn't you think of mentioning this to me?'

'Because,' I whisper back, 'they dropped it.'

'Dropped it?'

'Yes. They said NFA.'

She makes a note of this on her pad and returns to her place.

'Thank you, Your Honour. My understanding is that the stabbing that the Crown is alluding to with reference to Mr Squire was NFA'd by the police. In the circumstances it is completely improper for the Crown to attempt to influence your decision by that means. If there was evidence, they would have charged him. The fact that they didn't charge him, if anything proves that there was no evidence against my client. And finally, Your Honour, if Mr Shute was a danger and he did murder this victim, what we can be sure of is that he hasn't presented a danger to anybody since that time, nearly thirty years ago.'

The judge looks at me and then at the two lawyers.

'I'm going to rise to consider my decision,' he says, and leaves to the refrain of 'All rise'.

39

Friday

Although the judge is out of the courtroom, everyone else stays, like actors milling around waiting to perform. If they could, everyone would be lighting up; instead they chat. The woman in the gown is talking to the prosecutor about her holiday. The gaolers are talking to one another about some member of staff who has been fiddling with the rotas. And I am here in a well of light, behind glass, looking at my hands.

Jan finishes scribbling something and comes to speak to me between the gaps in the glass wall.

'He's just going to decide. Shouldn't be too long. Did you catch the rest of it?' she says.

'No. What's the rest?'

'Don't worry, I'll explain it all later but basically, whatever happens with bail, your case is being listed soon for pleas.'

I nod to indicate that I understand but I don't really. When? Now? Tomorrow? What if I plead guilty, can I change my mind? I heave it all away somewhere in my head. At the moment, this isn't information that I can process. All I have in my mind is bail. Every clean inch of thinking room is considering, calculating variations of the same data. If I don't get bail I will be taken to a prison. But I don't know for how long. I don't know if I can I try again for bail in another day or two or if there are limits. And I don't know how long can I survive behind high walls in a maze of ever-decreasing squares.

On the other side of the sanity equation, the fact is I have to be out. I need to be out so that I can find those dollars. I can't tell the police about any of it. They are past believing me and there is no way that Nina will tell them the truth. She stole a quarter of a million dollars and did God knows what with them. And even if, in some circumstances, she might tell the truth, she wouldn't do it to help me. She thinks I killed Grace, her best friend. What if the police get to her? What if they speak to Seb and he tells them about Nina and the money? When I think about it in this way, I am not sure where his loyalties lie.

But if there's the slightest chance that I can trace the money, I have to try. I need to speak to Nina, before the police do.

Jan drifts back to her seat and sits scrolling through messages on her phone and I remain, wilting between extreme alternatives.

Fifteen minutes pass agonisingly by. People walk in and out of court. Bored, all of them, except for a small Indian man who is clutching a paper and worriedly looking for the right court. He alone seems at all moved by the significance of this awful, cheap, blanched room. When the judge comes back in, the man ducks back out again silently. The room falls quiet and every-body eases once again into character. My breath stops. I hold it so I can listen to what he is saying, but all I can hear is a pulsing sound in my ears. Fragments of his words find their way across the court and snake through the glass. *Considered very carefully*

... balancing the interests of the defendant and the prosecution ...
seems to me ... met by ... imposition of ...

He finishes speaking and there is no reaction from anybody that allows me to deduce his decision. The gaolers aren't uncuffing me. The prosecution isn't complaining. On the other hand, Jan isn't either. She hasn't leapt to her feet to remonstrate or shout 'appeal'.

The lawyers spend some time mumbling to the judge who mumbles back at them individually. The minutes stretch. My breath catches as my body remembers it needs air. I gasp audibly but nobody reacts.

Finally, the judge turns to me and in a loud voice asks me to stand.

'You understand that your application for bail is allowed on strict conditions? You will live and sleep each night at the address notified to the court. You will be required to report to the local police station each Monday and Thursday. You are not to apply for travel documents. And you are not to go within five hundred metres of 42B Farm Street. If you breach any of those conditions, or if you fail to turn up to your next hearing, you will be committing a separate offence. Do you understand?'

I nod. The judge rises. And I am so grateful, despite the murder charge that has now crystallised around me, that I want to cry. Until the gaoler stands up and leads me back down into the cells.

'What's going on?' I say. 'He released me. Didn't he release me?'

She looks at me as if I have just materialised before her.

'Okay. Just quiet down for a second,' she says and leads me back into the cell and locks the door.

Blood wells up in my head and feels as if it is pooling behind my eyes. I don't know what is happening but I have an urge to scream.

I start pacing the cell until the floor begins to contract.

'I want to see my solicitor,' I shout. The words simply rebound back into my face. This room is designed to withstand more than I can give it.

I drop to the floor and begin to rock. There is a tide beginning in my head that I need to contain. He said bail. Did he say it? Have I imagined that? I replay the conversation over and over again and the certainty I had minutes ago is beginning to dilute. He might not have said that. I couldn't hear everything. I was straining to hear at points. So, what now?

Just as I unleash a scream, the door opens and a golden head looks in. It is a young woman. Pretty. Cheerful.

'Flippin' heck, what's eating you, love?' she says.

I leap to my feet and put my hands together. 'He said bail. I'm sure he said bail. Can't you go up and check?' I say. 'Please. I can't go to prison.'

'What? No, silly sausage. We're just processing you. I've got your bail form here. See,' she says, handing me a form that says 'Bail' on it. There are boxes ticked and others left blank.

'What, so, I can go?' I ask.

'Yes. Just give us, what, ten minutes and once we've done your paperwork, you'll be released.'

I sit on the bench and let the tears run free, until finally the door opens and I too am freed.

I walk through the iron door and into the court lobby and am met by Jan. I want to hug her but my condition, the state of my body, stops me.

'You waited,' I say.

'Yes, I waited. That's what I was telling you as you were being taken down to be processed. So now can we get the hell out of Dodge?' She indicates the front entrance with a tilt of her head.

I follow her on to a street lit by a bright, early spring sky. I have been away from the embrace of the outdoors for less than a day and already it feels like a homecoming. In the dust of the traffic, the memories flood back to me, remaking connections to the world and binding me once again to it.

'Not sure how we did that,' Jan says, walking briskly and scanning the road as she does. 'Good judge, shit prosecutor. Anyway, well done. You're out. Right, we have a brilliant QC lined up for you. You'll meet her next week, on Monday. She wants to see you in her Chambers as soon as possible.'

'That's quick,' I think it as I say it. I had the impression of cases grinding slowly through the legal system at Jarndycian speed.

'Well, as you heard, this case will next be up in two weeks and before then you'll need to be advised properly about your plea. It has to be quick and you're lucky that this Silk is free, to be honest.'

Two weeks seems so fast that I become unsteady just thinking about it. By March, I will be back in court entering a plea. I nod vaguely as I follow along behind her, struggling to keep up.

'Monday, 2 p.m. at 5 Pump Walk Chambers. I'll drop you a letter with details. Nasreen Khan QC,' she says, sticking her arm out. A taxi screams to a halt and almost before I can mutter my thanks, she has jumped in. She leaves the door open for a moment to speak to me.

'You need to find that money, Xander. It's going to be key.'

I nod and put my hand up to wave at her as she heaves the door shut.

'See you Monday,' she mouths through the window as the cab rumbles off.

Once the taxi fades into the distance, I turn and walk the other way. Seb's. I have to go there. That is my bail address now. He doesn't know yet that I have to live with him. He's too polite to object. But it can't be how he was hoping his life would turn out. And I have no way of making it up to him.

The ground is comforting underfoot. I need something firm and permanent as everything else around me seems to be washing away. I try to gather my scattered thoughts as I walk. The last thing I remember is Nina. The things she said. As I remember them again my pulse begins to quicken. *All you ever loved was a version of her that you had created.*

There was hate or something like it – spite, maybe – in her voice as she said it. This disturbs me most of all. That she would hurt me for no other reason than to inflict pain. But now as I consider her, I can't quite see her in those colours. Not truly. There was something else in her voice. More than grief. Some other quality. I play through the conversation I now have to have with her. I run it over and over across the roads and the roundabouts, along the wide pavements and congested bridges.

I have to get her to talk.

Seb's house. The late afternoon light catches it in a way that makes it feel like a memory. I knock on the door. Seb should be at work, I think, but a few seconds later the door opens and he is there. He looks terrible. He is wearing jeans and a blue-checked shirt that looks slept in.

I hold up a hand to stop whatever he might say. 'I've been charged with Grace's murder,' I say. 'They kept me overnight. I've just come from court. And I have to stay here. Court bail. I'm sorry. Really sorry, Seb.'

His face runs pale.

'You've been charged? But how?' he says, plainly shocked.

'They think I killed her, Seb.' Without warning, my eyes begin to redden.

'I've been trying to find out what happened to you all night, but those guys, the police, they can be real arseholes,' he says, and then holds me in a hug.

He leads me inside and to the kitchen. For a second, we look at one another saying nothing. Suddenly I feel exhausted and dirty. I fight the idea of a bath but I need one, my skin is itching hot in place. There's a part of me that thinks of this dirt on my skin as an amulet. Had it protected me until I had my first bath in years, just upstairs? There's so much I want to say, but my social skills, always uncertain, feel blown after a night in the cells.

'Come,' Seb says. 'I've got coffee brewed.'

'Look, if it's okay I'd just as soon go upstairs and—' I begin but he places a cup in my hand and sits.

'They charged you with the murder?' he says again.

I nod, gulping the strong coffee.

'What did you tell them?'

'Not much. I went mainly "no comment".'

'But you told them you didn't do it?' he says, looking into my eyes.

'I don't think I did tell them that. Not really,' I say, running over it in my head.

He visibly recoils as if he's been hit. 'What? Why not, Xand? I can't believe it. This is serious.'

'Because,' I say, and then catch myself in a thought. And then it solidifies. I look to catch my fingers trembling. And then my voice:

'Because I'm not sure I didn't.'

40

Friday

'I can't believe that, Xander,' Seb says, shaking his head. 'I don't think that you could have. I remember how you were about her – you loved her. There's no way you could have harmed her. Could you?'

'No. I mean, I don't believe I could have, Seb. I did love her – I still do. But they think it. And they're police.'

'Police can get it wrong, Xander. You'd know if you had. And importantly, we would know.' He looks at me and sighs. 'You look exhausted. Let's get some food inside you.' He starts to rummage around the cupboards for ingredients.

We would know. We. I think of Nina and how she reacted to me. 'I need to go and see Nina,' I say. 'Where is she living?'

He stops what he is doing and faces me over his granite worktop. 'Nina? Really?'

'I have to find out about the dollars. I need an explanation.'

'I'm not sure that's a good idea.'

'Why?'

'Well, I don't think you're going to get much mileage out of her. She was pretty angry after you left. And she wasn't having any suggestion that she took the money.'

'But we both know she did – the earring you found.'

'I know,' he says, holding his palms out. 'I'm with you. I just don't know how much good it'll do.'

The food comes but all I can see is the sky exchanging light for dusk. I fidget in my seat, on edge. I have to see her.

He finishes a mouthful of salad. 'I could call her. Press her a bit more maybe? I'm just not sure about aggravating her and making her even more difficult about it.'

I don't know why Seb can't see how important this is to me. 'I don't care about aggravating her. This is my life.'

'Okay, okay,' he says, holding up his hands. 'I'll phone. Ask her if we can drop round.'

'I'd rather just turn up. I don't want her fobbing us off.'

Seb considers this before nodding, resigned. We drive. Seb's hands are steady on the wheel and the smell of expensive new leather fills my nostrils. After ten minutes, we turn up a street that must be hers and slow down.

'I'll come in with you, Xander. I'm not happy about leaving you with her, especially going by her recent behaviour,' he says.

'I'll be fine, Seb,' I say, waiting for him to look at me.

He draws smoothly to a halt. 'Can I wait for you here?'

'No. Really. I'll be fine.'

He takes a deep breath. 'If you're sure,' he says. 'Red door.'

I get out and walk to the well-kept front garden. Although it is small I know that in this part of London, Dulwich Village, the price of this cottage would be eye-watering. She is obviously still working in finance or something else lucrative. My heart skips a little as I rattle the knocker. I wait. The evening begins to gather darkness around my shoulders. I shiver in the cold until the door opens.

Nina appears in the doorway, hair glossy and sharp. She's dressed as if she's just back from work. Navy dress in a thick woollen fabric – bouclé, is it?

'Nina.'

She sighs, taking me in. 'What do you want, Xander?'

'I need to talk you.'

'If it's about the money, I have nothing more to say to you,' she says, and crosses her arms.

'I didn't kill her, Nina,' I say softly.

'Didn't you? You might as well have.'

'Nina, I don't know what she told you, but I did not leave Grace. She left me, and it tore me apart.'

She shakes her head in supressed fury and turns to shut the door on me.

'Wait. Okay. I know you won't accept what I say. That's fine. I get that. She's your friend.'

'Was.' She's glaring at me. Willing me to challenge her.

'Was. I'd be surprised if you weren't loyal to her. But I'm not here about that. I need to know what happened to the money.'

She pauses in the act of shutting the door.

'I don't care whether you believe this or not, but I don't have the money,' she says, a hand on the door.

My heart sinks at this. 'Nina. If there were a way I could do this without asking you for anything at all, believe me, I would. But I can't, Nina. I can't do it without you. They're charging me with murder, Nina. I didn't do it. They think I killed her for the money.'

As I say it I feel my head swimming with the pressure of it all. I want to cry in frustration, make her somehow do the right thing.

She looks at me for a second and then closes the door. 'Bye, Xander.'

I stare at the shut door. I'm finished. But just as I am about to walk away, the door opens again.

'Look. If it matters, I know you didn't kill her,' she says. 'You haven't got the balls. Sorry – that didn't come across as I meant it.'

I nod at her and smile a little. 'Well, the police think I have.'

She considers this and I can tell she is weighing up how much she knows, which isn't much, against what she doesn't know, which is a lot. In the end she has no words to offer me.

'You should look at the boyfriend,' she says, and suddenly I am aware that my face has gone cold.

Boyfriend. That's what the police said. They suspected the boyfriend. But that the boyfriend was me. Even now, the idea of her having a boyfriend who is not me hurts.

'Who was the boyfriend?' I say. I think of the other man in the house that I saw, strangling her. There was someone else after all.

'You've forgotten?' she says, eyebrows raised.

'Did I know?'

'Yes. It was the yoga guy. You must remember. Ariel.'

It comes washing over me. The smooth, easy manner. The oiliness of him. That smile. That wafting about in fake serenity. Our arguments. My jealousy.

'She was seeing *him*?' I say, incensed.

'Oh,' she says, quiet now. 'You didn't know.'

I feel hot tears beginning to pool in my eyes as I shake my head. She stands behind my watery screen, not moving.

'She didn't love him,' she says. 'It was a rebound.'

The words reverberate. I can't believe it – after all the arguments we had about him. The baseless jealousy I was accused of. But she went to him. And then the pettiness of my reaction climbs in. She is dead. Grace. Gone – killed. And she could have been ended by him – that stabs at me most.

And then it seems to me that this can't be true. The man who killed her had a suit on as if he had been at work. It couldn't have been him. Ariel didn't wear suits.

'Ariel didn't kill her,' I say.

'I didn't mean he killed her. I meant I think he might have the money. He's the only other person who might have known about it.'

The words settle on me and then begin to soak through. And the truth of it starts to wake me. I close my eyes and sink to my haunches on Nina's step, eyes clenched, trying to think. There is something in the back of my memory about this. I try to reconstitute that evening. Those flickering flames against the wall. The song.

I've had trouble with my memory
And less with my back
But the vision of a girl on my mind won't go away …

I stoke up the scent of burning logs in order to revive the memory. He said something, didn't he, about money? I heard him calling across the room to her. *Champagne?* he said. Something about celebrating. *Celebrating what?* she said. And then it came out: *the money.*

She wished she hadn't told him, in my memory. She wished she hadn't mentioned it. It was the dollars. It must have been.

'But how did he get it?'

'I don't know about that. I do know that he disappeared pretty quickly after she died. Didn't even come to the funeral – cremation.'

'And you didn't mention it to anyone? Her parents I mean. About the money? About Ariel disappearing?'

'No,' she says. 'Sebastian wouldn't hear any of it until after the service. And when I brought it up afterwards, he insisted that it was your money and that you'd left it with him, in his charge. Only you could take it. Wouldn't even consider giving it up to anyone else. You know how bloody uptight he is about all that crap.'

'So, what, Ariel could have broken in and taken it?'

She considers this for a second. 'Who knows? We had a kind of wake for her. I looked out for him but didn't see him. We were half-expecting you to turn up,' she says then, and her face changes.

I hear the words and then the tears come. I am in mourning. For Grace. For our past. The loss of it all.

41

Friday

The need for new air in my lungs overrides my decision to make my way straight to Seb's. Some part of me is still feeling the effects of the last day or so layering themselves over the events of the last ten days. I'm struggling with the information. I haven't processed it yet.

The sun has set into the edges of the street and paints the houses in flame. But the beauty can't penetrate my anxiety.

I have to find Ariel. I didn't even go to her funeral. If I could remember where I might have been, that would be something. Perhaps there'd be something symbolic in what I had done that day if I could only put myself there. Did I think about her – specifically – that day? Or dream of her maybe that night? I wasn't there, but he was at the house. With the money.

And now the money's vanished. How am I going to get off this murder case? I described every detail of the house to the police, confessed to them I was there. It was as if I'd framed myself.

The idea of finding Ariel clamours in my head. Where do I even begin to look? What could I possibly say if I were to find him? I can't just accuse him outright of stealing the money with nothing more than an overheard slip of the tongue. I was there – I must have been – and even I can't be sure that it was him. And if it was, then it must also have been him that strangled her. The idea of that, and the possibility that it could have been him begins to flood my head with noise. Somehow, the notion that he killed her, while I stood by, is more horrific than if it had been a stranger. That I stood – *lay* – frozen in fear of him.

I make my way to the library as the daylight has all but leaked away, to seek out Amit's help. He'll know how to trace the history of a person with a name. He will be able to dive into that fathomless digital world and come up with pearls in his mouth.

The building is etched in the early evening and I surprise myself with the remembrance that I haven't read a book in months. Books have always been there as joists in my life. They've been shelter as much as, no, more than anything else. I always had a book in my pocket. Now the need to pick up a book and read something is returning.

The warmth of the library hits me as soon as I walk in. The glow of low light and bright lights in places adds optimism to the warmth. I cast around in search of Amit but now am quietly pleased that he is not here. I can breathe before it all starts. I go immediately to the French Lit section and flick my eyes across the M's – Maupassant, Mauriac, Molière – until I find him. And then there he is, my Proust.

I take up a volume and flip it open to a random page and am faced with his madeleine moment. He tastes a crumb of cake and suddenly old memories that were lost to him come unbidden. *But when from a long-distant past nothing subsists, after*

the people are dead, after the things are broken and scattered,
still, alone, more fragile, but with more vitality, more unsubstan-
tial, more persistent, more faithful, the smell and taste of things
remain poised a long time, like souls, ready to remind us, waiting
and hoping for their moment, amid the ruins of all the rest.

The smell and taste of things remain poised, but he failed
to mention the sounds. At that moment, as I'm reading this
passage, the memory comes rushing back: I'm sitting on a
bench in a park with a low wall. No, not a park – the grounds
of the Horniman Museum. The grounds my feet keep finding
again and again.

But I am there and Grace is beside me. I have this book in my
lap. This passage. I am reading, reciting, in fact, as she lies with
her head in my lap.

'It's too wordy, Xander.'

'Yes, but listen to what he's saying,' I said. 'He's saying that
what any of us has to say is worthy.'

She laughed at that point and lifted her head. 'Not *worthy* –
wordy. Nobody can have that much to say.'

Now I laugh. She was right of course. And nobody ever had
that much to say ever again: 4,215 pages.

But as I stare at these pages, something else comes back.

It's there, in shadow, ready to trigger a memory. All it needs is
a gentle pull and a deluge of these somethings stored will be
waiting to consume me. I grasp around the edges in frustration. Something wants me. Not a smell. Not a taste. Something
else is there tapping at my head. Or digging. Perhaps a sound.

'Xander?'

I look up and see Amit's face, in smooth innocence.

'Do you never go home?' I say, smiling.

He flushes momentarily at this and I remember that he has the librarian, Hazel, on standby to call him when I appear.

'I prefer it here,' he says, shrugging. 'Anyway, I kind of come in to check on you. How did it go with the lawyers?' His voice is low, not quite conspiratorial, but self-conscious – on my behalf.

'Hard to say,' I say, after thinking it through. 'I'm afraid I need your help again, if it's not too much trouble?'

He nods and without being asked, straightens his bag over his shoulder and makes a beeline for the computer terminals. I follow him in a way that makes me feel like a child. He sits, his face underlit by the glow of the screen. He tilts his head slightly.

'I need to find a person. Not missing this time at least.'

'Sure. Name?'

'Ariel.' I spell it out. He types it in and looks at me expectantly.

'Surname?' he says.

'I don't know it. But I thought since the name is quite unusual?'

He spins in his chair and gives me a deflated look. 'It's quite hard with a full name but with only the first name it's impossible. Look,' he says, pressing return, '262 million results.'

'He's a yoga teacher if that helps. Or he was, at any rate.'

He types in 'yoga' and sends the information into the machine. 'Still 36 million. And if I put in London, it's still 6.8 million.'

'Well, you at least managed to narrow it down,' I say.

He laughs for a second before becoming serious again.

'I'm sorry. You really need a second name or a date of birth maybe.'

'Thanks anyway,' I say. I hesitate, not wanting to impose on his time longer than I have to. 'You couldn't do one more thing for me, could you? I promise it won't take you long.'

He agrees and I tell him what I need. Within a minute he has given me the answer. 'Thanks, Amit. I appreciate it.'

He gets up and shoulders his bag again. 'No probs,' he says, and then stops in his tracks. 'Oh, just remembered.'

'What?' But he simply rummages in his bag.

After a moment he produces a book – the one I gave him. I am about to protest his returning it, but instead of handing it to me, he opens the covers and fishes out something from the pages.

'Here,' he says, 'I found this.' There's a folded sheet of letter paper in his hand. 'It was in the book. Thought you might want it back.' He hands me the yin and yang patterned sheet. I open it and begin to read.

'I'm sorry,' he says sheepishly. 'I read it. Wasn't sure if you'd want it back.'

In a daze I walk to the door, expecting him to have followed me, but he has already sat himself down at a desk and started to arrange his books. I look across to say goodbye properly. And then as I stand on the threshold, half in, half out, I look down to read.

My heart is thumping.

Dear Xander

I do hope that you will take advantage of the house while I'm away. It's going to be empty, after all, and I hate the idea of you being out in the cold.

Although you probably won't believe me when I say that I still love you and that I always will, it's true. In a way, we grew up together. I did so much of my growing with you, even if you didn't. You always seemed to me to have arrived fully-formed into the world.

I skip the next few paragraphs because what is in them makes me so desperate that I can't read them without feeling tears in my eyes.

And I wanted to thank you for the gift! Thank you so much, Xand. You know how much I love Jack and I know how much you hate him! So, I'll treasure it all the more. When I play it, I'll think of you. I want you to know that when I think of you, it's always fondly, and when I think of you in the future, it will always be with love. I still remember you when I am in the museum garden. When I close my eyes, I can still see you sitting on our bench – you remember the one by the —

My eyes dart a little and I move to the end of the page.

If there's anything that I can do to help you, please say. I'll always be your friend. I hope you can be mine. I hope that I find you again one day soon when your demons are behind you.

One thing, and I know you're not going to like hearing me say this, but one thing that A has taught me is that life is there to be lived. It's a gift and we must never waste it. Money can be wasted – should be, even. But time is there to be spent and enjoyed. That's why I've come to a decision about the money: I want you to keep it. Keep it. Buy yourself a place that you can feel safe in, and just heal. Do that one thing for me, if you do nothing else.

Your Mabel

I don't remember this letter. Not really. It lights a flame some-where in my mind. I must have read it at the time; after all, I kept it in my favourite book. I scour my head for some remem-brance of this. Not long after that day in the café, the next day or the next week, she must have found me, and given me this letter. I must have kept it in the book, until frightened I would lose it, I put it with the other things I gave to Seb to look after.

I did read this letter. But only once or twice. It hurt – I'm sure of that.

And reading it back now makes sure about one other thing.

I have my appointment on Monday with the QC. This letter surely changes everything. Or it could. And all of a sudden, my gloom lifts slightly so that a future that I had settled in my head is given light and is changing into something new.

42

Friday

By the time that I get back to Seb's, night has set in. I ring the doorbell and he opens it, looking harried.

'Everything okay?' he says, ushering me in.

'Fine. Why?' I say, following him.

'You've been gone longer than I expected Nina would tolerate you,' he says, walking into the living room. In the room I am conscious suddenly of my smell. He sits and when he beckons me into the matching cream chair, I hesitate.

'Maybe I should go and have a bath,' I say, and stutter in the doorway.

'It's okay, sit,' he says, reading my discomfort. 'I've got the good stuff open.'

There is a bottle of Macallan on a small ebony coffee table. That bottle. The one Dad liked. It's there on the table, half-full. Two glasses keeping it steady.

'So, what did she say?' he says, and pours out two measures. His hand shakes a little as he offers me the glass.

'What you said. She denied it.'

'Knew she would,' he says. 'But you were there for a bit. Did she say anything interesting?' The tone in his voice is one I haven't heard before. He's aiming for a nonchalance that he hasn't quite managed.

'Actually, I wasn't there long. Didn't even go in. But she did make me wonder about something.'

'What's that?' He takes a sip, wincing a little.

'Ariel. She thinks it might have been him who took the money.'

'Ariel?' he says, straightening in his chair. 'The yoga guy? What makes her think that?'

'Actually, I'm beginning to wonder if it was him, but it doesn't really add up in my head.'

'Why?'

'That night. The night it happened. I was hiding behind the sofa when they came in. I couldn't see much. But I'm sure I heard him say something about celebrating having the money.'

He leans back in his chair. 'Well, she was seeing the guy. And she went away with him. Maybe that's it. The simplest explanation. But how did he get it?' he says.

'I'm not exactly sure about that. Could he have broken in? After … after Grace?'

He considers this a while. 'Maybe. It's possible. We had so much going on around that time, if he had broken in while we were out, I can't say I would necessarily have noticed. And back then you could just breathe on that window and it would have fallen open,' he says, aiming his glass at the bay window.

'But it doesn't completely add up,' I say.

'Why not? He didn't come to the funeral. I'd say that every-thing points to him. Especially after what you just told me about what you heard.'

'I don't know, Seb. As much as I loathed him, I can't really see him breaking into your house in broad daylight to steal money. I didn't like the guy, but I don't see him as a cat burglar.'

He pauses for a second and takes another sip. 'Maybe he did it at the wake,' he says. 'I remember seeing him there and now I think of it he was lurking around upstairs quite a bit.'

My heart skips. Nina said he hadn't been at the wake. I want to believe this is just Seb's way of supporting me. To help confirm what I already think. I take a sip of the whisky. The liquid stings the inside of my mouth. 'But the man I saw,' I say. 'He had a suit on. Couldn't have been Ariel.'

'That's what's bothering you?' he says. 'You know he had a job?'

'Well, he was a yoga instructor. I knew that,' I say.

'No. A proper job. He was an insurance guy or something,' he says. 'It's true he was a yoga instructor but only ever part-time. I don't think Grace would have gone out with someone who was just a yoga teacher.'

He had a job? I sit back in my seat and take some more whisky in. So he killed her. Then he took the money. The thoughts swill around my head, trying to get traction on something.

'That's where I was this evening.'

He looks at me in confusion. 'What do you mean?'

'I was trying to track him down. What happened to him? Did you ever see him again?' I say, sipping some more. The whisky burns my chapped lips but the pain is welcome.

'After Grace died? No. He just vanished. Although—'

'What?'

'He wasn't really our friend. We didn't know him, as such, beyond what Grace told us about him. Met him twice in total, I think.'

'I have to find him,' I say.

He turns to me with a raised eyebrow. 'Good luck with that.'

'What do you mean?' I say.

'What are you going to trace him with? You don't even know his name, do you?'

'Ariel. It can't be that common a name. And now we know he was in insurance.'

'Xander. I don't think Ariel was his real name. I think it was like a yoga name. When I met him, he called himself something else, though I can't remember now what it was. It was something less frilly, like Harry or James.'

This stops me mid-breath. I haven't even considered that Ariel might not be Ariel. My body starts up a mild panic. 'What the hell am I supposed to do now?' I say.

I close my eyes and there is silence. All I can hear now is the pulse of my blood in my ears beating out a percussive drum. I stay this way, perched on an abyss until I hear Seb moving across the room. My ears wade through the sounds coming from the other end of the room and I look up. Seb is shuffling through records. I close my eyes again. How am I going to find a person without a name?

I hear the wisp of a record leaving its sleeve. A low static hum, velvety and rich. It is the sound of a cinema before the screen lights up. The sound of anticipation. A soft amplified thud. A hiss and then in glorious technicolour, sound comes rushing in waves across the room.

There's trouble on the uptrack
And trouble going back ...
But the vision of a girl on my mind won't go away ...

Opening my eyes, I see that Seb's back again in his chair. He catches my gaze and swills his glass sadly. Rory comes now tapping at the windows of my head. He wants to come inside. I can fight him back for now, but not for much longer. I clamp my eyes and a giddiness takes me over so that I feel as if I am trapped in an eddy of swirls.

Time slips from grey into deep black. The hiss of a stylus on a loop shakes me from the images flickering in my eyelids. I open them with a start. The night has fled. It is early morning. Seb is curled up on the sofa. I roll as quietly as I can on to the floor and then tiptoe out of the room.

In the bathroom I scrub myself with soap and a trickle of water, crouched in the bathtub. When I come back down, Seb is still sleeping, so I creep quietly out of the front door. The world in here is cloying but when I get outside the pavement has a light dust of frost that crunches as I cross it. Cool air in my lungs shakes the sleep from my body as I walk.

Rory, who has been holding on by the fingernails, has flown away. There is a difference in the two worlds, his and mine. A difference in substance, physics. He doesn't have the physical strength to hang on to me when I am moving. Even slowly. But he can fill my mind when I am inside and boxed in.

Grace now comes directly in view – just a shimmer. I stop and try to look at her but she is too insubstantial. But I see her smile, her eyes hollow. *You*, she points at me. It's *you* she seems to want to tell me. I smile back at her. I nod.

'I know,' I say. 'Me.' And she becomes air again.

I walk, aiming for the Horniman grounds once more. That's why she has appeared. She is calling me there so that we can talk this out. Me and her. She is calling me so that we can untangle it together, the thing that has been tugging at my brain.

Seb lied to me. I'm less sure about his motivation than I was last night, mixed as it was with his warmth and whisky. Was he just trying to confirm my suspicions? I don't think so any longer.

I walk through the main entrance since it is daytime. There are no walkers or visitors at this hour, though. Only a few pigeons, grubbing for food, and me. I make my way to a sheltered spot I sometimes sleep in. My feet are fleet. The air carries me.

Ariel didn't break in, did he? Grace says this but not with her mouth. It is all with a look.

He didn't.

Seb lied.

There is the hollow formed from dead branches and twigs, still unmolested. I made this a few weeks ago as a shelter, before all of this. Before Squire, when the world was clearer. There is slime and rotting mulch now under its awning, but I am alone here.

I shut my eyes and catch Grace's hand as she holds it out to me. She leads me somewhere deep inside a memory. The flames kick out at the wall. They glow and dance and crackle to the sound of a hissing turntable. I glance out from behind the edge of the sofa. He is standing over her, his legs steepled on either side. Can I see his face?

There are thoughts that are running through my head which feel as if they are chasing me or leading me somewhere. But they are there, with me.

I can't go back there to Seb yet.

I have the QC to see on Monday. It's Saturday now. Until then I can wait here.

Untangling. Collecting. Connecting.

If all the while, unravelling.

43

Monday

Nasreen's chambers are exactly as I had pictured them. There are clerks in a clerks' room busy on telephones and computer screens. The waiting room that I'm shown to has prints of hand-drawn caricatures of barristers on the walls. Through the glass door I see what must be the barristers, rushing past in smart suits. Then after a few minutes of waiting, a teenager in polyester comes to take us through to the conference room.

'Can I get you some tea or coffee, Miss?' he says to Jan as he leads us through a panelled corridor.

'A coffee would be great, Mike,' she says. 'Xander?'

'I'm fine with water, thanks.'

The words dry in my mouth. I am nervous here. This place is secluded like a Cambridge college, serious in a way that Cambridge wasn't.

He shows us into a handsome room where a woman is waiting with a restrained smile. I glance round. More wood panelling. Sash windows open out on to a cobbled courtyard, making the place feel like a parody.

'Mr Shute, I'm Nasreen. Do have a seat,' she says to me, before turning to Jan. 'How lovely to see you again, Janine.'

Jan smiles and sits next to me at the large glass table. Nasreen taps her laptop shut and leans forward to me.

'Mr Shute. Let's get to it, shall we? I've been through what the prosecution has served in terms of papers. There's good and bad news from what I can see.'

I find myself nodding even as I am dangling by a thread in her fingers.

'The good news is that there is no forensic evidence to link you to the murder whatsoever. By which I mean there is none anywhere near the body or even in the room as far as one can tell. Although you can be sure that they will be continuing to investigate and so you shouldn't be surprised if we are served with evidence last minute.'

'Okay,' I say, and I look across at Jan who seems relaxed now, in the hands of the expert.

'There are, however, your admissions in your interviews. I am bound to say, Mr Shute, if you had listened to advice in your last interview, they wouldn't even have that. I mean, I think we could have excluded the earlier admissions made without a caution having been administered. But we are where we are.'

'Where is that?' I ask.

'That depends on you, Mr Shute. If you stand by your admissions in the interviews, we have you at the scene of the murder as it is happening, with no good explanation for being there. Not to mention the emptying of a significant sum of cash from a bank account, weeks before the death.' She says this last part with a raised eyebrow as if expecting me to protest.

'What do you mean, stand by my interviews? I can't unsay what I've said.'

'Well, how can I put this?' she says slyly. 'Not all defendants maintain at trial the account they give at the police station. Often things are said at times of considerable pressure that on reflection aren't intended. Do you see? I mean here, for example, there is the admission on the one hand that you saw the deceased being murdered. And on the other hand, the fact that in your account you only visited that house on that street for the first time just *weeks* ago. On one view, you and the police are at cross purposes. You are talking about different things.'

I shift in my place. These are the same clothes I slept in, though I have washed in a public lavatory. My procedure is that I take a sock and wash it thoroughly in hot water and soap. Once it is clean I use it as a flannel before drying it again under a hot-air dryer. But clean skin under dirty clothes still makes me squirm a little.

'But, as I told Jan, I think I did go there. In 1989, I mean. She gave me a key. I'm sure that's what happened. I must have been there. It must have been her that I saw being killed.'

She tucks a biro behind her ear and darts a look at Jan who catches it deftly.

'Forgive me for being blunt, Mr Shute. But it's not a very confident account of yourself. I wonder whether on reflection you *didn't* in fact see Ms Mackintosh being killed. I wonder whether the years of being in the wilderness, shall we say, have dulled your memory somewhat? I mean it's not unheard of for people to become highly prone to suggestion when under stress. Can you be sure that this officer, DI Conway, is it, didn't take advantage of your suggestibility?'

Jan drops her head, bracing for what she knows is coming.

'I am not suggestible, Mrs Khan. It was me. I was there. I did not kill her and I saw her being killed.'

Nasreen pushes herself back from the table and exhales. 'Is that what we're going with?' she says, more to Jan than me.

'That's what we're going with,' I say, and then add, 'but I have some more information.' I am about to reach into the pocket of my coat when I am stopped.

'Don't worry about any of that for now,' Nasreen says. 'Why don't you start by telling me everything that you remember about that night?' She takes up her pen and writes in a soft-backed blue notebook as I talk.

I tell her how the door had been unlocked, and step by step what I had told the police about Ebadi's flat. Nasreen is deaf to the nuances of the drama. Instead she listens as if she is a hawk looking for mice, scurrying through the narrative. *Describe him. Everything you can remember. What did you see? What was he wearing? What was she wearing? Where were they standing or sitting? What was in his hand? Where were they when the argument started? Exactly where? What was playing on the radio?*

'The record player,' I say, correcting her. I want to tell her about how I think I know him, the killer, and that I know something about him. But I can't. I can't tell her what has happened to the cash. But I can tell her how Grace *gave* it to me. I reach into my pocket for the letter but I am held back by Nasreen's hand.

'The record player then, could you see who changed the record or switched the player off?'

'It wasn't switched off exactly. He, the guy, took the record and threw it against the wall. It broke in two,' I say, holding the letter out.

'How do you know that?' she says, suddenly alert.

'Because I heard it,' I say.

'You heard it break?'

'Yes.'

'In two? Pieces?'

'Yes. Why?' I say, puzzled by something that is obviously hiding in the question.

'In two,' says Jan. 'You couldn't have *heard* it break, *in two*.'

I feel my eyes roll. 'Then I saw it. What's the difference?'

'Where was it when you saw it later on?' Nasreen says.

'I don't know. On the floor, I think. Yes, on the floor. I think it ended up by the window somewhere.'

'And the sleeve. Did you see that?' she says quickly.

I close my eyes and try to claw the memory closer to the foreground. 'On the sofa maybe. Yes, leaning against the base of the sofa. I think.'

Nasreen looks over at Jan and beckons her over to her laptop which she opens.

'Look at these scene pictures they uploaded to the Digital Case System,' she says to Jan.

Jan looks over Nasreen's shoulder and then a look of realisation crests over her.

'Exactly where he says it was,' Jan mutters.

'Looks like he was there, all right,' Nasreen says.

'That's what I've been trying to tell you,' I say.

'But hang on, I can't see the record itself. Is there a picture of the room by the windows?' Jan asks.

'No, the photos only go to here,' Nasreen says, pointing to the screen. 'Okay. Jan, can you get a request to the Crown over please? Tell them that we want that record sleeve examined for prints and compared against our client's arrest dabs.'

Jan nods.

'And the record itself, too. They must have it as an exhibit somewhere, I'd have thought.'

Jan scribbles a note and looks back at the screen. 'Wait a sec,' she says, catching something. 'Enlarge that pic there. Isn't that a bit of a record, there? Looks like it could be.'

Nasreen frowns at the screen and nods. 'You might be right, Jan. Good eyes,' she says and then turns to me. 'We will do our best to get this information from the Crown. But you should be aware that we don't even know at this point what in terms of real evidence they have retained. The police did not initially have this as a murder. Some of the scene was photographed and preserved for the inquest. But we have no idea how much from the original scene exhibits they still have.'

'But how can that be? Aren't they relying on that for their case? I mean, to prove I was there. DNA, prints and all that?'

Nasreen laces her fingers together so the red polished ends are aligned.

'No, Mr Shute. That is not what they are doing at all. Their evidence of your presence at the scene comes entirely from your admissions in the interviews. If, and I mean *if*, they still have any of the items from the room, they might be able to do a fingerprint lift but DNA is out of the question. If they didn't do it at the time – and frankly, they wouldn't have even for most murders back then – any DNA would have degraded by now. And that's *if* they preserved it properly.'

'So why are we asking for things they probably don't have?'

'Because you never know. And the sleeve they could well have,' she says.

They then begin to draw the interview to a close. Nasreen puts her pens and her notebook into a neat stack.

'Wait. There's this. You have to read this,' I say, finally finding the space to show them the letter. 'It's from Grace.'

'Grace?'

'He means Michelle. She didn't like "Michelle",' Jan says.

I hand the letter to Nasreen. By the time she finishes reading it, her brows are crossed and she slides it across the table to Jan who skims through it.

'This is good, Xander,' Jan says, stabbing the letter with her finger. 'She'd given you the money anyway, so that won't hold as a motive.'

'It definitely helps,' Nasreen adds. 'I mean, the Crown doesn't have to prove motive in this country, Mr Shute, but if they have one it never hurts.'

'So, what now?' I say.

'I'd still like to know what happened to it,' Nasreen says, in a way that implies that she doesn't expect an immediate answer.

'You need to be ready to enter your plea at the next hearing,' she continues. 'I take it from you that is *not guilty*. We are not arguing diminished responsibility or insanity. Just a straight not guilty. Then we get some directions from the judge and wait for trial. In the meantime, the prosecution will serve whatever evidence they want to rely on, and once we have it we send them a document telling them what your defence is and then we can get some disclosure.'

'Disclosure?' I say.

'Yes. If they have anything which could help your case, they have to give it to us, disclose it. And, of course, we wait to hear about whether they have the record or the sleeve that we will have asked for and if they do, what the fingerprint tests show.'

'What are we hoping for?' I say.

'Well, best ways, there are prints on it that don't belong to you or the deceased but a third party, our alternative candidate. And even better if the Police National Computer turns up an identity for our man. Worst ways, we get nothing, but lose nothing. I'm assuming you didn't touch it, Mr Shute? Where you saw it and where it is on the photograph, is that where they left it? The deceased or her murderer?'

'Yes, that's right,' I say, but the truth is that whatever I do remember dwindles to almost nothing when I am scrabbling about, desperate to remember. I don't know what I touched.

'Then we are all good,' she says, and stands to shake my hand.

I offer mine but withdraw it when I see her face. She smiles at me instead and opens the door to show us out.

Jan leaves the building with me and we walk to Temple Station a few minutes away. 'That letter is good,' she says, once we get there. 'Same paper, same handwriting as the others the police have. And Nasreen. She's my first choice for your case.'

I manage a smile.

'But we still need to know where the money is. They could put you through the mill for that.'

I wipe a hand across my face and watch as she turns and disappears through the barriers and down the stairs, deep underground. Once she has gone I walk the other way towards the river. Now this is done, I have to speak to Seb. I don't want to, but he has left me no choice.

44

Tuesday

When I manage sleep, the memories begin to gather. They are liquid, like blood, pooling in places, coagulating in others. There is a kind of repair going on where the gaping patches are slowly, haphazardly, being stitched together. Since all of this began, I've started waking up sometimes with my fingers at the edge of something important, delicate. There are, for instance, cold ponds of recollection: long nights in squats. Fights over sleeping bags or sticky, collapsed mattresses. Fights over drugs. I couldn't function there in that world. The rules had all to be relearned. Hierarchies I had known were no longer recognisable.

And then the memories jolt forwards and backwards years at a time. But through it, that song is there like a shard in my brain.

There's trouble on the uptrack ...
But the vision of a girl on my mind
Just won't go away ...

And after meeting Nasreen, I know why. That record connects me to her life and death and I can't let it go. The image jabs, again and again. A broken record. The bench. There in the museum grounds. We sat on it together, Grace and I. *Our* bench. But when the images of those days collide, it's not the sunshine that filters through, it's the mud. I am clawing away at the wet earth, sinking my fingers deep into the mud, and I am desperate. There is an urgency in the memory or the dream, whichever it is. I am on all fours, digging, digging as if trying to uncover a dead body. And in my dream I pull the body out, wrapped in paper, only to discover it's not Grace. Or it is her, but a fractured version of her.

I haven't roamed as freely as I used to. Back then I'd go from night to night, shedding all the excess that I was carrying; now, instead, it just builds. Whatever is in here, in my head, feels like it has the time at last to multiply and colonise. It is as if I am the host for a disease. But I am tired of being in my head. I have to climb out. I bring myself to my surroundings and am relieved to find that I am in Seb's house, in 'my' room. The key he gave me sits on the bedside table. I leave it there when I go down to the kitchen so that it doesn't feel as if I've taken ownership of it.

I make a pot of coffee and take an extra mug into the living room for when Seb wakes up. As I walk in I hear a grunt and look to see Seb there, slouching on the sofa and staring into the ceiling. He flinches when I walk in but otherwise doesn't react. He's dressed for work but there's growth across his cheeks.

'You're up,' I say and pour him a steaming cup. He gets up to take the coffee.

'Yeah, well, couldn't sleep,' he says.

I sit in the matching chair and put the cafetière at my feet.

'Listen, Seb,' I say. 'I need to ask you something.' My heart is beating but I don't think the tremor reaches my voice.

He sits up so that he can better look at me.

'Ariel didn't take the money, did he?' I say.

He half-smiles at the question before he realises that I'm serious. 'I have no idea, Xand. That was your theory, wasn't it?'

'It was to begin with. Until—'

'Until what?'

'Until I spoke to you.'

'I'm not following,' he says. There is irritation leaking into his voice.

'He didn't break into your house and steal the money.'

'Right … So what's your new theory?'

I notice him swallow hard, staring at me too firmly. Agitation in the way he seems to concentrate on stilling himself.

'There was no sign of a break-in,' I say steadily.

'Well, there's the window.' He looks down briefly before looking up again. 'You remember how it rattled – it was that rotten.'

I am embarrassed for him – for us both – that I have to ask these questions.

'But he wouldn't have known that,' I say, watching him carefully. There is colour climbing up his neck.

'Then he could have done it at the wake. I told you he was hanging around upstairs a lot,' Seb says, shifting in his seat.

'And then what? Did he climb into your loft and carry out bags full of cash?'

'Maybe.'

'How did he know where it would be?'

'I don't know, maybe Nina told Grace, and she told him,' he says, reddening further.

'But Nina said she was sure he didn't come to the wake. She seemed annoyed at him for missing it – as well as the funeral.'

He cocks his head at me, waiting for what is next.

'You invented that earring, didn't you?' I say. 'I didn't see an earring up there by the box.'

'What? I was trying to get her to confess,' he says. 'We know she took it. You said it yourself.'

'You're not working, are you, Seb?'

'What?'

'I mean, every time I knock on the door, you're here to answer it. Whatever the time of day. You were even here when the police came. To arrest me. How are you always at home? Even now. Why aren't you getting ready for work?'

'I've had some days off. What are you getting at?'

He stands now and I do too, but I have two inches on him, and these bones. 'Days off from where?' I say.

'What?'

'Where do you work?' I press.

'You know where – Deutsche.'

I shake my head. He opens his mouth as if to speak but thinks better of it. 'I checked. Or, at least, I got someone to look it up at the library. You don't work there.'

He looks at me, his face red with anger. He makes a move towards me and then stops and holds up his palms.

'How long has it been?' I say. He considers the question and then sits back down with a sigh.

'Three years and eight months,' he says, deflated. Any fight he may have had in him has gone. 'The pressure to make decent numbers year on year ... But I don't need to tell you about all that, do I?' He pauses, as if on the edge of tears. 'And you never came back. It was just there, burning a hole in my roof for twenty-five years.'

'Seb ...'

'What would you have done?' he asks, desperation cracking his voice.

'Not that,' I say. 'I wouldn't have stolen.'

He stares at the carpet. I wait for him to finish accounting for himself.

'It was just a few thousand at first. Enough to feed the mortgage, pay the bills. And then the months went by and nobody was hiring after the banking crisis.' He shakes his head. 'It made sense to pay the mortgage off. It made sense, Xander, you must see that. The money was just up there, getting devalued when the dollar fell. And some of it had even begun to rot.'

I sit down again.

'Go on, ask what you want to ask me,' he says.

'No. I know it wasn't you who killed her.'

'Only just though, eh?' he says.

'You lied to me.'

'I never lied to you,' he says bleakly.

I let out an incredulous laugh.

'I was embarrassed,' he continued. 'After all these years you came back and we were ...'

'What?'

'The same,' he says. 'I thought – I thought I was better than you. But I wasn't.'

The words ring and lie suspended in the air for some moments, and I have to look away. When I turn back I see dust motes colliding with invisible forces, molecules directing them this way and that in the dying light. Brownian motion, I think, as we look at one another in silence. Tossed around by invisible forces. I'm shocked by how much I failed to see. 'Seb,' I say then. 'You should have—'

Then the telephone rings and the sound of it lunges between us, impatient. Seb waits for it to ring out but when it doesn't he answers reluctantly. A few seconds later he offers me the handset.

'It's for you.'

'Hello?'

'Xander? Good. It's me, Jan. Have you got five minutes? There's news.'

Immediately my heart begins to quicken. 'Go on.'

'It turns out they have the record sleeve, after all. They tested it for prints ... there's a partial print which probably belongs to the deceased.' She pauses. 'Then there are four dabs which the forensic scientist says are a good-to-strong match for yours.'

I feel the breath stall in my chest as the words filter through.

'They survived? All this time?'

'Not exactly. They did a routine set of lifts at the time.'

My prints. I hadn't expected that. I was expecting *his* prints. The murderer's.

'Were there others?'

'Some partials,' she says, 'but not good enough for a comparison.'

There is an answer to this lurking somewhere in the eaves of my brain. Jan carries on explaining about partial prints but I'm trying to focus on finding this reply. How could my prints be on there? Suddenly, there is a glimmer of something and when I tease it out the answer is there. 'Wait. My prints. Yes. Of course, there were my prints. The record. I bought the record for her.'

The line is dead for a second.

'*Okay,*' she says slowly.

'The letter,' I say. 'It's in there: *thank you for the gift*, she wrote. That was it – the record was the gift I'd bought her.'

'That could be any gift—'

'No, she says … *You know how much I love Jack.* She said it. Jack is the record – Jack T. And *when I play it.* It was the record,' I say.

There is a pause. 'We'd need to prove she was talking about that specific record.'

It is so obvious. But she sounds uncertain.

'All we have for certain is your prints on the record,' she says. 'That's the evidence.'

'No,' I say. 'Not on the record – you said *sleeve*. What about the record itself? I saw him throw the record. It will have *his* fingerprints on it, the killer's. It has to. That's all records ever do, attract fingerprints.'

'Unfortunately, they have some of the record. But they've lost some of it.'

'What do you mean?'

'They only have a piece of it and that doesn't have any prints on it.'

'What?' I say, my hopes crashing under the weight of the information. 'How could they just lose it?'

'It happens,' she says. 'Missing exhibits. Sometimes they don't even seize everything. They didn't think it was a murder, remember. It's a minor miracle they had any of it.'

I consider this and exhale.

'Okay,' I say.

'I've told Nasreen about all this, and I'll tell her what you said about the record. Needed to confirm your explanation for the prints. Okay. Better go,' she says, and hangs up.

I replace the handset and sit back down.

'Everything okay?' Seb says, concern written on his face.

I shake my head. 'Not really.'

45

Friday

It's been almost two weeks since my phone call with Jan and I have heard nothing more. I just wait, continuously flattened by the walls in Seb's house. I want desperately to leave but I can't. I have to train myself to withstand the weight of confinement.

Seb continues to pretend to go to work.

'You know I read once about those Japanese salarymen who lose their jobs but still get up every morning, get dressed and go to "work". They just go to the park. Rows and rows of them on benches. The article said that they pretended because they were ashamed of losing their jobs, but I don't think it's just shame. I think it's that pretending is the next best thing to doing.'

'You could get another job,' I say to him.

He nods sadly and straightens his tie. 'You could too,' he says.

When the day of my hearing comes, it is grey and flat. I wash thoroughly and dress in a suit Seb has lent me. The trousers are loose around the hips and the jacket is short in the sleeve, but I wear it gratefully. As I walk up the long path to Southwark Crown Court, I suddenly realise that it is familiar. I came out of it after my bail hearing, but I didn't see it then. Now I look and recognise it as a building I have seen before in the papers. Today there is no press, only shallow puddles and misty, driven rain. As I walk I see myself reflected in the huge windows lining the route. I am indistinct, a ghost almost.

Jan and Nasreen take me to a small room. There is enough space for a table and three chairs with their guts spilling out into the open. Nasreen, in her wig and gown, catches me looking at the furniture.

'Classy, isn't it?' she says, removing her wig.

'I've seen worse,' I say.

She smiles and spreads her diamond fingers at me.

'Okay. Remember your plea. Not guilty. You might hear me make a fuss about one or two bits of disclosure but apart from that it should be a fairly swift hearing. You will hear some dates, called stage dates; this is just a timetable for the service of papers, that kind of thing. The only date that you really have to worry about is the one at the end – the trial date. Okay?'

I nod. Jan updates me a little on the progress of the record, telling me that the prosecution haven't found the rest.

'What?' I say.

'Shit, we're being called on. Let's go, Nasreen will explain it in court,' she says, and we follow Nasreen as she slips her wig back on to her head and walks towards the courtroom.

This court gives me a sense of déjà vu. It is like a magnified version of the courtroom I was in before. This one is vast, and the judge so far away that when he finally comes in, I can barely see him. He is in red robes and smiles benignly at everyone. I am shown into a dock with glass walls and asked my name and nationality and then told to sit down.

'Ready for arraignment, Ms Khan?' the judge says.

'Yes, please, My Lord.'

'Very well. Mr Clerk, please would you put the indictment,' he says to his clerk.

'Alexander Shute you are charged on this indictment with one count of murder. It is said that on the 30th day of December 1989 you murdered Michelle Mackintosh. To this charge how do you plead?'

The court falls into silence and it is as if the world has stopped moving. They all wait, and a part of me waits too.

'Not guilty,' I say.

The remainder of the hearing goes exactly as I have been told before Nasreen gets to her feet.

'My Lord, we were surprised last week to be informed that one of the exhibits from the *locus in quo* has vanished.'

'Vanished?' the judge says. 'Is it a critical exhibit?'

'As far as we are concerned, My Lord, it is. It is our case that the defendant witnessed rather than committed this murder. My instructions are that he saw the murderer shortly before the act take a record off a record player and throw it across the room, where it broke in two. That record may, we say, in the circumstances and mechanism of the throwing, have captured the murderer's fingerprints.'

'Yes. And what's your point, Ms Khan?'

'My point, My Lord, is that although the Crown have been able to test one of the two pieces, without result as it happens, the police appear to have mislaid the other piece.'

'I see.'

'And we would like to put the Crown on notice here and now that there is likely in the circumstances to be an application to stay this case for abuse of process.'

'Yes. Mr Douglas-Jones? What do you say?'

'We are making enquiries, My Lord. The indications at the time were of an accident, and for that reason, the exhibits weren't treated exactly the way they might have been in a murder case. In a nutshell, My Lord, we have what we have. Frankly, we are surprised that there was any fragment of the record available for testing at all.'

'I see. Well, Ms Khan, you'll take your own course, but I will need some persuading to stay these proceedings on that ground alone.'

I am dismissed shortly after and find myself in the corridor being debriefed by Nasreen.

'Remember your bail conditions. Jan will be in touch. In the meantime, if you think of anything else, you must tell us sooner rather than later.'

I nod and then watch them both leave and turn towards the main road.

The adrenaline of being in court begins to subside and within moments of being in the open air, I feel flat. I turn the opposite way to get my bearings when I see a face that I know. My heart drops.

'You?' I say.

'Xander,' says Blake. I am close to her and for the first time I see her in the glare of daylight. She is younger in this light, and more attractive. But the pallor of her face betrays long hours under electric lights.

'So, you pleaded not guilty?'

'Yes,' I say.

'Good.' She turns to walk away, then stops. 'I know this is a strange thing to say, but if I can help you with anything ...'

'Thanks,' I say. I am touched that she believes me. No, more than that, I feel seen, and because of that it feels a little as if I could even find a path back to myself.

She smiles a half-smile and walks towards a parked police car.

Halfway across London Bridge I stop to look down into the water. There's nothing about the river that conjures any warmth or romance. The views either side of the bridge are impressive, but the waterway itself is a trail of slurry. There are no blues or greens in its spectrum. There is no emotion, no invitation to anything joyful. It's impassive and friendless.

My final walk will be here or somewhere nearby. When I dive into its cold bed, neither it nor I will weep for any lost time. Small waves will swill over me casually and stones in my pockets will pull me through its depths. I can do it. I've never doubted that for a second. If I have to. I can't stay another day in a cell.

I'm no longer as calmed by the thought of leaving nothing behind as I once was. To arrive with nothing and to leave nothing behind has a poetry to it, but now that I'm here at the threshold of an exit, I'm no longer sure about poetry.

It's not until I step on to south London earth that I feel the security of home. For nearly thirty years I travelled without borders and I managed to get only as far as here. We came here, Grace and I, just to feel separated from London and now I wonder whether you can be separated from London. Because the city is not under your feet but on your skin.

It's still before midday and I don't need to be back at Seb's for any reason that I can think of. I wander past the road that leads there and press on up Lordship Lane. Within a few minutes I am back at the Horniman grounds. Grace pulls me here again, but today I pull along in the same direction.

I need to find it.

When I walk through the gate, I do it as a person. For once I am not in hiding or exile. I can walk in with the other people and blend in with them. At first, I am self-conscious about my beard but then I realise that there are more bearded than clean-shaven faces around me. Fashion seems to be in a curious phase – suits without ties, and beards everywhere.

In this new disguise, in Seb's suit, I discover a thing. People smile at me. I want to smile back but the joy is trapped somewhere underneath, like an air bubble.

I pick my way around the perimeter of the grounds, skirt the edge of a sunken ornamental pool and walk uphill. When I reach the top, there is a view of London that stretches out for miles: the Shard, the Gherkin, the Walkie Talkie. London has changed so that there are now pinnacles of glass at every turn. All these buildings with names fit for children have sprung up as if from a giant pop-up book. Grace might have loved this change. Or hated it. Or accepted it, grudgingly. Instead she missed it.

There are a few people by a bandstand, taking in the view, as I crest the slope and walk round the edge. And then I see what I am looking for.

Still here, after all these years. I touch the edge and feel the grain under my fingertips. Our bench. The warm burnt-umber tones have given way to weathered silver, but it is unmistakeably the bench. The plaque is still here:

In memory of Dad.
So Much Lost Time

The memory of her warm body comes crashing back. From here the world is as it was, a pocket in time, she and I together, our nerves exposed and sensitive to the touch. The rush of memory paralyses me. I realise finally that she and everything she was, and all that she was promised to be, is gone.

And I sink.

Sitting on the bench, I feel a knot in my stomach being stretched taut. Here she is, next to me, warm and real, against all of this cold everywhere. Before I can control it, I am crying. And it's as if I'm being pulled across every second of my life and being burned by it.

When the tears finally peter out, I find myself sitting on the grass and leaning against the seat. I press my hands into the ground to lever myself upright, but the sensation of the damp soil between my fingers triggers something. In the memory I have, I am digging. Clawing into the earth with my fingers. There, just behind the bench. I know it is here. Whatever it is.

And so now I move behind the seat and crouch. There are walkers nearby but they look away, afraid, as if I am about to do something unthinkable. I plunge my hand into the ground and dig. I scrape away a handful of wet, hard soil. Then, before I know what is happening I am digging desperately. One after another clumps of soil are hooked out of the ground. I dig as though beneath this foot of grass, there is a treasure or a life or some precious thing that needs air. I claw again and again but I don't quite understand why.

Through the damp soil my hands touch plastic and I stop. The corner of something smooth and plastic is poking through the ground but it's too far below ground to see. I tug at it and it slides out before catching in the mud. Another pull dislodges

329

more earth and finally it comes free, cascading damp earth as it does.

I lay it on the ground and stare at it, as if a dream has suddenly taken on form. I remember this thing. A clear plastic sack. Thick. Inside there is something that has been carefully wrapped in newspaper. Something that *I* have carefully wrapped in newspaper. At the very outer threshold of my mind I remember this. It comes now in an avalanche. I remember wrapping these things. I recall the nervousness I'd felt as I did it. This has to do with Grace.

The mouth of the bag falls open and I put my hand in. I take a corner of the newspaper wrapping and tear it off. I read the date across the top:

30 December 1989

46

Friday

There is no doubt. Looking at this thing in my hand, there is no doubt. It was me. It was me after all.

I pick up the bag and tuck it inside my jacket and run out of the grounds. I have to get out of here.

I break out again into a run, my hands and sleeves covered in soil. My knees damp and dirty. I remember burying this but I can't remember what happened before. My head pounds as I run. The boundary wall draws near and I jump it. I don't want the exit now. These gates are meant for people. Thoughts riot in my head.

Did I know this? Did I know that I killed her? Am I perpetrating huge diversions against myself? Am I just playing chess against myself, pretending that I haven't seen the plan behind the move? I am drawing myself in tighter and tighter coils into a box.

I must have known it all along. This – what is in this bag – proves it.

After ten minutes of running, I am at Seb's. I push my way past him when he answers the door and barge into the kitchen.

'Xander?' he says, following me, puzzled.

I look at him and the ease drops out of his face like a bag of cement.

'Shit, Xander,' he says, taking in my muddied form. 'What happened at court?'

I walk straight to the table and begin to peel back the wet plastic in my hand.

'Xander? What's going on?'

I ignore him and carry on unwrapping. The newspaper-packaged bundle is dry.

'*Xander.*'

I peel back the paper carefully and expose what has been lying underneath it for nearly thirty years.

'The missing piece,' I say.

How can it be? And yet it is. The fragmented recollections aren't needed any longer and can't save me now. The proof is there in front of me.

'Missing piece of what?' says Seb, as I sit on the chair nearest to me.

'The record,' I say, looking up at him. He's my only friend, and now the sole witness to my unravelling. 'I killed her, Seb,' I gasp. 'It was me.'

It takes some time for him to cajole me out of my daze. In broken sentences I tell him about the evidence. The record piece, the prints, everything.

'This will prove it,' I say, lifting the piece to him with a scrap of the newspaper.

He looks startled, concerned – on the cusp of panic. 'You have to give it to them. It might help you.'

As he says this he starts to rewrap the thing in its paper.

'Help me? It *incriminates* me.'

He stops, mid-wrap.

'Why did I bury it, Seb? Why would I do that unless—'

'Don't,' he interrupts. 'No. There *must* be another explanation.'

He stops and runs his hands through his hair. He is astounded and casts about for what to do or say next, because there is only one explanation.

'Shit,' he says finally. 'Do you *remember* doing it?'

I shake my head and as I do I feel the tears. I try and blink them back. I don't deserve to cry at this. I killed Grace.

'I don't fully,' I say. 'Sometimes when I learn something new, it changes what I remember. I remember this now,' I say, pointing to the record. 'I remember burying it.'

'*Shit*,' he repeats. He pushes the record back into the bag. 'Wait,' he says then, spotting something at the bottom of it and reaching in.

'What is it?'

'I've seen this before,' he says and holds it up.

Seeing it sends a shiver down my spine. It's a pendant in the shape of a tiny gold shell.

'Chelle,' I say under my breath. 'Michelle.'

The plastic bag lies fat on the table, stained in mud. After a while it begins to shimmer in my peripheral vision. But it isn't alone. It is here with everything I had forgotten. It's here with things that I didn't even know I knew, let alone forgot. I stand up suddenly and push back my chair.

'What are you going to do?' he asks.

I close my eyes and take a deep breath. I don't know what I can do. 'I'm going to lie down,' I say at last and then make my way upstairs. I can't go now. He'll stop me. I have to wait till he is asleep.

My head throbs, but it's not clouding my thoughts. Rather, it's making them clearer. The threads of my life are being pulled together and there is only one thing left to be done. I see now that this has been stalking me for almost thirty years. Maybe deep inside I thought I could outrun it, but that was never possible.

47

Saturday

When I am sure that he is in his room, asleep, I go back down. In the kitchen, the time on the oven blinks 01:22. I reach for the bag.

I step into the night with the bag tucked under my arm. The walk to the police station feels like a death march and I feel a kind of undeserved nobility about it. The air swims around my face, reminding me of itself and of freedom, now lost. I can't keep running.

Before any suspicion of light, I reach the door of the police station and look up at the building. There's a world behind those doors that I don't want to open. And yet I must.

In the darkened sky, the street lamps flicker orange. I see a boy in the distance under a lamp that reminds me of Amit. His face glows in the sulphur.

I turn round and push at the door to a desk sergeant I haven't seen before. This one looks more awake and less irritable than the others have been.

'Is DI Blake here?'

He looks at his screen, takes my name and picks up a phone. 'Yes, Rachel. Someone here to see you.'

I put the bag on my lap and look at it. It has kept my life's secret. When I think of Grace and Rory, they are all in the centre of my life, whether I orbited around them or they me. But – and this hasn't penetrated me until now – they are gone. They are dead and the damage that I did to them still clings to me. I have been running, but I haven't been able to free myself from their guilt or their blame because I have kept them with me. How could I run away from them when they are inside me?

But now, I can escape. Knowing this, I look up.

'Xander,' she says. 'Twice in twenty-four hours?'

I stare at Blake and at the bag on my lap. This moment feels suspended between two outcomes.

'I have this,' I say, and show her the muddy bag. She looks at me, confused. 'It's the other bit. Of the record. I had it,' I say.

She is walking towards me but stops abruptly mid-stride and draws in a breath. 'Xander. I. Oh, shit. I need to caution you,' she says, putting a hand on her head and then sitting softly next to me. I can smell a faint scent of coffee and jasmine.

'I'm seizing this as evidence in the case,' she says at last. 'Wait here. I'm going to get an evidence bag and some gloves.' She rushes off through the double doors and is gone no longer than a minute or so. When she returns she has a large polythene bag in her hand and is pulling on surgical gloves. She takes my bag and seals it in the larger one. When she has written on the label, she turns to me.

'I can't ask you any questions about this without cautioning you and then interviewing you with your solicitor,' she says, levelling her eyes at me. She is signalling.

I nod and then get up to leave.

'Xander. You know we're going to test it, don't you?'

'Yes,' I say, and walk to the front door, pausing to raise a hand at her in goodbye.

'I can't not follow the evidence, Xander,' she calls to my back as I walk out.

There are things I have to do and I don't know how much time I have. The sky is darkened ink and there is no moon. Its absence feels personal, as if the moon has been plucked out of the sky to shame me.

I head quickly back, but even marching at double time and taking a bus part of the way, it still takes over an hour. By the time I reach Seb's door, dawn has begun to appear. After slipping off my shoes at the door, I tiptoe quietly up the stairs to bed.

I drop into a dark and dreamless sleep.

Morning light washes through the curtains but I shut my eyes against it. There is too much now going on in my head to be distracted by light. I need more sleep. My body and my pounding head crave it. When I wake again much later, shards of so many colliding dreams are still sticking to me that I feel groggy and disorientated. I head for the bathroom and run a bath, using bubble bath to dampen the sound of water against enamel as it fills.

I climb in and as soon as the water swaddles me, it is as if everything in my mind that isn't ordered or clear is jettisoned into the tub. As my body becomes cleaner, my head clears, too.

I stayed there. When I was lying broken on the street, she, my love, *ma belle*, appeared and offered me shelter. And I took it. I slept, there on that silken carpet, for days, maybe. I was there.

I saw her come in. With him.

She'd surprised me.

Perhaps I slept there behind that sofa out of sight as the fire warmed my bones dry. Maybe they argued and he left. I made that noise, and he, alerted to me, left. And then she turned to see me. We argued. I was stalking her. I disgusted her. I would have reminded her that I loved her and that I would have done anything for her. Reminded her that she loved me. That she gave me a key. I would have reminded her about the record – that she still played it, still cherished it. And something was said or done to make me fling it. I can see it now, breaking in two. Did I strike her then? And did I then stand over her and lose control? It feels likely now. That I watched myself, as if disembodied, as my anger flooded into her, and rage took me over. As everything reddened before my eyes.

There is a rituality to this act of bathing now. It feels like a last rite. I wash each part carefully before cupping water in my hand and pouring it over my body. Finally, I submerge my head and hold it under water until my hair floats freely. When I come up for air, I feel reborn. I wrap a towel around my waist and return to my room. Seb has laid out fresh clothes again and taken away the old. Dear Seb. We've spoken about the money a few times and I have reassured him that he is forgiven. Told him that it never meant anything to me in itself. When I am dressed, I go downstairs.

He is in the kitchen, busying himself at the stove. There are plumes of smoke coming from a blackened pan in his hand. He hasn't heard me come in.

'Blast,' he says loudly, and runs his hand under the tap.

'Seb. Come sit. We need a chat,' I say, taking a seat at the table.

He looks around startled and then hesitates, unsure where to put the pan. He drops it into the sink. 'Xander. Where have you been?'

'Seb, sit down for a second. We need to talk. I just wanted to say thank you,' I say.

He runs his hands through his hair. 'Xander. Where the hell did you go? And the bag – it's gone.'

'I wanted to tell you ...'

His face contracts in concern. 'You went to the police?' he asks. 'You gave it to them?'

'I had to,' I say. And then there is silence. We look at one another and I notice a tear in his eye and when he goes to wipe it, I realise that there's one in mine too.

'The money is yours,' I say. 'I don't want you ever worrying about it.'

'What?' he says.

'You can keep it. I don't need it.'

'But it's yours. I'll pay it back. I just need—'

'You let me in here when I needed you. That's – that's everything to me.'

I can't turn back now. I know that I can't go to prison, so there is really only one option left. I will of course feed out the line for as long as I can. There are still things about life that I can marvel in. I want to be warm, and then to be cold and shivering under a blanket of leaves, breathing air that is crisp enough to crackle. I want to mourn, and to submit to any redemption that is left to me.

'You kept that?' he says, looking at my neck.

I place my fingers lightly on the shell pendant and nod. Whatever mood I left him in has shifted to something darker. 'What now?' he says.

I don't know what to say to him so in the end I look down at my hands and say nothing. He doesn't move. The silence swells between us until he speaks again.

'When?' he says.

The question catches me. I continue breathing slowly until I have to swallow. 'Soon. A week, maybe.'

He rubs his eyes with the back of his hand. 'And you're certain?' he asks quietly. 'I just can't believe it, Xander. What happened?'

I have nothing to help him with this. Nothing I can give him can explain it. I loved her. I must have. But I couldn't live without her. Is that it? Was it that awful?

'Shit,' he says, coming to himself. 'Nina – what do I tell Nina?'

I reach across the table and take his hand. 'Seb.'

'You can't do it, Xander. It's a coward's way out.'

I smile as my throat catches more tears. 'That's me, Seb. Coward. A bridge. A jump.'

'No, Xand, that is not you. You're not a coward. You've held this so long now. You've suffered, you have, but you can't just leave. Not now. Not after all this time. When I've just got you—'
He breaks off, losing himself in tears.

'This isn't a thing to be sad about. You mustn't be sad about it. I had chances. I had a lot of chances,' I say. 'I fucked them all up.'

He shrugs off my hand. He looks at me, his face stained with tears and disbelief. Finally, he gets up and I hear footsteps as he goes upstairs to his bedroom.

I splash some water on to my face in the sink and return to the living room. There's a small bookcase in an alcove. And when I see the books I remember how I keep meaning to read and yet never seem to manage it. I run a finger along the spines. A few of the titles mean something to me. I pick out a Maupassant and study the cover. *Le Nœud de vipères. The Nest of Vipers*. Rory gave me this copy.

The Christmas that he gave it to me comes flooding back. We are in the drawing room. I am sixteen and sullen, he is innocent as he always was. The fire is flickering in the fireplace and Dad is sleeping in his favourite chair beside it. I remember the feeling of blackness radiating in waves from me. But there is a whisper of frustration through the hate. And it is love. The love won't be rinsed away. It won't leave me and him. It stains us both.

48

Tuesday

It has been three days since I delivered the bag to Blake. I know there's no longer any spare time.

I am in the kitchen, giving Seb some space. I need space, too. There are thoughts to pack and curate. Which to preserve and which to consign? The telephone rings, piercing the silence. I put down my mug and answer it.

'Xander,' the voice says. 'It's Jan.'

'Hi,' I say. 'I thought it might be you.'

'Did you? But you didn't think it might be clever to tell your lawyers before you walked into a police station with evidence in your own murder case?'

'I'm sorry,' I say. 'I thought you might have stopped me.'

'Too right I would have.' She breathes heavily into the phone as if composing herself. 'Anyway, they found a print.'

My heart sinks. In the gap of time that opens out, I see that today might be the day that I have to take those last steps. I was never expecting good news. The fact that I had the record at all after all these years is enough to convict me, but still the news shocks me. In the quiet of the line a ringing starts in my ears.

'The print would have degraded by now,' she says. 'But only a normal print. A surface fingerprint from sweat might last a few days,' she continues, 'but that wasn't your print. Your print was visible.'

Your print. My print.

'It was in blood.'

The chemicals rush to my temples and I want to drop the telephone but instead I hang up and sink to the floor. The silence begins to gather itself again and collect around my ears. The whine starts as a low hum and then steadily gets louder. Soon it is so loud that the walls around me are bouncing the sound of silence into my head.

I have to leave.

I walk faster and faster until I am almost running. People on the pavements slip and slide away from me as I bowl through. I can hear my voice, squeezed and scratched, shouting out at the pedestrians. 'Move! Move!' I say, ploughing through them.

This is wrong. Through that one piece of evidence delivered straight to the police, I had stopped and surrendered, confessed my guilt. Why, now, am I so surprised? The truth, I realise, is that even at the point I had handed the evidence to the police, I wasn't sure what was me and what was my imperfectly stitched-together memory.

I can't let this fractured mind of mine fracture my resolve, though.

Something like this happened before, with Rory. When he jumped. I remember it clearly now, how I felt when I heard about it. If only I'd been there, I might have been able to stop him. And now when I reconstitute the memory, I remember being there. I remember seeing it unfolding before my eyes.

I was standing next to him on his balcony. Night had descended across London but there, high up above the streets, it was somehow still light. Not light in a luminescent sense but in the meaning of lightness. There was a weightlessness there.

He was clutching the railing, his fists white against the night. He might have been drunk. And if I was there, I was in a cloud of dark anger. He'd said something to me and I something to him which he'd bitten against.

'You hadn't earned that. That *love*,' I might have said.

And he just drank and swallowed back his response. If he had one.

'You can wish I were dead,' he said at last. 'But I'm not. I am still here. I'm still your brother. I still love you.'

His eyes would have been red – *were* red. The water was building up in them from the wind here at the top of the building.

'You don't love me,' I said. 'You, none of you ever loved me. You were all oblivious to me. And this … this is just guilt.'

'Then I confess,' he said, turning to me, tears falling freely now.

I shook my head and walked back into the flat. The floors were smooth and warm under my socked feet. In the low fridge in the kitchen area, I found myself a can of something to drink. Clicking it open, I headed back out to the balcony.

When I got there Rory was straddling the balcony barriers. They were metal so they could hold his weight, but I was alarmed.

I ran and stretched out my hand for him. He pulled his own back and as he did he wobbled on the rail.

'No!' I shouted.

'Don't come closer,' he said. 'I haven't decided yet. I need to think it through. Wait.' He held out a hand in my direction. I stopped in my tracks but was on my toes, ready to leap out and grab him. He looked like that boy I remembered, the one who cried over crisps. All I wanted to do was comfort him, rescue him.

'Okay,' I said and held out my palms. 'Take your time.'

I waited and watched as the machinery in his head whirred. I followed him in my head, tracing the paths I knew he was taking and suddenly I realised where he was heading.

'But you know you can't redeem anything through death,' I said quickly.

'Ha,' he said. 'I'm not sure Jesus would agree.'

I swallowed. We were there – at Jesus – more quickly than I expected.

'You're Jesus now?' I said. 'Okay, then you'll have to be killed. Suicides don't provide redemption. Besides, an atheist like you? Come on, Rory. Stop being an idiot. Get off that wall.'

'Okay, brother,' he said, smiling from the corner of his mouth. 'Okay, I'll get off – but you tell me. What's the penance? There has to be one.'

He teetered for a second and then steadied himself with a hand. I was halfway to him by the time he was stable again. His hand flung out again by way of warning.

'You don't need redeeming,' I said, stopping. 'Not you, of all people. Come on. Back here.'

He laughed a little. 'But the oblivion. There's the oblivion I relegated you to. That's a crime,' he said, his voice becoming shrill.

'I was being dramatic.'

'No. Not dramatic. You were being truthful,' he said seriously. 'So, tell me, Xand, how do I recover from that?'

The wind up there felt strong. It came upon him suddenly, buffeting him and panicking me.

'You can live,' I said quickly.

'And then what? I knew it all along. I saw it. I saw how he was with you and how he was with me. And I did nothing. I didn't want to. I wanted it to be like that.'

'You don't know what you're saying,' I said and the words or half of them were carried away by wind.

'I do, Xander. What do you think all of this is? My life's misery hasn't just been about this,' he said.

He was crying then and tears ran down his cheeks in fat streams, and suddenly I was thrown back to that same day in the park, Rory on his knees, Wotsits sodden on the grass. I stepped forward and he yelped, holding out his hand.

'No!' he said, eyes blazing.

In a single step, I could be up against him. It would take just one step. I fixed my eyes on his. He was crying so hard that all I wanted was to hold him. He was crying so hard he was in danger of falling.

I took the leap and threw my arms around him. He stiffened before collapsing into me. He sobbed and as he did he clutched at me. I pulled him back over the rail and he crumpled to the floor. We stayed like that for some minutes.

'Come in, Rory,' I said, once he had stopped crying.

He looked up at me, his face wet and red at the eyes and pulled himself to his feet and allowed me to usher him in.

When I left late the next morning, he saw me to the door and embraced me.

'I'm sorry,' he said. But I didn't read any sorrow – only desperation.

When he dropped to his death some days later, I buried this episode in my head. And now it comes back to me.

And yet.

And yet there is a version of this memory in which I threw my arms around him and held him as he teetered on the balcony. I smothered his sobs and then once they had subsided, I wiped his eyes. My hand was there on his head, stroking his hair. I whispered to him, my love. And my forgiveness.

And as his breathing settled into a steadier, slower rhythm, I leant into him.

And, gently, I pushed.

49

Tuesday

It takes an hour to reach Waterloo Bridge. It is the one that I use more than any other to cross the border. It has none of the beauty or the fancy ironwork of Chelsea or Albert. It has no lights, or towers. There is only one thing to mark it out from every other: the view.

I avoid it, now, that view. But halfway along I stop and gaze into the river instead. The river's muddy faces swell and shift but they are still impassive, inscrutable. Tourists and workers in suits and coats pass behind me but don't give me a second look. I don't want to be seen. I could climb over this low barrier and slip into the water without so much as a turned glance. I would slide in like a knife and sink to the bottom with mouthfuls of river water in my stomach and lungs. The cold of it, the shock of it, will make me gasp. I will flail and when the water begins to claim me, I will rail and fight as my body's instincts overpower my will. But then, after a brief rattle of life, I will go.

When Rory died, he succeeded but I did not. I see that now – at last. The haunting of those years finally over. I see it. I know what it means to yearn for release in this way. To be free of the oppression of memory and action. I know what made him want to go and why he climbed on to the ledge. When you are there facing the eternal nothingness, it is overwhelming. It is all that it can do. It must overwhelm because that is its nature. So, he was overcome, as he was bound to be.

Now I am, as he was then, straddling the barrier. I swing a leg over until I am sitting on the wide wall that separates earth from air and water. The surface is slippery and sitting on it makes me feel giddy, as if on a downward swing. I swivel to face the water and feel the pull of the waves. When people visit high buildings and climb to the top, the thing they fear most isn't falling, but jumping. They are afraid that some urge will take them and they will jump. And now here I am fearing the opposite – that I don't have the courage to jump.

The river tugs at me. I inch forward, sliding on the smooth paint. There is tingling in my feet. I slide a little further until my legs dangle freely. The nerves in my toes sizzle with the sensation of falling, but my hands are still here, gathering sweat on the flat of the wall. I am aware of some people stopping, looking. A phone or two has come out to raise the alarm.

It is time.

I can see Grace now. Her face is there in the water. Now her arms. She is beckoning me.

'Xander!'

From behind me.

I turn my head and I am shocked to see that it is Seb. His car is parked opposite, the hazard lights blinking, and he is running towards me. I could go now, before he reaches me, but then there will be alarms and panic and commotion, and rescues. And I don't know if I can try again after that.

I spin back around and slide reluctantly on to my feet. 'Why are you here?' I say.

He comes puffing up, crossing the road quickly in between beeping cars. 'What are you doing?' he says, panting.

'You knew,' I say. 'You knew I was doing this. I told you.'

He nods frantically. 'Yes,' he says between breaths, 'but that was before.'

'Before what?'

'Xander. When you went haring out of the house after that call, I did last number ID and called the number. Jan.'

'So?' I say. She can't have told him anything – she would be bound by confidentiality.

'So, speak to her,' he says, handing me his phone. I stare at it momentarily before taking it.

'Jan?'

'What's that noise – I can hardly hear you. Is that you, Xander?'

The traffic crowds into the phone and I cup my hand around it to fend it off. 'Sorry. Can you hear me now?'

'Xander? Good. You hung up before I could tell you.'

'Tell me what?' I say. Already my heart is beating hard.

'Whose print it was. Our print was for a guy called Yull. Harry Yull.'

'Harry Yull?' I say weakly. And then the name begins to chime bells. As I say it out loud it strikes me.

'He went by a version of the name. Ariel,' she says. 'Anyway, the police, your friend Blake especially, have been busy following up this guy. Turns out he was in the area on the date of the murder. He was working just around the corner from her address. So, the Crown are reviewing the case.'

For a few moments, I stand there in silence. I am sure I cannot have heard this properly and yet, there she is on the other end of the phone, almost laughing from the news.

'But,' I say, 'I was *there*.' Seb looks at me expectantly, the wind blowing tears into his eyes.

'Well, they're not saying it wasn't you. It's more that they're saying they can't be sure it was you. They can't disprove your defence. You said it was another guy, and, well, it turns out another guy's print was on the record fragment. In blood.'

'So, what about this guy, Ariel?' I say. 'Harry Yull?'

'Nothing. He's dead. Died of a heart attack in 2000.'

Dead.

The bridge has resumed its usual pace. People walk past, immersed in their own presents.

'It wasn't my print,' I say to Seb, handing him back the phone.

'It wasn't your print,' Seb says, holding me by the shoulders.

'But that doesn't mean I wasn't responsible,' I say.

'What do you mean?'

'I mean, I'm not sure any longer. When I bring it back, it's not as I told it.'

'What do you mean?' he says into the wind.

I look back into the river, inviting me to become a part of it. I turn away from Seb and make off up the bridge, heading to the northern side. He follows me and after just a few strides, I feel his hand firmly against my arm.

'Stop running. Xander. Just stop.'

'I have,' I say. Tears gather behind my eyes and I am so angry that they are there. I don't need tears. I need resolve. I take in a deep breath and look into Seb's eyes. I don't want to burden him with this. I want to take the weight with me. When I go I want to leave the world behind me lighter. But when I look into his eyes, I see that it's too late.

He stares at me and there is fear and anger there. But he waits.

I sling my mind back to the night it happened. I am there once again, lying behind the chesterfield holding my breath, afraid of being caught. The flames are making shadows on the walls and that song, playing no more, lies broken in two on the floor.

'Shut. Up,' the man says.

He has leaned her back over the table, covering her mouth with his hand. I see her wriggling then. She is fighting to get upright. Fighting to get his weight off her body. Fighting to get his hand off her mouth.

Her legs kick out, but reach only air.

I get to my knees. From this position I can see that she is changing. Her face, her neck, are changing colour. Perhaps, I think, I can make a noise. Distract him. I cough loudly and then just as he turns, I duck back down. It has worked. He has released her. He turns back towards her. She gasps loudly, clutching her throat and then levers herself off the table.

He has forgotten what distracted him and has now turned to her, holding her gently by the elbows.

'I'm so sorry. I'm so … I'm drunk,' he says, and then he gathers up his belongings. As he does he knocks over a glass which shatters on the hard surface of the coffee table.

'Oh, shit,' he says, and begins to collect up the shards. 'Oh, shit,' he says again, his finger is in his mouth and he hops around trying, drunkenly, to clear up the room. At the other end of the room, Grace is breathing heavily but has returned to herself.

He straightens up from where he has been rooting around on the floor. I can see from the sofa that he has gathered up the broken record pieces. He proffers them, pathetically, to her.

'Just leave!' she says.

He drops the pieces softly by the window, and then he is gone.

And now I am on my feet. Her sobbing has brought me out and I think, ridiculously, that I can comfort her. That she wants me. I pad softly to where she is standing by the dining table. She is crying softly into her hands. I put my arm around her and she bristles suddenly.

'You nearly killed me, you. You fucking, you fucking weak, pathetic,' she says. The words have struck me before I have registered what they mean. Before I have understood that they are meant for him and not me. She will think that I'm him, until she can see me. But she can't see me, it is too dark. It is too much of a stretch for her mind to make sense of me, here. When she realises it's not him but someone else, she screams out in terror. She lashes out frantically, in fear, slapping at my face. As soon as the blows land – almost before the sound waves reach my ears – I react. As if bound by the laws of physics. Every force. An equal and opposite reaction. As soon as her hand whips my skin, my instinct for survival pushes mine back at her. It happens before I can stop it. It is that quick.

Her head snaps back on her neck with a crack. She freezes then as if between decisions. Her face is a pale, perfectly still surprise. My heart stops. In that gap. When all things still remain possible. My life, then, flashes before me in a kaleidoscope.

Bright-light moments. Heavy sadnesses. Regrets, all of them. Mistakes. My mind gathers as many as it can in that divided infinite sub-second, as if fleeing from a burning building with my last possessions.

Then her knees buckle, as if the bones in her legs have vaporised. As she drops, another dull crack. Her body pulls the back of her head down hard on the edge of the table. And then, a final thud, and she lies scattered on the floor.

I remember dropping to my knees and whispering her name over and over.

I remember walking in circles, frantic. Parts of my brain are imploring me to wipe surfaces and things I might have touched. And then I see the record pieces and the world stops spinning. I am caught in that nowhere time. One of the pieces is smeared with drying blood and I know that he has touched it, his finger cut from the broken glass. The working, calculating part of my brain impels me. I should take it. In a light daze I grope around for something to wrap it in and find some newspaper.

There is the wine. She was drunk. She fell. I pick up the bottle and pour some of it on her shirt. I study the angles. What will work. I see her pendant next to her on the floor.

And then, I run.

I hear the door at the end of the corridor slam. And as it does, at last, I too am slammed, back into existence.

I am here. On this bridge.

'I didn't mean to do it,' I say, crying.

'It wasn't you,' he exclaims.

'It's been so long, Seb.'

He holds me then until the tears finally subside. He releases me from his embrace and puts an arm around my shoulder.

'Come on. Let's go home,' he says.

We dodge the traffic to cross the road. The car is sitting against the kerb edge, waiting to take us away. But I know as I climb in that it can never take me far enough.

The road opens out before us. Seb reaches out and touches my arm as he drives. I think I see somebody behind us, and I turn around to look in the back seat. It's empty.

ACKNOWLEDGEMENTS

To Mama without whose prayers and support nothing good that came my way would ever have reached me. Thank you for everything you gave me without counting any of it. Thank you for life. And for love. And for more than I will ever know. I love you.

To Dad who wanted me to read – always – to make up for the reading that wouldn't come to him. Thank you for the stories. And for that smile. And for being proud whether I deserved it or not. We will come to you one day not too far away.

To Sadia, my wife. My life. And the third best lawyer in the World. Thank you for all that faith that you somehow still have in me. Thank you for the daily blessings bring into my life. I love you. One day I will repay you with twenty-two point two million somethings. What those somethings are though is not yet clear. I'm beginning to think it might not be pounds. I really hope by now you're getting some sleep though I'm not hugely optimistic. Thank you for your belief and your ideas and that believable optimism that you infect everything with. I couldn't do any of this without you. I wouldn't want to.

To my brothers and sisters, Kash, Omer, Khurrum and Aiysha. I miss you all. To me each of you is a compass point that helps me find my place in the world. Thank you.

Now to ones who make this thing happen … the Book GIANTS.

To the matchless Camilla, my agent. If my first draft had been a portrait then Camilla was the one who said, gently, 'you know I feel that we should stick to having just the two eyes. And maybe lose the third arm. And add a nose. Definitely add a nose. And a neck.' Thank you for making the book recognisable. And of course, for all the championing you do and do so well. I couldn't have asked for a better guide and friend to navigate that water filled with all those sharks!

To all those others at Darley Anderson who combine their energies on my behalf. Thank you. And especially to Sheila for all her efforts in launching my screenwriting career! Thank you also to Mary and Kristina and Georgia. You are all brilliant and lovely and enormously talented people.

To Sara Helen, my amazing and talented editor. Thank you for taking away rough edges and for the polish and for understanding the book in ways that even I didn't. I've always said that there's no point in having an editor unless they're cleverer and more imaginative than you are. And although it's a low bar in my case, you've flown over it. Thank you for taking me on and welcoming me so warmly to the Raven and Bloomsbury families. Thank you to all the brilliant minds there who do such sterling and difficult but masterful work. There are countless sales and publicity and marketing heroes who work behind the scenes and have done so much to bring this book into being and I am indebted to you all.

To Greg Heinimann who designed such an evocative and striking cover, thank you. And to Lin Vasey for her work on the copy edit and to Catherine Best for her work on the proof edit who just prove that every single book is a collaboration of many. Thank you for your efforts.

I am grateful too to Ben Douglas-Jones QC who not only did me the privilege of allowing me to fictionalise him for a moment but who also kindly (together with Chris Parker) allowed me permission to reproduce and reprint (and change for the worse) an extract from the marvellous Fils de la Terre © Ben Douglas-Jones and Chris Parker. Thank you for your encouragement and giving me faith in the story.

I reserve a huge store of gratitude to Alex Tribick. In many ways there would be no books at all without Alex's support. He knows why this is true and I want to say a deeply heart-felt thank you to him. Alex, *bonnet de douche*, my friend. It's such a privilege to work with you. Sadia adds her thanks but also her commiserations to Sue (I'm not sure why).

Next the Chillies. The Red Hot Chilli Writers host a delicious podcast if you're ever in the mood for one, but they are also my writing support group. By turns they are patients and therapists. I can't count the number of times that their wit and humour, their support and solidarity have rescued me from the pits of writing despair. So. Reluctantly. Thank you in totally random (picked out of a hat order) Amit AA Dhand, Ayisha Malik, Nadeem Khan, Abir Mukherjee, and absolutely least of all Vaseem Khan. Each of them are talented and brilliant writers and have given me something to aim for. Thank you, people. I should add a second thank you to Ayisha who edited an early version of the book and in the process taught me how to write betterer. Thank you.

Thank you to all the readers and the reviewers and the bloggers. The ones who tweet and the ones who silently read and breathe life into dusty pages. I fully and readily acknowledge what a huge privilege it is to be able to write at all and be published but also that it is the readers who bring the books into existence as stories. Thank you.

Finally, to Zoha and Shifa. I am so proud of you both. If I have written this book just for the pleasure of being able to say that, then it was worth it. I love you both to somewhere past heaven and back.

Also – you guys are very annoying A LOT of the time. Let's not forget that.

A NOTE ON THE AUTHOR

Imran is a practising barrister with almost 30 years' experience fighting cases in court. He hails from Liverpool but now lives in London with his wife and daughters. His debut novel *You Don't Know Me* was chosen by Simon Mayo as a BBC Radio 2 Book Club Choice for 2017 and longlisted for Theakston Crime Novel of the Year and for the CWA Gold Dagger, and is currently being adapted for screen in four parts. When not in court or writing novels he can sometimes be found on the Red Hot Chilli Writers' podcast as one of the regular contributors.

@imranmahmood777

A NOTE ON THE TYPE

The text of this book is set in Minion, a digital typeface designed by Robert Slimbach in 1990 for Adobe Systems. The name comes from the traditional naming system for type sizes, in which minion is between nonpareil and brevier. It is inspired by late Renaissance-era type.